40 and Waiting

A NOVEL BY

KAI JAE

Book designed and formatted by Melodye Hunter

Editing by JenWestWriting Editing & Marketing Services

Printed and bound in the United States of America

First printing March 2020

Published by Well Done Publishing, LLC, Washington, DC 20011

This book is dedicated to Donna Darlene - the best mom in the whole wide world. Thank you for sacrificing so much, loving so hard, and for showing me what a strong relationship with God looks like. I am so honored that He thought enough of me to bless me with you as my mom. I love you with all my heart, and I miss you immensely.

40 and Waiting

A NOVEL BY
KAI JAE

Well Done
PUBLISHING, LLC

Chapter 1

Peppered with head to toe goosebumps, Morgan rubbed her bare, butterscotch-hued arms as she awaited the gynecologist. The brisk, early autumn breeze sent a draft creeping through the window of the dimly lit examination room. Her swollen eyelids tightened over her light brown eyes as she traced the orange, brown, and gray asymmetrical wallpaper border around the room to avoid staring at the mint green walls. She thought, *who in their right mind would think this wallpaper complements the paint color? On second thought, maybe it's supposed to distract patients expecting bad news….Come on, doc… can all of this be over already?*

The longer Morgan sat surrounded by diagrams of women's anatomy and public service announcements about practicing safe sex, the more her nerves unraveled. The ticking of the wall clock's second hand was much-needed background noise in the eerily silent room. With the long, skinny fingers of her right hand, she tapped the edge of the examination table in unison with the clock. With her left hand, she tugged at the paper-thin robe that barely tied in front of her. A bona fide Paranoid Patty, Morgan often lived inside of her head, commentating her life through a dark lens. Although she sat in near silence, her mind raced as it replayed the events that led to this dreaded appointment.

All Morgan ever wanted to do was meet her Mr. Right, fall madly in love, get engaged, then marry and live happily ever after. She often fantasized about her wedding day, complete with tears of joy cascading down her fiancé's face at the sight of her walking down the aisle in a custom white satin mermaid gown that accentuated all of her God-given curves. Although she was now thirty-eight years old, her dream of a fairytale romance never wavered. She longed for the type of relationship her parents had before her father died nearly four years ago from complications of diabetes. Her parents enjoyed a union spent with one's best friend, protector, confidant, champion, lover, and ultimate life partner. When Morgan met Justin two years ago, she thought he was God-sent— not because she heard from God, but because Justin seemed to check the boxes of all things she asked God for in a man. As a Christian, she knew that God gives believers the desires of their hearts. By age 36, she was clear that she needed to approach God boldly to ask for a man because time was ticking away, and she needed to seal her fate as a married woman instead of winding up as an old spinster. Given her current disposition, she may have left off some key attributes in her prayer.

* * *

It was a Sunday morning in September 2015—the type of day when people with convertibles let down the top, throw on some shades, turn up the music, and cruise at high speeds as the wind whips through their hair. As autumn leaves cascaded to the ground, Morgan pulled up to a pump at her local gas station as she did every Sunday morning after church service. She couldn't sing a lick, but that didn't stop her from belting out the Fred Hammond song playing on the radio as if she were the lead soloist—until she noticed the suit. There was something about a man in a suit that made the hair on the back of her neck stand at attention.

Morgan turned off the car and tugged at her tight, dark brown natural curls which normally rested neatly on her shoulders, but were now in complete disarray after her impromptu praise party. Standing at the next pump in a pinstripe navy blue suit was Justin, filling up the tank of his black-on-black, twenty-four-inch chrome-rimmed Range Rover. As Morgan walked past him to pay the gas attendant, they made eye contact. And just as she always did in awkward situations, Morgan darted her eyes to the ground and bit her lip. She never knew what to say around attractive men, mostly because the few guys that she had ever found attractive never reciprocated her feelings. Instead, they left her feeling insecure, just like Douglas Jackson did ever since the second grade.

Morgan gushed over him, laughing at all of his jokes and even letting him cheat off of her homework. It all fell apart one day in fifth grade during a dodge ball game at recess. There Morgan stood, all alone, with her pigtails, uniform, and knee-high socks, waiting desperately to be picked for a team. Douglas was team captain and got to make the final selection, and although Morgan didn't like being called last, she was sure to be on his team. Just when she thought Douglas was going to say, "Morgan, you're with us," in front of the entire fifth grade class, Douglas yelled, "Who wants lame Morgan? I don't want her; y'all take her." And the entire class burst out in laughter.

That day of complete humiliation and rejection— May 12, 1989—was burned in Morgan's brain. Yes, she was naturally cute, average height with flawless skin and curves in all the right places, but she was a Plain Jane, and she had limited experience in the relationship department. Was Morgan the total package? In her mind, no. Mindful that her current state of singleness was partially due to her insecurity, Morgan was ready to take action. As she headed back to her car, she convinced herself to make eye contact again, but this time to speak. *Morgan, say something, for goodness sake. Or at least smile. Don't look pissed off; men don't like that.* But then she noticed that "the suit" was no longer standing at his side of the pump—Justin was standing right there beside her 2007 royal blue Toyota Camry, pump in hand, unscrewing the gas cap. In her head, the conversation went something like:

"Hi. Thank you, but you really don't have to do that."

To which he replied, "I know, but I want to."

But that's not how it went—instead, Morgan blurted out, "What are you doing?"

"Pumping your gas," Justin said sarcastically.

Morgan couldn't get out of her head quickly enough, so she continued to spiral down *Attitudinal Lane.*

"How do you even know what type of gas I use?"

Laughing, Justin said, "It's a Camry. I've never heard of putting high octane in a Toyota, but I guess to each his own."

Morgan prayed that she'd get swallowed up by a sinkhole. She realized that this whole conversation could have been avoided had she simply said, "Hi," and "thank you." She took a deep breath, nodded in agreement, and said, "You have a point. Thank you."

This handsome, five-foot-nine, chicken-nugget-golden-brown-skinned man with curly black hair and a slight gap between his two front teeth smiled, nodded, and introduced himself as Justin Nichols. Morgan asked if he went around pumping everyone's gas, to which he responded, "No, not everyone."

Thoughtful, Morgan noted. She proceeded to ask a series of questions that quickly filled out her mental checklist:

Where was he coming from or going all dressed up? Church. *Jesus lover - check.*

Where did he live? He owned a condo in Prince George's County. *Homeowner, self-sufficient - check.*

Children? None. *No baby Momma drama - check.*

After filling Morgan's gas tank, he walked her around to the driver's side car door, opened it, and waited for her to get in and buckle her seatbelt before gently closing the door. *Chivalrous—check.* Before returning to his car, he asked if he could call her sometime, indicating that he was interested in taking her out. *Confident and direct - check.* In her thirty-six years of living, Morgan never experienced anything like that. She was flattered, impressed, and completely caught off guard. This was a sign from God.

After just four months of dating, Morgan was head over heels about Justin, and he seemed to be smitten with her as well. He always surprised her with sweet gestures, like dropping off lunch at her job in the middle of the day, saying it was just an excuse to see her beautiful face. Although Morgan was in strong like, she thought the ultimate test would be when she disclosed to Justin that she was abstaining from sex. Men who were only out for one thing would ghost her after such news, but not Justin. His reaction sealed the deal for her. He nodded, said, "Cool, I respect that," and then invited her to spend Christmas Eve with his family at his Aunt Rochelle's house, which was a Nichols family tradition. *Cool with abstinence - check.*

The Nichols family was a large clan. Justin was the youngest of five boys and the only one without children. He had six maternal aunts, two maternal uncles, four paternal uncles, and three paternal aunts. Sadly, his father was never in the picture. His mother, who was in her early fifties, only acknowledged being thirty-five years old. She was Ms. Fly Betty with long, blond tresses of weave flowing down her back and a bright neon yellow gel manicure with rhinestones. She looked good for her age and made it a point to always accentuate her assets—boobs, butt, and waist—in everything she wore. Christmas Eve was no different. Justin's mom, Ms. Rolands, wore a red-and-white Santa hat with a one-piece red pleather catsuit and a thick black belt that showed off her thirty-two-inch waist. She finished off her outfit with black, thigh-high, four-inch stiletto boots.

As Justin maneuvered through his aunt's three-story, 1200-square-foot townhouse filled with nearly a hundred relatives posted up in every corner of the house, he maintained a firm, yet gentle grip on Morgan's hand. Every few steps, he would acknowledge his family and then turn and introduce Morgan as his girlfriend. Morgan couldn't keep up with all the names and faces because everybody looked alike. Inside, she was tickled by how proudly Justin claimed her as his girl. When Justin got around to introducing Morgan to his mother, Ms. Rolands pushed Justin out of the way, grabbed Morgan, and embraced her in a bear hug.

"It's about time I met you. This boy won't stop talking about you!"

Morgan's skin started to tingle. *Bragging to his mom about me? Family-oriented and loves his Momma - check.*

Things went so well with meeting Justin's relatives that it never dawned on Morgan that things might go differently when meeting her family—specifically, her mother. Morgan grew up without siblings but with two parents who were also only children. When her father passed away, Morgan insisted that her mother move in with her. Morgan loved having her mom as a roommate for the past four years, despite her overbearing motherly ways and her keen ability to call it like she saw it. They were best friends, so Morgan was eager to hear what her mother thought of her man. An opportunity presented itself one evening when Morgan returned home from a date for Justin to meet Mrs. Barnes for the first time.

"So, what you think?" Morgan asked.

"About what, honey?"

"Justin, Momma. Justin," Morgan said.

"Oh. He's a… pretty." Mrs. Barnes seemed to be at a loss for words. The only problem was that she always had an opinion.

"What's that supposed to mean?"

"Morgan, he is very well-groomed. Looks like he spends more time than the average woman getting ready. You sure he plays on the right team?" Mrs. Barnes asked.

Morgan was highly offended by her mother's remarks. How dare she question his sexuality?

"Really, Momma? So you gonna question the man's sexuality 'cause he takes pride in his appearance? That's really superficial coming from the woman who raised me to look beyond the physical and get to know the person behind the mask."

"Mask. Interesting choice of words," Mrs. Barnes said.

"How so?" Morgan cocked her head to the side.

"Morgan, the man you brought in here for me to meet today, wasn't Justin. It was his representative. Now, did his representative show well? Yes, but I wouldn't expect anything less. Any grown man coming to meet a young lady's mother for the first time better be on his best behavior, or else he's an idiot. So, you are asking me what I think of him? I don't know him. The verdict is still out. Only time will tell, baby."

Her mother's read on Justin blew Morgan's mind. She valued her mother's opinion and wanted her to like him just as much as she did, especially since Morgan was sure that he was the one. Morgan made it a point to take advantage of every possible opportunity for Justin and her mom to interact.

As the months went by, although Justin's behavior toward Morgan remained consistent, she began to notice some of his traits that she was oblivious to before. It started with his cell phone. Justin always kept it on silent and always kept it in his possession. He never disclosed his password, but he would allow Morgan to use it from time to time when the battery on hers died. Having experienced very few relationships, Morgan couldn't discern if this was normal behavior. It wasn't like his phone was completely off-limits to her. She asked her best friends, Renee and Stacy, about it, but they were divided on the issue. Renee, who was smart beyond measure and extremely analytical, suggested that Morgan monitor his behavior. Stacy, on the other hand, who was a little rough around the edges and extremely blunt, pretty much insinuated that Morgan was being insecure. Then there was his drinking. Justin didn't drink often, but when he did, he always got wasted. Morgan tried not to appear as a holier-than-thou Christian, acknowledging that everyone has vices, but she was definitely on guard whenever they'd go out where there was an open bar.

That July, Morgan invited Justin to an office cookout at a park along the DC waterfront. It was a kid-friendly, alcohol-free event. Every summer, Morgan's employer, DC's Child and Family Services, hosted a "Family Day" where the city would celebrate foster and adoptive parents and their kids. The park was filled with moon bounces, volleyball nets, obstacle courses, and other fun-filled activities for the entire family. The DJ was on the ones and twos, playing every line dance, encouraging attendees to get out of their seats and onto the makeshift grass dance floor. D.C. Mayor Victor Byrd walked around the park shaking families' hands and took a photo op flipping burgers on the 55-gallon drum BBQ grill.

Since Morgan arrived early to help set up for the festivities, Justin agreed to meet her there by 2:00 p.m. When he finally showed up at 3:45 p.m., Morgan immediately tasted alcohol when she greeted him with a kiss as he explained that he had just come from meeting up with an old college classmate at a nearby restaurant. *Dang, again? Does he have a problem? Morgan chill. Did the man have a few drinks? Yes. But is he drunk? No. Tipsy? No. Thank goodness this is an alcohol-free event. He will be fine. Chill out,* Morgan thought.

Two hours later, as Morgan checked on the popcorn and cotton candy vendors, out of her peripheral view, she saw a crowd forming near the dance floor. As she approached, she could see the crowd laughing and pointing at something or someone on the dance floor. Morgan's heart dropped. *Please don't let it be Justin,* she thought. To her disappointment, Morgan found a drunk Justin on the dance floor, bumping and grinding with somebody's seventy-five-year-old, three-hundred-pound grandmother. Justin was bent over, butt in the air and hands on the ground to stable himself. Many people watched with phones in hand, live streaming the whole ordeal on social media. Morgan was beyond embarrassed. She exhaled, approached the dance floor, head down to avoid being recognized on camera, grabbed Justin by the arm and attempted to pull him off the dance floor. He managed to break free from her grip, turned, whipped out his "john," and relieved himself right there in the grass in front of everyone.

Morgan never felt so humiliated in her life. *This grown man did not just do that. In public? In front of my coworkers? Who does that?* She ran to the parking lot as the thoughts began to flood her throbbing head, leaving Justin behind to stagger his way along the fence toward the parking lot. Morgan jumped in her car and pulled up to a somewhat-passed-out Justin, who, after moseying on down to the end of the parking lot, had posted up against an eight-foot white picketed fence. Morgan looked around to see who was looking, jumped out of the car, ran around to the passenger side, opened the door, grabbed Justin, shoved him in her car, got back into the driver's seat and sped out of the parking lot. In her head, she started making a to-do list: *Update my resume and get a nice power suit for interviews because I can never show my face at work again.* She cussed Justin out the whole ride to his condo, although he wasn't conscious enough to hear any of it.

The next day, Justin arrived at Morgan's house with flowers and a bottle of her favorite fragrance. He was beyond apologetic. Apparently, some of Morgan's male coworkers snuck rum in plastic soda bottles to the cookout. Having drunk scotch earlier in the day with his classmate, Justin forgot not to mix dark and light liquor. He was concerned about his behavior and realized that he needed to get it in check. He was not an alcoholic and didn't want to become one, so he was going to give it up for a while. After giving him a piece of her mind, what else could Morgan say? The man acknowledged his mistake and agreed to take the action that she was requesting. *We are all works in progress,* Morgan thought. Justin's dry spell lasted a good month and a half before his next alcohol-induced debacle that, thankfully, happened in the privacy of his home.

Nearly eight months into the relationship, the butterflies in Morgan's stomach began to dissipate. Justin was sweet and kind, but for some reason, occasionally, she found herself wondering, *is this it, God?* Having prayed for a man, Morgan didn't want to seem ungrateful. But if she were honest with herself, she would admit that something was missing. One evening, while cuddled on the couch in Justin's living room watching *Love and Hip Hop*, he initiated "the talk."

"Hey bae, can I ask you a question?"

Morgan sat up and turned to face him. "Sure."

"So how long is this celibacy thing going to last?"

"Huh? What do you mean? You know I'm abstaining until marriage. We talked about this. Why? What's wrong?" Morgan asked.

"Nothing. It's just, you know, a brotha got needs. You know I love you. You know I want to be with you. You know we gonna get married one day. I just need to be honest with you. I want you. I need you; like, really need you. I'm not trying to mess this up. I'm not trying to make you do anything you don't want to do. But, for real, it seems like you want it, too."

"What do you mean?" Morgan asked.

"Whenever we make out, your body be feening for me. It's like you be teasing me 'cause your body is definitely saying yes, but then you pull a hard stop. And I'm not about games. We grown."

"So, what are you saying?"

"I'm saying I want you, and I know you want me too," Justin said while he caressed Morgan's shoulder.

"And if I say no?"

"You say no."

And that was the end of the conversation. Did Justin give her an ultimatum? No. He didn't say that he would cheat if she didn't sleep with him. Was his assessment incorrect? No. She knew her body had a mind of its own. She admitted that, given her age, their teenage make-out sessions were a bit immature, but it was within her comfort zone. Could she blame him for bringing up the conversation? No. If anything, she wanted them to have a relationship where they both felt like they could discuss anything and everything honestly and openly. Was it realistic to expect a grown man to abstain from sex until marriage? No. *I knew no grown man would be ok with this celibate thing,* Morgan thought. *Men are physical beings.* Was marriage really in their future? Despite his flaws, Morgan was convinced that this man was God-sent. And besides, in recent weeks they talked about marriage more and more. With that, Morgan gave in, let down her guard, and let Justin in. Literally.

* * *

With her fuzzy socks on and ashy knees exposed, Morgan waited for Dr. Chao to enter the room. About fifteen minutes later, in walked a short, petite Asian lady in a white doctor's coat, accompanied by a timid, stringy-blond-haired assistant. Dr. Chao greeted Morgan with a warm handshake. Looking down at Morgan's chart, Dr. Chao said, "So, Morgan, it looks like you are two months shy of your annual. What brings you in?"

Over the embarrassment of the situation, Morgan blurted out, "My boyfriend," she paused, "ex-boyfriend cheated, and I want to be tested for everything. We always used protection, but I need to know for sure."

"That sleazebucket."

Morgan looked up at Dr. Chao with surprise and respect. *Yessss, Dr. Chao! Team Morgan, I see you. Sleazebucket is an understatement, but I'll take it.*

"I am so sorry, Morgan. Of course, that is the wise thing to do. I know how nerve-racking this can be, so I will expedite the results." Although the exam lasted less than ten minutes, for Morgan, it felt like an eternity as she lay on the table, feet in stirrups, legs spread as wide apart as her thunder thighs would allow. Dr. Chao instructed her to relax, but Morgan couldn't help thinking that this whole ordeal was completely avoidable. *Why did I give in to having sex with this man?*

Dr. Chao tried to put her at ease. "You know, before I met my husband, the last guy I dated cheated on me with his roommate, Steve. Girl, we've all been there. You want to talk about it?"

"Not really. I mean, I was blindsided. I thought he invited me out to propose. Instead, he tells me that he is expecting a baby with his ex-girlfriend, Courtney, whom he described as crazy, delusional, and needy."

"Oh, wow. I'm sorry, Morgan."

"But, get this: she's seven months pregnant. He swore that it was a mistake. It only happened once, and he was sure that he and I could work through this. He doesn't want to be with her. He wants me."

"Men are dumb."

"Aren't they? I mean, I stood there, wanting to punch him in the face as he continued to spew revolting crap from his mouth."

"You should have. I would have. I may be small, but I pack a heavy punch. I grew up with four brothers." Dr. Chao stood and said, "Well, Morgan, we are all done here," as she removed her blue plastic gloves. "I will call you when your results come in. Don't stress about it. It's his loss. And if anything, it sounds like you dodged a bullet."

* * *

The next day, Morgan nestled into her extra-cozy, plush couch to binge-watch *The Haves and the Have Nots* on OWN. She also treated herself to raw chocolate chip cookie dough from the Nestlé Toll House tub. After devouring half of the bucket, her cell phone rang.

"Hello?"

"Hi. Is this Morgan?" a woman asked.

"Yes, it is," Morgan replied.

"Hi, Morgan, it's Dr. Chao. Do you have a few minutes?"

Although the test results were all she could think about after her doctor's appointment, at the very moment before the call, Morgan almost forgot that she was waiting for the test results. Morgan tried to focus on the voice on the other end of the phone, but she couldn't help but try to remember if Dr. Chao told her that she would call with the results, whether positive or negative, or only call if the results came back positive.

"Yes." Morgan paused. "Is everything okay?"

"Morgan, I have some good news," Dr. Chao hesitated, "and some bad news."

"What?" Morgan asked.

"Morgan, I need you to take a deep breath and hear me out." You could tell that Dr. Chao gave these types of talks often. "We tested for HIV, herpes, gonorrhea, syphilis, HPV, and chlamydia. Your results came back negative for all of them, except for chlamydia."

Morgan sat up straight and gasped. "I don't have any symptoms. How is this possible?" Morgan's mind started wandering from the color of her urine this morning to the pain she felt in her lower abdominal during her last menstrual cycle.

"Now, Morgan, chlamydia is one of the most common forms of sexually transmitted diseases and often lies dormant in people with little to no symptoms. The good news is that it's completely treatable with an antibiotic." There was a pause in Dr. Chao's voice. "The bad news is that chlamydia can cause sterilization, and there is no way to know for sure until you start trying to have kids."

Up to this point in life, Morgan wasn't convinced that she wanted kids, but in that very moment, with Dr. Chao telling her that there was a chance she could never have kids, she realized that she wanted the option. The remainder of the conversation was a blur. Morgan couldn't believe that her greatest fear had come true. *Why me, God? Why?* She kept asking herself. She wasn't promiscuous. Was this punishment for not abstaining? Because she gave in to temptation, she now had to watch her ex have a baby while she endured a monthly cycle for absolutely no reason. Now that she was barren, she feared she was destined to live life alone? Morgan couldn't decide who she was angrier with—Justin or herself. She thought for a split second to call and tell him about the STD, but that would be too embarrassing.

* * *

As another weekend arrived, Morgan moped around the house in a flannel onesie looking absolutely pathetic. She had tear stains tattooed to her face, and her untamed curls hadn't seen a brush or comb in days. Her mother was fed up.

"Morgan Elizabeth Barnes, have a seat young lady," Mrs. Barnes demanded as Morgan closed the kitchen pantry door after retrieving her third honey bun for the morning.

Startled, Morgan obliged. "Yes?"

"Morgan, you've been mourning the loss of your relationship with what's his name for the past two-plus months. It's time you pick up that shovel in the garage, dig a hole, and bury him and your relationship with him six feet under. Justin ain't no more thinking about you than the man on the moon. Why in the world are you giving that man so much power and control over your life? You are one hundred percent free, but you are walking around this house as if you are in shackles. It doesn't make sense."

In all honesty, Mrs. Barnes was a little disappointed that Morgan was still wallowing in her feelings. She must have gotten that sensitive trait from her Dad. Mrs. Barnes was one tough cookie. She would have told Justin off, deleted all connections to him on social media, flipped him the bird, and moved on—'cause you only get one opportunity to disrespect Mrs. Barnes. Instead of being angry or relieved that she dodged a bullet, Morgan was wearing this cloak of shame and defeat. Her mother just couldn't understand.

"Momma, you don't understand. Justin checked all of my boxes," Morgan began.

"All your boxes, except for honest, loyal, respectful, trustworthy. Should I continue?" Mrs. Barnes was not for the pity party.

"You're right, but I prayed for a man, and God sent me him. It's not fair. Here I am all alone, possibly sterile, and he and Courtney are out there living life as a happy family and throwing it all up in my face."

"Morgan, do you hear yourself right now? They are out here living life to the fullest, and the only person stopping you from doing the same is you. Ain't nobody throwing anything up in your face. Until you decide to stop tormenting yourself and stop snooping on their social media stuff, you are gonna feel slighted. And don't get me started about the facades people put on social media. Baby, you over here mad that some girl got your sloppy seconds when God has clearly told you he ain't the one. You know what your problem is, right?" When Mrs. Barnes was on a roll, there was no stopping her. Before Morgan could even answer the rhetorical question, Mrs. Barnes continued. "You say you believe God, but you don't. It's easy to say you have faith, but it's when you are tested that you know whether or not you are indeed walking by faith."

"I do believe, Momma." By this time, tears were rolling down Morgan's face. Mrs. Barnes handed Morgan a tissue. As always, she hit the nail on the head.

"Baby, if you believed the God who blessed me with your Daddy and forty-two years of marriage, the God who blessed me with you, after four miscarriages and after doctors told me that I could not have children, the God who answered your prayer of wanting to be a homeowner and exceeded your expectations in what you not only wanted in a house but also what you could afford in this area, you'd know that God has never let you down and that He always shows up and shows out. Yes, He brought Justin in your life for a reason. Figure out the reason and move on. Heck, you should be excited to know that God heard your prayer and answered it. It means He is in the neighborhood. And while Justin may have checked several 'boxes,'" Mrs. Barnes said with air quotes as she rolled her eyes, "you'd know that God has someone for you that has ALL the boxes checked off, plus some you didn't even know you wanted. That's how God does, baby. But you got to know that in here," Mrs. Barnes said grabbing Morgan's hands tightly and gently placing them on Morgan's chest over her heart.

By this time, Morgan's tears turned into a waterfall. Everything her mother said was right. Morgan knew that God always showed up, maybe not when she wanted, but always in the nick of time. Why did she doubt Him? Morgan's inner voice began narrating, *God, I am thirty-eight years old. If not now, when will I meet my husband? You know the older I get, the less desirable men my own age will find me. These forty- and fifty-something-year-olds only entertain twenty- and thirty-year-old women. How much longer do I have to wait? When will it be my turn?*

That night, while sitting up in bed, Morgan couldn't help but think about what her mother said, "Sweetie, you do know that God can't bring you Mr. Right as long as you are still hung up on Mr. Wrong, right?" Morgan knew in her heart of hearts that she experienced this relationship for a reason and that God had something better in store. This was merely a chapter in her life and not the finale. While she could rationalize the situation, it would be easier to grasp her circumstance if she knew the end of the wait was in sight. *Lord, just give me a sign,* she pleaded with the Father. Turning on the lamp sitting on her cherry wood nightstand, Morgan pulled out a leather-bound journal from the drawer and opened it to a blank page. She closed her eyes, took a long, deep breath, and began to envision her future. Beside her, gingerly holding her hand was her husband. She couldn't make out his face, but she felt loved, protected, and adored. And in their watchful gaze were two healthy little kids, a boy and a girl, running around playing in a grassy field.

Morgan opened her eyes and began to write.

"Dear Heavenly Father, please help me to be open to receive the man that you have put on this earth just for me. This man will be honest and forthright, God-fearing, dependable, hardworking,

family-oriented, chivalrous, intelligent, handy, fiscally responsible, fun, and handsome. God, please help me not to be barren. I do want kids, with the right man, of course. God, help me to stay out of Your way, stay out of my own head, and just continue to do what You are calling me to do. And God, please help me to know when You've sent the one. I need a sign or two, please. And, I don't want to rush You, but if you could expedite this request, I would most appreciate it. I thank You in advance for hooking me up beyond my wildest dreams. I ask these things, in Jesus' name, Amen."

* * *

Little by little, Morgan began to change her perspective and see the brighter side of things. It helped that the holiday season was approaching, which was her favorite time of year. As was the tradition in the Barnes' household for as long as Morgan could remember, today, Mrs. Barnes and Morgan would head out to find the perfect Christmas tree. They stopped at a local sandwich shop for hoagies and fries and a slice of carrot cake to share before taking on the challenge of picking out the perfect tree. With full bellies, they stopped at two different Christmas tree lots, only to be disappointed with the selections. Upon arriving at the third location, claiming victory that this would be their last and final stop, Mrs. Barnes and Morgan began to canvas the endless rows of freshly cut trees as their nostrils filled with the pleasant smell of pine and firewood. Dividing and conquering, they both yelled out, "Found it!" at the same time. Morgan looked up and down a few rows before finding Mrs. Barnes standing in front of a tall, full, green, white pine. Morgan admitted it was pretty.

"Nice, Momma, but come take a look at the one I picked out."

Mrs. Barnes examined Morgan's tree, which met

the same criteria as her own, and she admitted that it, too, was a good choice. Feeling like they chose two good options, they decided to go with Mrs. Barnes' tree. Morgan and her mother proceeded to follow the scrawny worker bundled up in layers under a gray hoodie to the cutting station where Mrs. Barnes gave specific directions on where she wanted the trunk of the tree cut. Just as the man put the saw to the tree, Morgan abruptly stopped him and turned to Mrs. Barnes, saying, "Momma, that's too short."

"No, it's not. That's where I want it cut." Mrs. Barnes was a little stubborn in her old age. The man looked at Morgan and then again at Mrs. Barnes to confirm the placement of the saw on the tree. Morgan nodded and he proceeded to cut the tree as directed. Once he finished sawing, he stood the tree up. Mrs. Barnes looked at the tree and said in disgust, "Oh, that's too short."

"What?! I told you that, and now we are stuck with it," Morgan said. *Didn't I just tell this woman not to cut the tree there? Now we are stuck with this darn tree meant for Barbie's playhouse. Really, Momma?*

"Oh, no we aren't," Mrs. Barnes said assuredly. "I don't want that tree. Morgan, go show the man the other tree." She didn't bat an eye or miss a beat because she knew she wasn't taking home that abnormally short tree.

The man who just performed surgery on the white pine interrupted and said, "Ma'am, company policy says that you can't return a tree once it's cut."

Mrs. Barnes looked at the young man, eye to eye, and politely said, "Young man, my daughter is going to show you the tree that we want. Please, go retrieve it. Thank you," Morgan's mother smiled. She began to walk around the lot until she found a young newlywed couple. She overheard them talking about the trees in the lot being too big for their one-bedroom apartment. "Excuse me," Mrs. Barnes interrupted. "I don't mean to eavesdrop, but I think I found the perfect tree for you." She walked the couple over to the tree she no longer wanted, and the couple agreed it was a perfect match. Just then, Morgan and the young worker returned with the other selection. Mrs. Barnes explained to the man that the couple wanted the mini tree and asked Morgan to direct him where to cut her pick.

Morgan and her mom couldn't stop chuckling about the whole ordeal. It was just like Mrs. Barnes to get what she wanted, despite the minor setback. Morgan pulled into the driveway of her house off the dark alley. It always seemed like the streetlights in the alley were on sensors; however, they went out as cars approached instead of turning on. Morgan jumped out of the car to go inside the house to make room for their perfect Christmas tree. Mrs. Barnes quickly got out of the passenger seat and came around to the driver's side, where she got behind the wheel of the Camry. She looked through her rearview mirror and noticed a black sedan with smoked out windows slowly creeping down the street. "Alright, Jesus, peace be still." Her instincts kicked into force and she immediately locked the doors and prayed that Morgan would stay in the house until the car passed. The driver in the sedan quickly pulled into the alley, turned off its headlights, and stopped abruptly behind Morgan's car parked in the driveway. Mrs. Barnes' eyes scanned the car through the rearview mirror, trying to burn a description of the car in her head. Two young boys wearing ski masks jumped out and approached the car on both the driver's and passenger's sides. With their hands on the car doors, they yelled for Mrs. Barnes to open the door. One boy pulled out a gun and began giving orders.

"You better open this damn door, old lady!"

The sound of Mrs. Barnes' heartbeat rang in between her ears as she began to honk the horn profusely. With her foot on the gas pedal, Mrs. Barnes revved up the engine while the car remained in park. The neighbor to the right of Morgan's house turned on the porch light over their back door and peeked through the curtains. Just then, the driver of the sedan pulled down his window and hollered for the boys to get back in the car. In frustration, the boys turned and ran back to the car, but not before one of them smashed the passenger side back window with the back of the gun. Mrs. Barnes flinched at the shattering glass. Morgan thought she heard a commotion, but by the time she came outside to see what was going on, the car sped off. Morgan couldn't believe it. In less than two seconds, Mrs. Barnes' life could have been taken.

To Morgan's surprise, it didn't take long for the police to arrive. Her persistent mother insisted that the young officers help Morgan bring in the Christmas tree that was tightly tied on top of her car before she would give them her statement. Despite Mrs. Barnes' calm demeanor, Morgan made them some hot tea to calm their nerves. Morgan knew that her mom was beside herself. Just one week before Christmas and these boys plotted to rob an old lady at gunpoint? While sitting at the kitchenette, the two police officers shared that there were a series of armed robberies in the neighborhood and warned them to be on the lookout. *Thanks for the late-breaking news, officers,* Morgan thought. Morgan's favorite holiday, with their family tradition of picking out a tree and decorating it together while listening to oldie-but-goodie Christmas carols, was now clouded by the image of Mrs. Barnes nearly being carjacked.

Once the nice officers left, Mrs. Barnes grabbed

Morgan's hand and said, "Baby, we got to count our blessings. He got us." She returned to sipping her tea and added, "We got to remember why we celebrate Christmas, 'cause it has nothing to do with a tree—or us, for that matter. All we can do is pray for those young boys and say thank you, Dear Heavenly Father, for letting us see another day."

Morgan nodded in agreement. "Amen," she said quietly. She then grabbed her mother and held her tight. She didn't know what she would do if she lost her.

Chapter 2

Beep. Beep. Beep. The alarm clock on Morgan's nightstand went off.

Shoot. It's 5:00 a.m. already? Morgan thought. She slammed the snooze button, rolled over and buried her head in her pillow for an extra five minutes of sleep. In her mind, she contemplated how much longer she could stay in bed before absolutely being late for her spin class. *5:15 a.m....fifteen more minutes.* It was a new year, and Morgan wanted to start it off right. This was the year for Morgan to get her sexy back. She questioned whether she ever quite mastered sexy, as she spent most of her life hiding behind loose-fitting clothes because she hated her body. But enough was enough. If she didn't like her love handles, sagging booty, and thick thighs rubbing together, she needed to do something about it. Renee and Stacy invited Morgan to go to this spin class for the past year and a half, but she kept putting it off. Within the past year, Stacy lost fifteen pounds, which was great because she weighed in at over two hundred fifty pounds. During that same period, Morgan nearly gained fifteen pounds. She couldn't confirm the theory because she refused to get on the scale, but the dance she did to get into her skinny jeans intensified over the holidays.

Two years passed since her breakup with Justin, and despite her efforts, she was still as single as ever. She thought that last year was going to be her year with turning forty and all, but it turned out to be another uneventful year. Tired of waiting for life to happen, this year, Morgan was determined to focus on what was in her control: becoming the best version of herself, mind, body, and soul. With absolutely no prospects over the past two years, Morgan was determined to change her dateless life this year. She recognized that she needed to put herself out there. No guy was going to ring her doorbell and ask her out, except for maybe the UPS guy, who walked with a limp and suffered from halitosis. With the pressures of starting the year off with a bang, Morgan finally accepted a date with Damian, whom she met a couple of weeks ago on Bumble, an online dating site. Stacy and Renee took the lead on creating her profile and even initiated a few conversations with some potential guys. Damian was the only one that didn't scream serial killer to Morgan. It was hard to tell if he was attractive because he rocked baseball caps in all of his photos, but on the bright side, he was employed—worked for Metro, was 42 years old, never married, no kids, and loved Jesus—or at least that's how his profile read. They agreed to meet for drinks at 5:00 p.m.

Beep. Beep. Beep.

"6:15 a.m.!" Morgan yelled while jumping out of bed. She tried to remember if she hit the snooze button again, but it didn't matter. Either way, she messed up day one of "Mission RYS – Reclaim Your Sexy!" As she came to the realization that she couldn't possibly get dressed and make it across town for class by 6:30 a.m., the aroma of fried bacon filled her nostrils. There was something about the smell of bacon. After getting dressed, Morgan pulled her hair into her signature high bun and headed downstairs. To no surprise, Mrs. Barnes was in the kitchen, frying up a feast. Dressed in a long, tan housecoat, slippers, and a scarf, Mrs. Barnes was in her zone. Morgan quickly scanned the room and found her target—hot, crispy bacon on a grease-soaked paper towel. She picked up three slices and headed toward the kitchen table. As she took her seat, she curled up in a ball, like she'd done for as long as she could remember, to eat her bacon.

"Momma, I thought I asked you not to fix all this food. I am trying to eat healthy this New Year."

"Well, Ms. Morgan Elizabeth Barnes, morning to you, too. I call myself trying to fix my daughter a good, hearty breakfast before she heads off to work. You young folks think coffee is a substitute for food, and I'm here to tell you that it ain't," Mrs. Barnes said as she rolled her eyes upward and prepared Morgan's plate. Morgan chuckled to herself at the thought of being categorized as "young folk." At forty, she didn't feel young.

Not wanting all that good food to go to waste, Morgan examined her hefty plate of scrambled eggs with cheese, bacon, French toast, and grapes, and blessed her food while her mom sat beside her at the kitchenette reading the morning newspaper.

Looking up from the paper, with her reading glasses resting on the tip of her nose and silver hair peeking through the edge of her scarf, Mrs. Barnes reminded Morgan of her doctor's appointment. Morgan's mom liked to keep her fine silver and gray hair short, laid down on the sides, and just long enough on the top to curl and feather out.

"What's it for this time, Momma?" Morgan asked sarcastically. Honestly, it seemed like ever since her mother turned seventy, she stayed in a doctor's office. At seventy-two, Mrs. Barnes, small in stature, standing at five feet tall, and rounding out a size twelve dress, was still in good shape and didn't look a day over sixty. She was still as independent as ever and wouldn't hesitate to remind you of it either.

"My eyes," said Mrs. Barnes.

"Oh, you need me to take you?"

"No, Mr. Thomas said he'd take me," Mrs. Barnes said, blushing.

"Momma, I swear you have more men chasing you now than I have ever had in my entire forty years of living. What's the secret? Please share." Morgan was ashamed to admit it, but her mother's social life far exceeded her own. There was Mr. Thomas (Stanley) from church, Mr. Jenkins (Walter) from bingo, Mr. Pickney (Jimmy), the plumber, and Mr. Bailey (Morgan didn't know his first name) from Mrs. Barnes' computer class at the library. Even Mrs. Barnes referred to him as "Mr. Bailey," which led Morgan to believe that he must teach the class.

"What can I say, honey? I'm like a fine wine; I get better with time," Mrs. Barnes said, winking at Morgan as she got up to walk to her room.

* * *

The air outside was crisp and chilly. Mrs. Barnes, dressed in a navy-blue cardigan sweater to match her blue-and-gray tweed slacks, was wrapped up warmly in a tan wool shawl that was a little too warm. As her forehead started to perspire, she asked Mr. Thomas to turn down the heat in the car. As with all her doctor's appointments, Mr. Thomas dropped her off at the front of the hospital and told her to call him when she was ready to be picked up. She knew that Mr. Thomas never left the parking lot. He would park in the rear of the lot, read his paper and listen to the news on the radio.

First thing in the morning, the hospital always reeked of cleaning solution. It never smelled quite as nice as Pine Sol's Lavender Clean fragrance that Mrs. Barnes used at home, but the hospital air had not yet been contaminated with trillions of germs and turned stale yet. As a result, Mrs. Barnes made all her appointments for first thing in the morning. She walked through the cardiology wing of the hospital and entered the doctor's office. Approaching the window, Mrs. Barnes signed in and said to the receptionist, "Good Morning, Nancy. How are you? Is my doc in yet?"

Since being diagnosed with Dilated Cardiomyopathy in July of last year, a condition in which the heart's ability to pump blood is decreased because the heart's main pumping chamber, the left ventricle, is enlarged and weakened, Dr. Derek Patterson moved Mrs. Barnes' appointments to every other week. Given that she was as stubborn as a mule, Mrs. Barnes refused to consider alternatives like a pacemaker or defibrillator, or any type of surgery for that matter. Although her age was not ideal for the surgery, the fact that she was in good health otherwise made her a viable candidate. But Morgan's mother wouldn't entertain such foolishness. As far as she was concerned, God gave her seventy-two long, healthy, and joyful years of life. When He called her home, she would be ready. There was no reason to postpone the inevitable. She would continue to live out her last days with family, friends, and good food. It was for that reason that Mrs. Barnes lied to everyone about her bi-weekly doctor's appointment. Bad eyesight was common for aging adults, so she used that as her guise. She didn't want people to treat her differently upon finding out about her diagnosis, especially Morgan. Morgan took after her father when it came to worrying about things and people. She was a worrywart. Morgan spent all of her years worrying and caring for others. It was about time that Morgan started living for herself.

After Mrs. Barnes was taken to the examination

room, in walked the handsome, Hershey Kiss skin-toned Dr. Derek Patterson. He was forty-three years old and tall with a broad-shouldered athletic build. And his pearly-white smile formed dimples that stabbed his cheeks like an extra-fine point pen. He possessed a sincere, yet professional disposition that Mrs. Barnes always teased him about. Over the course of a few months, she was able to break down Dr. Patterson's guard and get to know the man behind the white coat. "Finally, it's about time you showed up. You know I have a hot date waiting for me outside," Mrs. Barnes said jokingly.

Dr. Patterson laughed and politely responded, "I do apologize for keeping you waiting. I asked my assistant to check to see if your labs were in yet, and she didn't do it. I followed back up myself."

"Sounds like you need a new receptionist. I can help you out, but it will cost you. I'm thinking, a fully paid vacation to Fiji."

"Fiji, huh?" Dr. Patterson pondered the thought then responded. "Mrs. Barnes, I don't think I can afford your services." They laughed.

"When's the last time you took a vacation?" Mrs. Barnes asked.

"Hmm. I think the last vacation I took was to Vegas. A friend from college was getting married and had his bachelor party there."

"And when was that?"

"Uh, 2015? 2016?" He guessed while scratching his head.

"Baby, you need to go have some fun. God did not put us on this earth to work all day. It's 2019. You have no legitimate reason as to why you have not been on a vacation in nearly four years. This is the prime of your life. You don't have chick nor child. Your health is on your side. You are financially sound. Please don't let all that fineness go to waste." It was funny; every time Mrs. Barnes went to the doctor's, she always ended up diagnosing Dr. Patterson and prescribing a remedy. Since his mother passed away ten years ago, Dr. Patterson developed quite a fondness for Mrs. Barnes' maternal wit.

"I hear you, Mrs. Barnes. It's just…" he paused. "I'm a beach man. I love the beach. And I'm not trying to do a guy's trip. Those always get out of control. And I'm not trying to take any ol' female. They would definitely take it the wrong way. So, until I can take my dream vacation, I'm content working hard. It keeps me busy."

"So, if I'm hearing you correctly, you're single and looking?" Mrs. Barnes believed in being direct.

"Yes, I'm single. I wouldn't say I'm looking, but I think I'm ready to settle down. Should God present the right woman in front of me, I think I'd know what to do and not hesitate," he blushed.

"Well, baby, I don't know what you think is gonna happen. Mrs. Right isn't going to show up at your door or your office for that matter and say, 'Yooouuuwhhooo, I'm here.' You have to get out and meet people. My daughter has the same dilemma, and I tell her, Morgan, get your behind out of this house. I don't understand what's wrong with your generation. Back in my day, we used to throw house parties, rent parties—shoot, any reason to throw a party. It was all about socializing and having good, honest fun. It might have helped if Morgan wasn't an only child."

"Me, too," Dr. Patterson interjected.

"But the point is, life is short. Life is what you make of it. I don't care how much fulfillment you get out of work, what's the point if you don't have someone to go home to at night to share it with? What is the purpose of your hard work and labor if you don't have future generations to pass your legacy on to?" Dr. Patterson nodded. "Now, I don't want to toot my own horn or anything, but I've been known to set up my daughter from time to time. Nothing serious has panned out yet, but I know one of these days, God will answer my prayers. Let me know if you ever want me to set you up on a blind date. I know some really nice women at my church."

"I think I'm good. Thanks anyway. Now, about your lab results. It appears your heart remains enlarged, and I am concerned that there may be some fluid in your lungs. I want to run another echocardiogram and CT angiogram immediately. I also want to change your beta-blocker and see how your heart responds. Have you been exercising and eating a low sodium diet like we discussed?"

"Dr. Patterson, I am not going to lie to you. I am seventy-two years old. If walking up and down the stairs in my daughter's house counts as exercise, then yes. As for sodium, I refuse to eat tasteless food in my last days. Now, I'm not going overboard on the salt, but I would be lying if I said I read the back of food labels for the sodium count."

"I appreciate your honesty. How have you been feeling lately? Fatigued? Experiencing swelling anywhere? Are you having shortness of breath or chest pains?" He asked these questions in quick succession while listening to her heartbeat with the stethoscope placed on her upper back.

"No, not any more than normal. You know I get a little winded going up and down the stairs, but I just take my time and sit down on a step if I have to. Thank goodness for ginger ale, because I keep indigestion. If I stand on my feet for long periods at a time, my ankles will swell, but that's about it," Mrs. Barnes said nonchalantly.

"Okay, well, please monitor these symptoms. I want you to head to the lab when you leave here, and I want to see you back in here next week. Ok?" Dr. Patterson said.

"Ok, doc. And the next time I come in here, I want the 411 on your date this weekend?"

"Date?"

"Yes. Date. You heard me correctly. You're giving me homework. Well, your assignment is to go out with a young lady between now and my next appointment. I want to hear all about it." Mrs. Barnes gave Dr. Patterson a hug and left the office.

* * *

Life as a social worker was not what Morgan expected. As she read case files, interviewed families and visited homes, she empathized with the kids and counted her blessings that God gave her such great parents. Coming to a stop, Morgan downed her lukewarm coffee before placing it in the cupholder and putting her car in reverse to parallel park. This morning, Morgan conducted a site visit for Tra'maine Edwards. He was a thirteen-year-old boy placed in foster care at the age of four after his father was locked up for aggravated assault and his mother abandoned him. Over the years, Tra'maine dreamt about being adopted, but after two unsuccessful adoption fairs, he gave up on the idea and instead got placed in one foster home after another. Three years ago, Morgan placed Tra'maine with an older couple who could never have children. This was the best foster home Tra'maine ever lived in. Tra'maine had himself a set of parents, the Stevensons, a golden retriever named Buddy, his own spacious bedroom, and something he had never experienced before—nightly family dinners. Things were great, until four months ago when Mrs. Stevenson was rushed to the hospital for shortness of breath and heart palpitations. She later died from a pulmonary embolism.

Mrs. Stevenson's sudden death took her husband and Tra'maine by surprise. They were both grieving the loss as best they could. However, Tra'maine's school contacted Child Protective Services for suspicion of neglect when he appeared to come to school in dirty clothes two weeks in a row. As Morgan walked up on the Stevenson's porch, she noticed a pile of newspapers that accumulated over the past couple of months lying scattered to the right of the door. Morgan took a deep breath and pushed the doorbell. After a few minutes, she pressed the doorbell again and could hear Mr. Stevenson making his way to the door. When he opened the door, he looked as if he had been sleeping. Once his eyes adjusted to Morgan standing there before him, he quickly rubbed his eyes and wiped the drool from his bottom lip.

"Uh, hi, Ms. Barnes. I wasn't expecting you," he said as he ushered Morgan to come inside.

"I know. Sorry to drop in on you unannounced, Mr. Stevenson, but I got a call from Tra'maine's school, and I needed to follow up."

As she walked through the front door, she was greeted with a musty smell of body odor, trash, and spoiled milk. Mr. Stevenson immediately began picking up dirty clothes that laid on the couch. "Can I get you something to drink?" he asked. "Did you say you got a call from Tra'maine's school? About what?"

"Mr. Stevenson, no thank you. I am fine. Can you please come have a seat?" As Morgan's eyes canvassed the house, she observed that the home that was once managed by a woman who took pride in maintaining a well-kept home was quickly turning into a pigsty. *What in the world happened?* Morgan thought. There were empty fast-food cartons and wrappers strewn across the dining room table, dishes piled up in the kitchen sink, and a film of dust layered the coffee table. Mr. Stevenson, a man in his early sixties, appeared to have aged nearly ten years since she last saw him. Usually closely shaven, he adorned a full peppered white beard.

"Mr. Stevenson, some of Tra'maine's teachers noticed that he has been wearing dirty clothes for weeks at a time."

"Dirty clothes? No." Mr. Stevenson refuted. "I mean, look, he is a teenage boy, and you know, if he is set on wearing something over and over again, who am I to stop him?" He rambled on.

Sitting directly across from Mr. Stevenson, who rocked in a Lazy Boy recliner, Morgan tapped his knee to force him to make eye contact with her. With a slow and calm tone, Morgan said, "Mr. Stevenson, I can only imagine what you are going through right now. You were married to Mrs. Stevenson, for what, twenty-plus years?" Just then, Morgan noticed a black and white photo on the end table of a young Mr. and Mrs. Stevenson laughing and holding hands while wearing roller skates.

"Thirty-four," he clarified.

"Thirty-four years? Wow! That's a lifetime. I'm assuming Mrs. Stevenson took care of the laundry."

Mr. Stevenson nodded while looking out the living room window.

"Okay. I can show you how to use the washing machine and dryer. It's simple. Do you have detergent?"

"I....I, I think so," Mr. Stevenson got up from the chair and walked to the laundry closet in the hallway off of the kitchen. Morgan followed him, and to her surprise, there were two full containers of liquid Tide, along with bleach and fabric softener. Morgan waited patiently as Mr. Stevenson rounded up dirty clothes from his and Tra'maine's rooms. Morgan explained how to sort the clothes by color and how to determine how much detergent to use. As she concluded her visit, she candidly shared, "Mr. Stevenson, I know you have a lot going on right now, but you need to get your house in order. There is obviously milk that needs to be thrown away and your trash hasn't been taken out in weeks. You have a minor, a son, living in this house and you need to tend to him and make sure he is living in a clean, flourishing environment. It's ok to ask for help. I can make some recommendations if you need them for a cleaning service or meal delivery service. But you have to do better."

"I know. I know. Tra'maine is a good kid. Marlene loved that boy as if he were her own flesh and blood."

"She did. And she is expecting you to do the same."

"Okay. Can you send me that information?"

"Of course."

* * *

Later that afternoon, Derek went to the hospital cafeteria to grab some lunch. He usually tried to miss the lunch crowd by eating around 11:30 a.m. This way he could snag his favorite seat in the dining hall that looked out toward the hustle and bustle of downtown. Unfortunately, today, his 11:00 a.m. appointment ran late, so by the time he made it to the cafeteria, seating was limited. After paying the cashier, Dr. Patterson, with a tray in hand, looked in the direction of his favorite seat and saw a group of twelve giggling interns, bunched together around three small square tables and engrossed in conversation. Slightly annoyed, he looked in the opposite direction only to find more tables full of medical professionals and family members of patients. Just when he was about to head to the to-go counter to wrap up his food, one of Dr. Patterson's new assistants, Lauren, waved her hand and motioned for him to come join her. Lauren, a twenty-six-year-old from a small town outside of Atlanta, came highly referred by Derek's mentor, Dr. Davis, who recently retired. She was short, round, and all made up. Her makeup was heavy, loud, and inappropriate for work. Specifically, her foundation was one shade too light for her chocolate brown complexion. She wore a glossy bright bubblegum pink lipstick that matched her manicure. Her fake jet-black hair was bone straight, parted down the middle of her forehead and rested slightly below her shoulders. She spoke with a heavy southern drawl.

Glad to see a familiar face and seating so he could eat his lunch, Dr. Patterson quickly made his way over to her table.

"Hi, Dr. Patterson. Please join me," Lauren said.

"Thanks, Lauren. You really saved me here. This placed is packed."

"Yeah, it is. I like it!" she said. "Dr. Davis' practice was small and near a residential area. I pretty much always brought my lunch. At least the cafeteria here has a vast selection of options."

"Good point. Although I am a man of habit and typically order the same thing every day."

They both looked down at Derek's boring tray of Caesar salad with shrimp. They laughed at the sight of it. "So how are you adjusting to the city? How is your housing situation?" Derek asked.

"Better. I was able to find a new roommate through a mutual friend from the ATL. I can't believe my first roommate stole five hundred dollars from me within the first seventy-two hours of me moving in," Lauren said.

"Yeah, that's crazy. When the receptionist, Nancy, told me what happened, I couldn't believe it. That's definitely not an accurate depiction of the people of my city, for sure."

"I know. I didn't take it personally. Just a serious wake-up call that's like, 'Lauren, you ain't in Eatonton anymore.' I mean, in hindsight, I should have known better than to leave a fat envelope full of cash with the word 'rent' on my dresser." Lauren shook her head in disbelief at such an elementary mistake. "When I got home that evening and saw that the door to my bedroom was left open, the envelop gone, and my roommate, Charity, had gone on a shopping spree, I nearly lost it. I felt so violated. I called my mom, and she was able to get in contact with a congregant whose family lived in Maryland. I packed up what little stuff I had and left that night."

"So, she didn't say anything to you?"

"She just kept going on about how it was her lucky day and how her boyfriend was going to flip when he saw her in all her new outfits."

"Did you call the police?" Dr. Patterson asked.

"I did, for what good that did me. It was my word against hers. I couldn't decipher whether the cop was in disbelief that I had five hundred dollars in cash or that I was dumb enough to leave it out. He took a police report and said that I could take her to court. After I left and calmed down, I spoke to my parents, and they said it was best I leave it be. It was only money. I mean, it was five hundred dollars, don't get me wrong, but it was a valuable lesson I learned the hard way."

"Wow. Yeah, some lesson. So, do you get along well with your new roommate?"

"Yeah, Keisha. She's cool. Howard alum or what I like to call, Ms. Socialite. She knows everybody and gets invited to all the events around town."

"Well, that's convenient. You get the inside connect to all the hottest parties in the DMV," Derek said.

"Yeah, she is definitely the life of the party. I am more of a homebody. She keeps saying she is going to break me out of my shell. She is supposed to be taking me to Young Flip's birthday party this weekend at the Stardom Club."

"You mean, Stadium Club?" Derek said.

"Yeah, that's it. The Stadium Club."

"You know that's a strip club, right?" Dr. Patterson asked.

"I know. Keisha said it's cool, though."

"Well, be safe. You know not to set your drink down, right?" Derek wasn't sure if Lauren's naivete carried over into social settings.

Lauren giggled, "Yes, Dr. Patterson. I know. I'll be fine."

The lunch hour went by pretty fast. Before long, Dr. Patterson and Lauren headed back to the office. As the day progressed, Derek couldn't get something Mrs. Barnes said out of his head, "Life is short…what's the point of it, if you don't have someone to go home to at night to share it with?" He laughed at the idea of her giving him "homework." Since giving up his playboy days more than five years ago, he had had only one serious relationship, which lasted three years and ended with his ex cheating on him with her personal trainer. In all honesty, he had no prospects. Bubblegum lipstick-wearing Lauren quickly popped in his head. *Absolutely not. Young. Dumb. And way too close to home,* he thought. Dr. Shelly Booker, the podiatrist, crossed his mind next. Shelly was a colleague he met at the hospital's holiday party last month. She was attractive, bi-racial—Asian and black—with long, bone-straight black hair. She was a transplant from somewhere on the west coast, and he sensed that she was in her late forties. Her skin was fair, and she had a round, flat face with freckles. During the party, Shelly approached Derek in a skin-tight, low-cut, red slip dress, insisting that he dance with her. Derek obliged, but after two songs, he excused himself, citing that he wasn't feeling well, but not before Dr. Booker slipped her business card in his pants pocket, with a whisper in his ear to call her sometime. There was something about her forwardness that Derek did not find attractive. Since they worked in different wings of the hospital, their paths had not crossed since. But now, with Mrs. Barnes all up in his head, he was wondering if his instinct was wrong; maybe he should give Shelly a chance. Before the workday ended, Derek found himself dialing Dr. Booker's office after searching the hospital directory for her number. By the second ring, Derek contemplated hanging up instead of leaving a message, but she answered.

"Hello. This is Dr. Booker. How may I help you?"

Clearing his throat, Derek responded, "Uh, yes, Dr. Booker, this is Dr. Patterson, Derek, from the holiday party. I hope I didn't catch you at a bad time."

"No, not at all. How are you? It's been a while; I thought you lost my number."

"No, no, not at all. I apologize for not reaching out sooner. I just had a lot going on. I was calling to see if you would be interested in grabbing coffee sometime?"

"Coffee?" Dr. Booker smirked as if insulted by the amateur invitation. "I don't drink coffee, but I do drink a nice glass of Chardonnay. How about we meet for drinks this Thursday after work. Let's say 6 at The Drone around the corner from the hospital?"

Derek wasn't sure what just happened. This woman completely hijacked the call and the invitation. He was leery of being around this inebriated woman who obviously was used to taking charge and getting what she wanted, but despite his better judgment, he responded, "Sure. Sounds good. I will see you then."

* * *

As she sat on the Metro train to meet Damian for drinks, Morgan tapped her Samsung cell phone to check the time—4:45 p.m. While she knew she should keep her expectations low, it was hard for her not to anticipate that maybe he could be the one. It was a stretch, but at the rate she was going, she would still be single by forty-three. She calculated in her head that it would take a year of dating to become engaged and at least a year to plan a wedding. With forty-one approaching and no prospects in sight, forty-three would be here before she knew it. Despite the possibility of being barren, Morgan couldn't help but fantasize about what she would tell her future kids about the day that she and their dad went on their first date. *God, please let Damian have potential. This wait is exhausting. It's been two years. Actually, it's been 837 days, but who's counting? I've been faithful. Haven't I been faithful, God? Please give me a sign,* Morgan thought. She thought back to his Bumble profile and continued her internal conversation with the Lord: *Damian doesn't even have to be the one. He can just be Mr. Right Now. At this point, I'll take that. God, I don't even remember what a man smells like. Is it so wrong to want to be held by man? Well, if that is asking too much, I will settle for holding hands or even locking arms while walking down the street. Come on, Jesus, hook a sista up. I need a sign of hope to hold on.*

As Morgan approached the escalators to exit the

Metro at 4:55 p.m., Damian texted her to say that the restaurant didn't open until 5:30 p.m. Strike one. The man didn't do his research before suggesting a meeting location? *Come on, dude, really?* The next text said that he was running behind because the train was delayed. Strike two. *Man, you don't keep a woman waiting. Well, there goes the possibility of a Mr. Right for Now.* Instead of turning around and hopping back on the Metro to go home, she surrendered to her appetite and made her way to Ben's Chili Bowl. She was going to be flexible and less rigid in this new year, which in turn would result in more dates. *Besides, worst-case scenario, a girl could get some good ole fries and veggie chili,* Morgan thought, chuckling to herself.

Ben's was packed as usual. The line extended to the door, so she excused herself all the way to the first empty booth she found. Morgan intentionally sat on the side of the booth facing the front door so she could observe Damian walking in. Although he hid behind his baseball cap in all of his online photos, Morgan could make out that he had a nice smile and dimples. Twenty minutes later, the door opened, and a Hispanic man entered. His looks reminded Morgan of the handsome actor, Jay Hernandez. As she observed further, he was cheesing from ear to ear as he held the door for what appeared to be his lady, a cute Latina with a tiny waist and a video vixen booty. As she passed by him, he couldn't help but follow her behind, literally. *What's the fascination men have with butts?* Morgan asked herself. Behind him entered a short, round black guy wearing a baseball cap.

Immediately Morgan's anticipation deflated. *Short and stumpy? Really, God?* She replayed her ask of God and realized she didn't specify physicality. *Shoot.* While engrossed in this conversation in her head, Morgan failed to notice the short, round guy standing in front of her at the table and extending his hand to her. Internally, Morgan reminded herself to be nice. She tried to be mindful of her facial expression, but she wasn't sure it was working. She finally focused, shook his hand and introduced herself. "Hi, nice to meet you. In-person, that is."

As Damian took his seat in the booth, he removed his Nationals baseball cap, which was fresh with no crease, to reveal a severely receding hairline. Morgan tried not to stare and nonchalantly check him out - *Height: five foot four at best; weight—two hundred pounds with a beer belly, and come on, dude—it's time to go bald already.* He wore wrinkled khakis and a short-sleeve polo shirt. His facial hair needed some attention. There was stubble above his lip as if he were a thirteen-year-old boy going through puberty. His beard was a different story. It was patchy—thick and prominent in some parts and not so much in others. It didn't appear he shaved anytime that week. *Did this man forget that he asked me out today? What happened to dress to impress? Was I not worth that? Geez.* Strike three.

Damian apologized for being late and offered to place their order. Ten minutes later, he came back to the table with fountain drinks in hand. He quickly jumped into interrogation mode, which Morgan didn't really appreciate. The first question out of the gate was, "Why are you single? What's wrong with you?" He tried to finesse the question by saying it appeared she was too good to be true. Morgan found the question insulting. Why must something be wrong with her because she was single? Is something wrong with her because she has standards? Is something wrong with her because she's not desperate enough to settle for mediocrity? And furthermore, who did this guy think he was even to ask such a question? For the life of her, she didn't understand why men who look like dirt were as confident as Denzel Washington, but women who could win Miss America had little to no confidence at all. Either way, Morgan tried to change the subject and not get upset since she was still waiting for her food. It was apparent that her chili fries were going to be the highlight of her evening.

Morgan proceeded to ask him what he did this past weekend. He shared that he took his son to a Wizards game. "Wait—what? You have a son?" she asked.

"Yeah. He's six," Damian said.

"Oh, that's cool. But when we were talking earlier, I asked if you had kids and you said 'no.' Why lie?" Morgan asked.

"Oh, naww. I never said that. It never came up in conversation. You must be getting me confused with someone else," Damian responded, shrugging it off.

"Yeah, we did. We were…" Just as she was about to recall the details of their conversation earlier, the food arrived. The waiter interrupted the conversation to ask if Morgan was Ethiopian, to which she responded, "no." They chatted for about five minutes about how she gets asked that question all the time by fellow Ethiopians. It must be her high cheekbones and red undertones. Meanwhile, Damian scarfed down his fries and burger.

When the waiter left, Damian jumped up from the booth, "Will you excuse me for a second? I have to use the bathroom." While he was gone, she began to go through their conversation via text messages. It was bothering her that she was almost one hundred percent certain that this man said he didn't have any kids, yet now he was trying to make her seem as if it were a figment of her imagination. Why lie about not having kids? What kind of man disowns his kids for a woman? Strike—she'd lost count. As she was scrolling through her text messages, she found it.

12/22/18 8:52pm

Morgan: "So how many kids do you have?"

Damian: "None, and you?"

"This negro right here," Morgan said underneath her breath, shaking her head.

Damian returned to the booth but didn't sit down. He actually looked flustered. "Hey, I'm sorry, but I got to go. I'm about to miss my train. The last train leaves Union Station in 15 minutes." He grabbed her hand and squeezed it. "Thanks for a great evening. Let's do this again sometime." He quickly went in for a half-hug, then turned and walked out. The abrupt ending to their date caught Morgan completely off guard. Just when she was about to tell him about himself, he dipped.

Just then, the waiter came over and handed Morgan the bill. "What's this?" she asked, confused.

"Oh, it's your bill. The guy's card didn't go through. He said you would pay the bill after you ate."

WTF?!? Strike one hundred!

Morgan replayed the date on her train ride home. She was trying her best to embrace the fact that everything works together for her good, but she couldn't see how this situation was anything other than a waste of time, energy, and a cute outfit. God was definitely in the neighborhood. He saved Momma from the carjacking, but why couldn't He just bring her a man already? Wasn't two years of singleness long enough? She wasn't getting any younger. Maybe He really was preparing her for a life of solitude. If He was, at least she didn't have to worry about someone dining and dashing on her if she was alone. Although she would never admit it, she wished God would just give her a sign if she were meant to be single forever, that way she wouldn't get her hopes up for something real and forever. Thinking back on today's date, she thought to herself, *Why me Jesus? Thanks for nothing.*

Chapter 3

At 6:00 p.m. on the dot, Derek entered The Drone, a quaint, swanky upscale bar tucked between an abandoned storefront and a Boli's pizza joint. From the outside, the average person would assume that the bar was a dive because of its location, but it was the perfect guise for the who's who of DC—politicians, influencers, lobbyists, and the like—to frequent every night of the week. The entrance was extra dark, but as Derek passed through some heavy black drapes, light emerged and he was greeted by a maître d' and the sound of a bass guitarist going to town.

"Good Evening, I am meeting Dr. Shelly Booker. There should be a 6 o'clock reservation." Derek looked around, taking in his surroundings. The establishment was packed with men and women in power suits. All were engrossed in deep conversations. Most people were coupled off, but there were a few in groups. No one was paying any attention to the four-piece band, which consisted of a bass player, a saxophonist, a pianist, and a drummer. They were playing a song that Derek had heard before but he couldn't put his finger on who performed it. He made a mental note that this was definitely a place that he should check out again. He loved live music.

Without hesitation, the maître d' responded, "Oh, yes. She has been waiting for you. Please follow me. I will take you to her booth." The gentleman stressed the word "her," as if her name was etched in the booth. Dressed in a white button-down and black bowtie, the frail Caucasian man walked Derek over to a secluded booth off to the right of the stage where the band played. As he approached the table, he felt Shelly looking him up and down. *Did she just lick her lips? Tell me this woman did not just lick her lips? Shaking his head, he thought, I'ma need an exit strategy.*

"Hi. I hope I didn't have you waiting too long." Derek leaned in to hug Shelly.

"Long enough, but that's ok."

Derek sat across from Dr. Booker while nonchalantly checking his watch - 6:03 p.m.

"I took the liberty of ordering you a drink. You look like a bourbon man." She slid a glass of brown liquor closer to him.

Really, lady? Derek slid the drink to the side and motioned for the waiter to come over.

"Thanks, but I don't really drink," Derek said to Shelly before turning to the waiter and ordering an iced tea.

Chuckling and pointing to her nearly empty glass of wine, Shelly said, "You aren't about to make me drink alone, are you? That's not very gentleman-like. What are you—a recovering alcoholic or something?"

"I am."

Dr. Booker's eyes got big. "Oh, I am so sorry. I didn't know." Just then, the waiter returned with Derek's cold beverage, and she immediately handed the waiter the bourbon she ordered. Then she swiped her wine glass from in front of Derek.

"Shelly, it's fine. I am not an alcoholic per se. Alcoholism runs in my family, and, well, I've had my fair share of benders in my heyday that in my older years, I've decided alcohol isn't for me. But please don't let me stop you from enjoying your Chardonnay. Please."

Shelly grabbed her glass and guzzled down the

remaining wine as if to ease her nerves from Derek's big reveal. Changing the subject, she leaned in across the table, stared Derek in the eyes, and batted her lashes. "You know, it's about time that you asked me out. Do you remember what you said to me at the holiday party?"

Are you serious? Do I remember what I said? No. I remember how I was trying to leave you on the dance floor but you kept pulling me in closer. This was a big mistake. Man, never do this again. "Ah, no, sorry, I don't. What did I say?" Derek tried his best to seem interested in this line of conversation.

"You said, 'you are working that red dress.' You remember, I was wearing that red silk dress that was cut down to here," she motioned slowly with her finger down her sternum to right above her navel.

I doubt those were my exact words, Derek thought, *but I'm sure I was just being polite.*

Shelly continued, "And I was thinking, that's not the only thing I'd like to work." Just then, her size seven Christian Louboutin red bottoms began to slide up Derek's inseam.

"Wow. Shelly, please stop." Shelly laughed while her foot continued to navigate north. With bass in his voice, Derek demanded, "Stop!"

Shelly jumped, and her foot retreated to the floor. "Shelly, I asked you out for coffee because I was thinking that maybe I misread you when we first met. But thank you for confirming that I didn't. This," Derek pointed to her and then back to himself, "isn't going to happen." Shaking his head, he said, "Have a good evening and be safe getting home." And with that Derek got up, pulled out his wallet, placed a hundred-dollar bill on the table, and walked out of The Drone with his broad shoulders back and head held high.

* * *

Despite missing day one of Reclaiming Your Sexy, Morgan was proud that she consistently made it to the gym at least three days a week for the past two months. She didn't realize how much she'd enjoy the spinning and HIIT classes. They made her feel strong and powerful.

Instead of focusing on her singleness, she decided to focus on her mentorship program. Once a month, Morgan, Renee, and Stacy would host "Real Talk," an interactive session with teen girls, ages ten to eighteen, to discuss a range of topics from bullying, sex, and politics to peer pressure and more. Morgan, with her exceptional planning skills, worked it out with her pastor, Pastor Johnson, to host the one-Saturday-a-month sessions in the rectory of the First Baptist Church of Gwynn Oaks. To sweeten the deal, the seniors in the hospitality ministry would prepare a warm breakfast for the girls, which always guaranteed a good turnout.

The arrangement with Pastor Johnson required Morgan to take the lead on organizing the church's annual bake-off. Nearly twelve years ago, the church started a bake sale where all the congregants would make pies, cakes, and every other diabetes-causing baked good and sell them quarterly to raise money for the church. About six years ago, Morgan suggested to Pastor Johnson that the church turn the bake sale into a bake-off contest similar to MasterChef. With a bake-off, they could include several local churches in the area, which positively influenced the community and raised more money, not only for the winning church but also for the first runner up. Pastor Johnson was a little hesitant the first year, but after the First Baptist Church of Gwynn Oaks received significant media coverage and saw an increase in membership, he looked forward to the annual bake-off. The concept was simple—participating local churches would put together teams of two, secure a coach by way of a professional chef, and make three original desserts within three hours, based on a list of undisclosed ingredients. Every year, local churches would alternate hosting the event, which brought celebrities and media coverage. In turn, the ticket sales helped raise money for the winning churches. To some, this may not have seemed like a fair deal, but Gwynn Oaks was the reigning champion of the bake-off for four years running. Pastor Johnson took his title very seriously. This year, it was Gwynn Oaks' turn to host, and Morgan promised to get celebrity chef Bart Vimeano of the hit TV show, *Flour King*.

Morgan looked forward to the Saturday sessions with the girls, many of whom were foster kids that she previously placed in foster homes. Some people in her office concluded that Morgan was vying for a promotion and only came up with the idea to impress her supervisor. In reality, Morgan saw this as a way to give back. Her mother instilled so much love and knowledge in her that she couldn't keep it to herself. Besides, Morgan learned so much from these young girls—from their outlook on life to their perseverance, despite some of the tragedies in their home lives. These girls were as much a blessing to her as she was to them. She was hoping her initiative would rub off on some of the guys in the office to host a similar series for young boys, but it hadn't caught on yet.

This Saturday's topic, entitled, "Removing the Mask," was on self-esteem. Morgan purchased a full-length mirror from Target and strategically placed it in the middle of the room with a metal folding chair facing the mirror. As the girls arrived, Renee handed out index cards with numbers poorly written on them. Renee was supposed to have prepared the index cards before she arrived, but in true Renee fashion, she waited until ten minutes before the girls arrived to write the numbers out. Renee was smart as a whip and dependable, but she lacked timeliness and organizational skills. *At least she remembered to purchase the index cards,* Morgan thought. Stacy stood opposite Renee and directed the girls to go fix their plates. Morgan loved Stacy's outgoing, in-your-face personality. The girls could easily relate to Stacy. The only problem was making sure Stacy didn't snatch up any of the girls if they became disrespectful. Stacy would have no parts of that. Morgan strolled by the dining tables to greet the girls with her infamous bear hug. After twenty minutes of eating and chit-chatting, Morgan began her discussion.

"All right, ladies, let's gather 'round. Can anyone tell me what today's topic is?" Morgan asked.

"Removing the Mask," one girl answered.

"Self-esteem," a few girls blurted out.

"Right. We are here to have a real conversation with ourselves about who we see when we look in the mirror. How many of you know just how important it is to like who you see in the mirror?" Morgan asked.

A few girls dropped their heads; others giggled. Cedré, a fifteen-year-old girl with really bad acne and braces, raised her hand and said, "Ms. Morgan, I know I'm supposed to say it's important, but I don't get it. In life, everybody else's opinions matter. Look at social media—likes are important. If they weren't, no one would post."

Cedré wasn't known for being outspoken. The fact that she had the courage to vocalize a valid point impressed Morgan. "Cedré, that's a good point. Can you do me a favor and come have a seat right here?" Morgan asked, pointing to the chair in the middle of the room. With some reservation, Cedré stood up and walked over to the seat facing the mirror. "Now, I am going to ask you a series of questions, and I want you to continue looking at yourself in the mirror, even when responding to my questions. Okay?"

Cedré nodded.

"Cedré, are you smart?" Morgan asked.

"Yeah?" Cedré said.

"I can't hear you."

"Yes," Cedré said more assertively.

"Are you sure you are smart?"

The girls started to giggle. Cedré looked around the room.

"Keep looking at the mirror," Morgan said, and then she asked the question again. "Are you sure you are smart?"

Cedré responded with some attitude. "Yes, I am sure. I'm smart. I got straight A's last quarter."

Morgan tried to hide her smile at how Cedré confidently responded to the question. "So if I said, you're dumb, how does that influence your answer?"

"It don't. You're not in school with me; you don't know what kind of grades I get." Cedré started to look at Morgan but remembered she was supposed to be looking at herself in the mirror, so she quickly spun around to face the mirror again fully.

"Right. So what you are saying is that your own opinion of yourself outweighs that of others because at the end of the day, the only person that truly knows you, is you. Is that right?"

"Yeah!" Cedré said emphatically.

Turning to the rest of the girls in the room, Morgan

said, "You see, at the end of the day, we have to know who we are and like who we are because the world is mean. There are going to be a ton of people in this world who don't like you for one reason or another, who are going to lie on you, who don't want to see you succeed. But if you believe in yourself, if you love yourself, if you know your potential, you can do just about anything."

While Cedré sat in the chair, Morgan made her identify three things that she liked about herself. Morgan then asked the girls in the room to shout out things that they liked about Cedré. Cedré then decided if she agreed with the comments. Unbeknownst to the girls, Stacy was in the back of the room, taking notes of all the affirmations that the girls said about Cedré. Right before Cedré was about to get up from the seat, Morgan handed her Stacy's notes and asked her to read them in front of the mirror.

Cedré briefly examined the sheet of paper and smiled. Looking at herself in the mirror, she read off the sheet of paper, "I am smart. I like that. I'm gonna have straight teeth in a month when these braces come off. I am a good big sister. I'm a good listener. I dance well. I can do hair. I give good advice. I'm funny." Cedré started giggling.

"What's so funny?" Morgan asked inquisitively.

"I got it going on." Everyone in the room burst out laughing, including Morgan.

"Yes, yes you do. And don't forget that. No matter what anybody says about you, I want you to continue to remind yourself of all of your good qualities."

One by one, the girls took a seat in the chair and participated in the exercise. By the time they read their sheets of paper, they were sitting a little taller and reading with attitude. Morgan challenged the girls to go home and recite their affirmations in a mirror each night before going to sleep.

* * *

As Morgan brushed her teeth that night, she began to examine herself in the mirror. She was exhausted but completely satisfied with the day's activities. What did she like about herself? She never posed the question before. As her eyes began to scan her body from head to toe, she realized that she could easily identify what she didn't like about herself. It took her a minute to think of something that she liked. She quickly wiped the toothpaste from her mouth, ran to her room to grab her phone, and opened the Notes app. While gazing in the mirror, her eyes first scanned her face. It was oval, with high cheekbones, a long nose, and full lips. Her thick, dark brown, shoulder-length natural curls rested on top of her head in a pineapple. She began to type, "I like my clavicle. And my nose. I like my height—five foot six, not too tall or too short. I like my even skin complexion. I'm a good daughter. I pray I'm a good mentor after today." Morgan began to think about what Renee and Stacy would say about her. She agreed, "I like my small waist. I'm funny. I'm a good friend… protective. I'm kind and giving. I'm good at my job. I'm smart." She began to think about her mom. "I am loved."

That night, Morgan committed to reading her list in the mirror before bed. She didn't want to be a hypocrite, telling the girls to "do what I say, not what I do." She saw where she needed to work on her own self-esteem. Instead of focusing on men or the lack thereof, in addition to getting right with God, she needed to focus on herself. She really was going to be forty-one and fabulous this year, out here living her best life. *God, help me to love me - all of me. And help me work on being the best version of myself. Amen.*

* * *

It was a rather warm Saturday evening in March; temperatures reached the high fifties after two weeks of blistering cold weather. Derek just arrived home from the gym. This was the first Saturday in three weeks that he didn't have to work. Between performing emergency surgeries, subbing for colleagues, and taking care of his monthly on-call responsibilities, Dr. Patterson forgot what it was like to sleep in late on a Saturday, run errands, head to the gym, return home, and catch up on basketball. He was looking forward to doing a little bit of nothing except lounging around the house, ordering some takeout and enjoying the games.

Although he knew it didn't have much nutritional value, he couldn't help but order his favorite, chicken wings with mambo sauce and fries, from the China Sub joint around the corner from his place. With a full belly and the soothing sound of Golden State destroying the Lakers blaring from his seventy-two-inch ultra-flatscreen television, Derek dozed off. He woke to the sound of his cell phone ringing. It took him a minute to realize the sound that awakened him was his phone and then another minute to find it between the cushions of his oversized bisectional couch. He missed the call. The room was pitch black except for the light from the television. He looked at his phone: 3:00 a.m. Hmm. *I guess someone butt-dialed me. I know it ain't no booty call.* Derek shrugged. Just then, the phone rang again.

"Hello?"

"Dr. Patterson, help me!" A drunk girl cried.

"What? Who is this? What's going on?" Derek demanded.

"Dr. Patterson, it's me, Lauren. Can you come get me? Keisha left me at Stadium to go to some after-party with Young Flip and n'em. I don't have a way of getting home," Lauren begged.

Dr. Patterson politely said, "I'll call you an Uber. Sit tight, and I'll call you back once I've ordered..."

"No. I need you to come get me. I... I.... uhh, I don't have my keys to get into my place. I'm new in town and don't know many people. I thought I could crash with you for the night. I drank too much, and these guys are staring at me. I'm scared. Please hurry," Lauren said and quickly hung up the phone.

"Hello? Hello? Helllllooo?" *No this girl did not just hang up the phone.* Dr. Patterson wasn't new to the damsel in distress routine, but why Lauren would jeopardize her career to try him, he couldn't for the life of him figure out. Was she young and naïve? Yes. Was she new to the area? Yes. Is it possible that she drank too much, trying to keep up with her peers? Yes. But something about the way she insisted on him coming to get her and then quickly hanging up the phone certainly felt like entrapment. Being the gentleman his mother taught him to be, Derek got up from the couch, wiped his face, grabbed his keys, and headed for the door.

The club wasn't in the best part of town. It was in the warehouse district, which once flourished, but now overflowed with abandoned buildings, making it an ideal spot for crime, drugs, and prostitution. As Derek pulled up on the block where the club stood, he saw a line of people still waiting to get in the club at 3:30 a.m. Two burly bouncers stood at the club entrance patting people down and looking in purses with flashlights. *Dang, I don't miss those days,* he thought to himself. Dr. Patterson canvassed the line to see if he could make out Lauren.

As his eyes scanned the line, he caught something in his peripheral—a group of about four guys in the parking lot at the side of the club. These guys were encircling something or someone. Derek had a bad hunch, so he quickly parked his car. Jumping out, he popped his trunk to see if there was any semblance of a weapon he could use in case things got rough. There was only one of him and at least four guys in the parking lot. He took a deep breath and reassessed the situation. *I am not going to jail for this girl. And I'm definitely not about to damage these hands for this chick. Lord, cover me.* He closed his trunk, empty-handed.

Derek hesitantly but assuredly approached the group of guys in the parking lot. He tried his best to identify physical characteristics in case he had to point anyone out in a police lineup. Out of reflex, his hand began to flex and ball into a fist, just in case he needed to swing on them. He couldn't believe he found himself in this situation.

"Aye. What's good?" Dr. Patterson said with authority as he approached the group of guys.

The guys first looked up at Derek, and then at one another, like "who is this dude?" Derek could see that behind the guys sat a girl, legs spread apart, either unconscious or sleeping, shoes off, and resting her head on a green dumpster. The smallest guy in the group, turned to Derek and asked, "Can we help you?" as the other guys stepped closer to Derek to intimidate him to retreat. But there was no backing down now. Derek stood his ground and placed his hand in his back pocket as if to pull out a weapon. From the outside looking in, he looked as calm as a cucumber, but he was sweating bullets inside. *Lord, please don't let me die trying to help this dumb girl. I am not trying to be on the ten o'clock news as the doctor found dead in the strip club parking lot.*

Derek's nonchalant disposition caught at least one of the guys off guard. He didn't seem to be phased that the odds were four to one. Dr. Patterson heard one of the men whisper to another, "Yo, I think he's 5.0. Let's bounce."

As Derek got closer, he confirmed it was Lauren on the ground. Her skimpy black spaghetti strap spandex dress rode up her thick thighs, exposing her Spanx as she lay there not moving. He prayed she was asleep and that he got there in time. He couldn't fathom how or why she would put herself in this situation. Derek finally responded to the petite dude's question, "Yeah, actually, you can." He broke through the group and leaned in to check Lauren's pulse. She was breathing. He turned to the little man, "She's with me. Thanks for looking after her until I arrived." As the group dispersed, Derek shook Lauren's face. "Lauren, wake up. Can you hear me? Lauren?"

Blinking to make out what was in front of her, Lauren opened her eyes. She started to cheese, "You came! I knew you would save me."

"What are you doing out here in the parking lot? Do you know what almost happened to you?" Dr. Patterson asked.

"I was tired. I needed to lie down," Lauren said.

Dr. Patterson shook his head in disbelief, helped Lauren to her feet, and escorted her to his car. *What is wrong with this girl?* It was obvious that Lauren was indeed drunk. There was no way someone would go to this extreme of pretending to be drunk, resting on a filthy dumpster, and almost getting assaulted to pull off a damsel in distress act. In the car, Dr. Patterson handed Lauren a bottle of water. "Drink!" he shouted. Lauren took a few sips and put the bottle down. Dr. Patterson insisted,

"Finish the bottle. You are dehydrated." As Derek drove, he got more and more upset. "What were you thinking? Do you know what could have happened if I showed up three minutes later?"

"I know. It was dumb. I know I'm going to feel like crap in the morning. I should take some aspirin tonight, huh?" Lauren asked. It was clear that she didn't get the magnitude of the situation.

"Lauren, you got to do better. You ain't in the country no more. There are serious repercussions for your actions, and I can't be your Kevin Costner to save you from every stupid decision you make." Just then, Derek pulled up to the Courtyard Marriott and parked the car.

Lauren looked around then looked at Dr. Patterson, confused. "I thought we were going back to your house?" Lauren asked. She leaned in toward Dr. Patterson's face and placed her hand on his inner thigh and squeezed it.

"Woman, get the hell out of my car!" Derek snapped. "You have lost your everlasting mind. Go inside. I reserved a room in your name. Get some sleep and take Monday off."

Lauren's eyes widened, then she quickly got out of the car and headed for the hotel's revolving doors. With her black stilettos in hand, tugging to pull down her dress as she walked, she turned back to see if Dr. Patterson waited for her to enter the hotel, but she only saw his taillights as he sped off.

* * *

On Tuesday morning, as Mrs. Barnes sat patiently in the waiting room to see Dr. Patterson, her spirit felt something wasn't right in the office. When she greeted Nancy, the receptionist, with an Easter basket full of candy, all she got was, "Thanks, Mrs. Barnes. Please have a seat; the doctor will be with you shortly." There was no small talk like normal.

When Mrs. Barnes went back to the examination room, Lauren barely spoke as she took her vitals. When Mrs. Barnes asked if everything was okay, Lauren mumbled that she was fine. As soon as Dr. Patterson walked into the room, Lauren's head dropped, and she quickly finished up her notes and left the room. Before he could even greet Mrs. Barnes, she blurted out, "Okay. What's going on Doc? And don't tell me nothing 'cause all of you'll are in a funk and it's messing with my vibe. I don't appreciate it." Mrs. Barnes tried to make light of the situation, but Dr. Patterson didn't laugh. Instead, he sat on the stool by the computer screen and scooted closer to her.

"Mrs. Barnes, it is rather unprofessional of me to disclose office business, but I could use your advice."

"Sure, baby. What's up?" Mrs. Barnes asked.

"I am contemplating firing one of my employees over an inappropriate act."

"Now look, I told you to go out there and date, but I never told you to hook up with Lauren, one of your employees," Mrs. Barnes said. "She's a baby, for goodness sake."

"What? No. Why would you...? How did you guess it was Lauren?"

"Doc, I'm seventy-two years old. There ain't much you can pull over on me, and besides, Stevie Wonder could have seen the tension in the air when you walked in here. Now, I ain't no lawyer, but you don't want to get caught up in no sexual harassment lawsuit because she denied your advances."

"No. Mrs. Barnes, that's just it. She assaulted me," Dr. Patterson admitted as he lowered his eyes.

"Say what?"

Dr. Patterson proceeded to walk Mrs. Barnes through the events of the previous Saturday evening. When he finished, Mrs. Barnes reflected on the young lady who took her vitals, who seemed so sweet.

"So, what's your dilemma? Because from where I stand, it's clear what you need to do."

"I'm torn because I told Dr. Davis that I would give this girl a job, and my word means something."

"That's admirable. But I would like to point out that you kept your word. You gave Lauren a job. You have no control over her actions to get herself fired. Look, I can't tell you what to do, but what I can tell you is that you need to accept people for who they show you they are, not who they say they are. Actions speak louder than words. You hear me?"

"Yes, ma'am," Dr. Patterson said.

"Not only that, but you are talking about your finances, your livelihood, and your reputation. You've worked too hard to let some young, thirsty thot jeopardize that."

Derek laughed, "Thot? Mrs. Barnes, really?"

"What? You think just because I'm old, I don't know slang. Don't underestimate me. I'm down," Mrs. Barnes said with a chuckle. "I don't know why it's so hard for y'all to find good, quality people. My daughter, Morgan, went on a date recently, and the man came up with some excuse to leave early and stiffed her with the bill!"

"Are you serious? Guys still do that at our age?" Dr. Patterson asked.

"You know, times have truly changed. It's hard to meet people nowadays who are genuine and not trying to live the life of reality stars. Relationship bars are set so low. Women are content being side pieces. Men are looking for mothers to take care of them. I mean, don't

61

get me wrong, that's been going on since the beginning of time, but it didn't seem like the norm like it does now. I remember when I met my husband at a rent party. Y'all young folks don't know anything about that. We'd all pay fifty cents to get into the party, and that money helped us pay each other's bills. Anyhow, we arrived at the party at the same time, but when I went to pay, Donald looked at me and said, 'Now, I know you don't think I'm going to let you pay, now do you?' And from there, we danced and talked all night long. That man courted me. He got to know my family and me. We took the steps necessary to determine if God was calling us to be one. And in the end, we heard that indeed He was."

"That sounds pretty amazing, Mrs. Barnes. That's what I want," Dr. Patterson said.

"And that's what I want for you and my Morgan. You two are so deserving. It's a shame it's so hard to find quality people."

As Dr. Patterson went over Mrs. Barnes's lab results, Mrs. Barnes began to think about Morgan and Dr. Patterson as a potential couple. She wasn't sure why the thought never crossed her mind before. *Better late than never,* she thought. As the session wrapped up, Mrs. Barnes asked, "So Doc, when you were in the Dominican Republic, did you dance any?"

"Did I? I couldn't get enough salsa and bachata. Why do you ask?"

"Morgan and her friends go salsa dancing every third Thursday of the month. Thought you might like to join her." Mrs. Barnes said.

"Mrs. Barnes, are you asking me to take your daughter out on a date?" Dr. Patterson asked.

"I'm asking you to clean up this mess at work, and once you have your stuff together, if you are inclined to want to go out with a real woman, who happens to share your love for dance, then be at my house next Thursday at 7:30 p.m.," Mrs. Barnes said with a wink, and she gave Dr. Patterson her burly goodbye hug.

As Mrs. Barnes opened the door to leave, Dr. Patterson asked, "What should I bring?"

"Orchids. Morgan loves orchids. Oh, and Doc? You aren't allowed to talk about my medical condition because of HIPPA, right?" Mrs. Barnes asked.

"Right," Derek said.

"Okay, good. See you next week, sweetie."

* * *

The smell of greasy fried chicken, smoked turkey neck and collard greens permeated the ventilation system, making its way into Morgan's room. It was a Thursday evening, and it was unlike Mrs. Barnes to fix such a heavy meal that typically was left for Sundays, but all Morgan knew was that there was no time to eat because she was getting ready to go out. Once a month, Morgan and her girlfriends would meet up at the local lounge El Fuego for salsa. Morgan and Renee loved to dance, while Stacy loved to flirt for free drinks. Though her dance skills diminished some since college, Morgan could still carry her own in all things salsa, merengue, and bachata.

In order to get into the club for free, ladies had to come correct. So, Morgan struggled with finding something to wear that was cute, yet comfortable. As she tried on yet another dress, the doorbell rang. And then it rang again.

"Momma, there's someone at the door!" Morgan yelled from her bedroom.

"Morgan, can you please get it? My hands are covered in flour."

"Really?" Morgan mumbled to herself as she ran down the stairs in her bare feet with a dress on that made her feel that she would be shot dead if seen wearing it in public. She peeked through the front door peephole and recognized Mr. Thomas patiently waiting on the porch. She opened the door. "Hi, Mr. Thomas. Come on in."

Mr. Thomas was an old school cat—charming and suave. He arrived with flowers and immediately removed his hat upon entering the house. "Good evening, Morgan. Don't you look beautiful this evening? You going out?"

"Why, thank you. I sure am," Morgan said as she spun around to make sure he got a good look at her dress. "Momma's in the kitchen," she said as she dashed back upstairs to change. Almost convinced she had nothing to wear, Morgan remembered the pencil skirt sticking out of her hamper. She thought to herself, *I can get one more wear out of this before I take it to the cleaners.* After another fifteen minutes, she was nearly ready in the black pencil skirt and mauve top that buttoned in the back. Stacy was with her when she bought the top and schooled her about the proper way to wear it.

"Girl, don't button the entire top, you are only supposed to button like the first two. It's okay to expose your bra. That's sexy."

Tonight Morgan buttoned the first six which covered her bra and then some. She left the last three buttons undone. *Stace, that's all I can give them tonight,* Morgan thought as she snickered to herself while putting on the finishing touches of lip gloss and hoop earrings. Just then, the doorbell rang again. This time Morgan didn't have to ask if her mother was going to get it because she knew she wasn't. She was too busy entertaining Mr. Thomas. Morgan tiptoed down the steps in her two-and-a-half-inch T-strap heels (anything higher and Morgan would fall completely on her face). She peered through the peephole but didn't recognize the person on the other side of the door. She yelled to the kitchen, "Momma, are you expecting someone else for dinner?"

Mrs. Barnes poked her head out the kitchen, "Oh, yeah baby, Dr. Patterson."

Morgan opened the door and there stood a real-life six-foot-tall Hershey chocolate bar in a baby blue casual button-down shirt and slacks. It took her a second to compose her thoughts. He really did take her breath away. "Hi. You must be Dr. Patterson."

"Yes, I am, but please call me Derek," he said, showing all of his pearly whites with a beautiful, wide grin and dimples to match.

Dang Momma, Morgan thought, *where have you been keeping this man? Morgan, chill out. Don't overthink it. Whatever you do, don't say anything dumb.* "Well, Derek, come on in. My mom is in the kitchen."

He walked through the doorway and turned and handed Morgan a potted orchid. "This is for you." Derek was naturally observant, so it didn't take long for him to assess the woman that stood before him. *Wow, Mrs. Barnes, you failed to mention that your daughter was gorgeous and THICK! Why am I just now getting an invite?*

Confused, she accepted the orchid, "Thank you," she said. Orchids were her favorite flower, and the only way he could have possibly known was if Mrs. Barnes blabbed. This moment reeked of her mother trying to play matchmaker.

Just in the nick of time, Mrs. Barnes turned the corner and grabbed Derek. "Hi, Suga. Thanks for coming."

Suga? Please don't tell me that Momma landed this fine young man. Morgan knew she could pull men, but really? There was no need to be Stella out this camp because she and her groove were doing just fine.

"Thanks for having me, Mrs. Barnes. These are for you." Derek handed Mrs. Barnes a bouquet of yellow roses.

As Morgan stood there dumbfounded, her mother offered up, "Morgan, I invited Derek to dinner. Can you join us this evening?"

After forty years, Mrs. Barnes and Morgan's communication extended beyond verbal interaction to in-depth conversations held just with their eyes. Anyone else looking at them would not know the meaning behind the looks. "Really?" Morgan said, raising her right eyebrow. "Well, I wish you would have told me earlier because I have plans this evening. You know, like I do, every third Thursday of the month?" Morgan overtly gave her mom the evil eye combined with the "I know what game you are trying to pull, and it's not going to work" look.

"Oh, that's right. I guess I got my days mixed up. But you normally go out around eight o'clock and it's only 7:30. You can oblige us for a half-hour, can't you? Especially seeing that dinner is ready." Mrs. Barnes said with a grin.

Dang, she's good.

Everyone headed to the dining room, where Mrs. Barnes prepared a feast of fried chicken, mashed potatoes, collard greens, and homemade rolls. The table was set for four, and she even used the good china—the ones they only brought out during the holidays.

Mr. Thomas got caught up in the news which played on the television in the kitchen. "Stanley, it's time to eat," Mrs. Barnes called out.

Mr. Thomas turned the corner and was surprised to see Derek standing there. "Oh, I thought it was just the two of us tonight?" Mr. Thomas blurted out.

"So, did I, Mr. Thomas, so did I," Morgan said, shaking her head.

The conversation over dinner flowed surprisingly well. Derek proved to be intellectual, staying abreast of the latest news and weighing in on political matters. He even passed Mr. Thomas' sports trivia questions. It was over this mother-designed dinner that Morgan learned that Derek was Mrs. Barnes' cardiologist. She never mentioned going to see a heart doctor, but Morgan guessed with age and numerous doctor visits, it only made sense.

At 8:15 p.m., Morgan stood up from the table and said, "Momma, sorry I can't help you clean up, but I have to get going. The girls are waiting for me. Derek, it was a pleasure meeting you. I hope you are taking good care of my mother."

"Honey, why don't you take Derek with you? I keep telling this man he needs to get out more. I've been inviting him to dinner for weeks now. Who knows when he will get out again?" Mrs. Barnes gave Morgan that motherly look that only she could give, which essentially said, *Don't question me; just do as I say.*

My Momma is a gangsta. That thought kept running through Morgan's head. While the thought of spending the evening with such a handsome, eligible man was literally an answered prayer, the pressure and fear of not embarrassing herself in front of this man weighed out. Third Thursday was the one day out the month that she looked forward to because she could let loose and just be because dancing was her thing. She turned to Derek and said, "Me and my girlfriends are meeting up at El Fuego. Its salsa night. I know most brothers don't know the first thing about salsa, let alone bachata or merengue, so if you don't want to go, I'd more than understand."

"I'd love to," he said, wiping the corners of his lips with his napkin and getting up from the table.

Morgan excused herself and quickly ran upstairs to brush her teeth and to text Renee and Stacy that she was bringing a man with her "so behave."

Derek displayed chivalry, insisting on driving and opening her car door. When he started the car, a black on black Acura MDX, Kendrick Lamar blasted from the speakers. He apologized and quickly turned the music down. He asked for directions to the club and then followed up with a series of questions that ranged from college to social work, to orchids being her favorite flower. The interrogation could mean only one thing: Mrs. Barnes talked about Morgan to him.

"My mother seems to have told you everything about me. Did she, by any chance, mention that while I love orchids, I always seem to kill them?"

He laughed. "So no green thumb, huh?"

"Nope," Morgan smirked. Why didn't her mom tell her about this doctor? She knew Morgan didn't mind being set up on blind dates. She had done it before. But this caught Morgan completely off guard. "It seems you know everything about me, and I don't have the first clue about you. So Derek, tell me something about yourself."

"Like?" he asked, grinning.

Morgan rambled off, "Like… where are you from? Where'd you go to school? How long have you been treating my mom?"

"I'm from D.C. Born and raised. I went to Howard for undergrad and then to Johns Hopkins for medical school. I've been treating your mom for a minute now."

"Is everything okay? Is there something I should be concerned about?"

"You know HIPPA precludes me from discussing

patient matters. What I can say is that your mother is amazing. She has so much life, and joy, and wisdom, and spirituality wrapped up in that small frame of hers. My life has been blessed just being in her presence." The admiration he felt for Mrs. Barnes was genuine. It was sweet. "I tell all my patients and their families that the heart is only meant to last so long. Its job here on earth is powerful in so many ways, but at some point, it must come to an end. We never know when it will stop, so take advantage of the time you have with one another now."

"Wow, that's deep. Good advice. Oh, take that parking space right there." Morgan pointed. "The club is around the corner."

* * *

As always, the lounge was packed with a diverse crowd of people. That's why the girls typically got there early to grab a table because it filled up fast. It was almost 9:00 p.m. Thank goodness Renee and Stacy got there around 7:30 p.m. to save a table. Morgan spotted them at a table with a perfect view of the dance floor. Renee and Stacy saw her approaching. Stacy rolled her eyes at Morgan for being late while Renee got up to give her a hug. In her ear, she whispered, "Is this fine man behind you the doctor because all of a sudden I am not feeling too well. I think I may need mouth-to-mouth resuscitation."

Morgan embraced her and whispered back, "Yes. And he is off-limits…I think. I don't know. Well, yes for tonight, he's off-limits," she said.

In the split second of their embrace, Stacy quickly approached Derek. "Hi, I'm Stacy, Morgan's best friend. And you are?"

"Derek." He extended his hand. "It's nice to meet you."

"I'm a hugger." Stacy bypassed his hand and wrapped her arms around him in a big ole hug. Along the way, she felt down his broad shoulders to his lower back. Upon releasing him, she said, "And it's nice to meet you, too."

Embarrassed, Morgan quickly apologized. "Derek, I'm sorry. Please don't mind Stacy. She's crazy. And this is Renee, my other best friend." Renee and Derek shook hands like normal people do when meeting for the first time. Derek asked if the ladies wanted something to drink. Renee asked for an amaretto sour; Stacy asked for a shot of Patrón, and Morgan ordered ginger ale with grenadine. Typically a man would look at her sideways when she ordered that drink or tease her and say, 'you mean a Shirley Temple?' But no, not Derek. He just smiled and said, "Sure. I'll be right back."

While Derek was still at the bar, one of Morgan's favorite songs of all time came on – "Suavemente" by Elvis Crespo. Morgan and her girls hit the dance floor as was the tradition every third Thursday of the month. During the song, they each eventually got swept up by men. Stacy's dance partner was a short Asian male with a man bun and goatee who didn't have a clue how to dance merengue. They were the epitome of an odd couple. Neither seemed to mind her large frame against his short, skinny one. His head rested comfortably on her chest as she led. Renee's partner was of Dominican descent. You could tell by the ease of his quick steps and flamboyant turns. He kept Renee in suspense as to what move he would pull next. Morgan's partner was an older man, late sixties. His dance moves were okay; she could keep up, but he wouldn't stop talking, firing off question after question.

"Where are you from? You are so beautiful." He took her ring hand and said, "You are not married? I'm taking you home with me. I'll treat you right."

Morgan quickly came back with, "No, I'm not married yet, but my boyfriend is right over there," pointing to Derek, who was manning the table. Derek and Morgan made eye contact and he waved, which was enough to get grandpa to stand down.

The song ended, and they all headed back to the table where their drinks awaited. Derek got them extra napkins which they eagerly used to dry their wet faces. Wiping her face, Morgan said, "Thank you for the drink and napkins. This is right on time." The girls chimed in saying "thank you." Stacy wasted no time on interrogating Derek.

"So Derek, what's your deal? Married? Divorced? Widowed? Gay? Bisexual?"

Chuckling, he said, "None of the above. I'm single and hetero."

"Mmm. Kids?" Stacy was going to get dirt on this man one way or another.

"No kids."

"Atheist? Jehovah Witness? Muslim?"

"Christian."

Renee chimed in, "Really? What church do you belong to?"

In that instance, Hector, a regular at the club, approached Morgan and asked her to dance. Morgan always looked forward to dancing with Hector because he was a really good dancer who never tried to push up on her. He was patient with her missteps. Morgan would always apologize for missing a step here or there and he would say, "Stop apologizing. You know if you miss a step, it's my fault. The man leads, so if you mess up its because I'm not leading you properly."

Before Morgan knew it, she and Hector danced

at least four songs. Renee and Stacy were both on the dance floor with random guys while Derek patiently waited at the table. From time to time, Morgan would glance over in his direction and she would see different females approach him. He would engage them in short dialogue, and they would walk away looking dejected. Morgan started to feel guilty that she abandoned him. She didn't know what her mom thought would happen having him tag along with her. She knew how much Morgan looked forward to dancing. Morgan excused herself from dancing and went back to the table to check on him. "Hey, are you having any fun?" she asked.

"Yeah. I'm glad I came out. I see why you and your friends like to come here. You are a really good dancer. Your face lights up when you dance. It's refreshing to see."

Morgan didn't really know how to take such an observant compliment.

"Thanks."

"Did you or your friends want anything else from the bar?"

"I'm good. We're good. Please don't ask Stacy, because she will ask for another shot. Thanks for asking, though."

"No prob. Then can I have this dance?" he asked with his hand out, ready to accept hers.

Morgan always hesitated to salsa with a brotha because they never knew what they were doing. For many, they somehow thought that shimming their shoulders and moving their hips from side to side was dancing salsa, but it's wasn't. To relieve herself from the guilt of abandoning him earlier, she accepted. As they approached the dance floor, the song changed. Since the music was loud, Morgan leaned in and said to him, "This is bachata." He nodded and gingerly grabbed her by the waist. Before she knew it, they were moving effortlessly in sync with the song and in step. *This man knows how to bachata? What?* As he spun her around, she saw the slight grin on his face. "You know how to bachata?" Morgan asked.

"I do. It's been a minute. I wasn't sure if I still had it, but apparently, I do," he said with confidence.

Three songs later, they headed back to the table where Renee watched for some time.

"Where's Stacy?" Morgan asked.

"Over there talking with that Asian man." Turning to Derek, Renee asked, "So Doc, you dance salsa, bachata, and merengue? Where'd you learn?"

"Yes, where did you learn? Girl, he pulled some move I've never seen before," Morgan said.

"I learned in the Dominican Republic a long time ago. Wow...like ten years ago? After medical school, I spent a year in the DR with Doctors without Borders. I don't think I've danced since I've been back in the country. I'm surprised how quickly it all came back to me."

Stacy walked up from behind Morgan and interrupted the conversation, "You guys ready to roll? We have spin class in the morning, Morgan!"

They gathered their things and headed out of the club. Derek and Morgan walked Renee and Stacy to their cars, respectively. Stacy watched as Morgan set her phone alarm for 5:00 a.m. before pulling off. The car ride home was quiet. Morgan kept stealing quick side-eye glances at Derek while replaying the evening and the numerous surprises that occurred. They both rode in silence, listening to the gentle breeze as it brushed across the car window. Derek flashed back to his date with Dr.

Booker and how his instinct told him to abort. But now, sitting in the car with Morgan, his gut was saying, this definitely has potential. Derek pulled up to Morgan's house, parked, jumped out, came around, and opened her car door. After walking her up the steps, they both started talking at the same time, but being the gentleman he was, he stopped to let her speak.

"Thank you for this evening. I had fun. You are full of surprises, Dr. Patterson," Morgan said, smiling.

"The pleasure was all mine. Do you think we could maybe do this again sometime?"

"Sure. El Fuego's salsa night is every third Thursday of the month, but there are a couple of other spots around town that have salsa night on other days of the week. Like Lucky Strike has salsa on Sunday nights." Morgan always rambled when she got nervous, and this was no exception.

"Oh, good to know. I just meant in general. You know, coffee, a movie, dinner… something like that?" Derek said.

Of course, you did, Morgan laughed. "Oh, that? Sure."

"What's the best way to reach you?" he asked.

"By phone," Morgan said as he pulled out his cell phone. "Are you asking me for my number?"

"I am," he said as he nodded.

"So, are we going to pretend that my mother didn't already give you my number?" Morgan asked sarcastically.

"We are," he grinned.

Derek's smile was contagious. Morgan felt the corners of her lips lifting until all thirty-two of her teeth were exposed. They exchanged numbers and embraced in a short hug. Her nose was met with the smell of freshly folded laundry in the middle of a forest. *And he smells good too,* Morgan thought as she watched him pull off. She quickly ran upstairs to get ready for bed.

Hearing Morgan come in, Mrs. Barnes made her way to Morgan's bedroom and knocked on her door. Before she could say enter, her mother was already in the room. She plopped down on Morgan's bed as Morgan tried to salvage her hair from the frizz that formed after all of her sweating and dancing. "So, did you and Derek have a good time?" Mrs. Barnes asked.

"Yeah, but Momma, who is this dude? I mean, you have never talked about this man. You definitely never told me that you had a fine, handsome doctor. I mean, are there more? Do I need to start taking you to your appointments?"

"Morgan, I love you. You know that, but sometimes you get in your own way. You overthink things too much. Derek is a good man. If I told you about him, you would have sized him up before he even arrived for dinner and come up with some excuse not to give him a second thought. I would have loved to see your face when he broke out those moves on you on the dance floor," Mrs. Barnes said as she burst into laughter.

"So, I was right. You purposely invited him to dinner on a third Thursday? Momma, I never knew you to be so sneaky. I now realize I need to watch out for you," Morgan said, shaking her head. She couldn't believe her mother pulled this off and went to these measures to have her go out with Derek, but inside she was grateful. She was pleasantly surprised by the night's events.

"So, how did the night end?" Mrs. Barnes asked.

"He said he would call."

Mrs. Barnes kissed Morgan on her forehead, smiled while touching her face, and headed to bed.

At Morgan's bedroom door, her mom turned and

said, "Derek is a really good guy. His mom raised him right. I think you two could truly complement one another. But hey, what do I know? Night, sweetie."

That man is fine. He probably has a girl that Momma doesn't know about, or maybe a few. I can't even be mad at him if he did. Just then, Morgan's conversation with God prior to her date with Damian snuck up out of nowhere. Could Derek be her Mr. Right for Now? Could he be the sign of hope that she prayed for? In the moment, her paranoia would not allow her to accept this as a possibility. At some point, the other shoe was bound to drop for Dr. Hershey Kiss, and she wanted to be ready, but the butterflies swarming in her stomach wouldn't subside.

* * *

As Derek drove home, he replayed the night's events. He wondered why he never asked to see a photo of Morgan as much as Mrs. Barnes talked about her. He was stunned by her grace and beauty when she opened the front door. Little to no makeup, flawless skin, banging body—thick in all the right places, beautiful smile, and eyes of honesty and modesty. Her dance moves were also enticing. She was quick-witted and smart. He knew if she was of Mrs. Barnes' stock, she was a good woman and was absolutely blown away that Morgan was the total package. Literally. Pulling up to his house, his phone rang.

"Hello."

"Derek, I hope it's not too late for me to be calling you. I've been meaning to call you for a few weeks now, but it kept slipping my mind. Blame it on old age," Dr. Davis said apologetically.

"Hey, Dr. Davis. How's it going? How's retirement treating you?"

"Oh, it's great! I sleep in when I want, I play golf when I want. Me and Missy get to see the grandkids down in Florida often. So how's Lauren working out? Man, she was by far my best assistant ever. Top-notch! When I was planning my retirement, I knew I needed to look out for her. You were my first choice. I knew you'd look out for her and she would learn so much from you," Dr. Davis rattled on.

Derek was torn as to how to respond. It was obvious that his mentor thought highly of this girl who not only demonstrated poor judgment on more than one occasion but who also came on to him. Derek wanted to say, "She's on probation after groping my balls." Instead, Derek took a deep breath and said, "She is doing fine. Good. She seems to get along well with my other two assistants." Derek decided that he would be honest and omit the negative truths.

"Oh, I'm glad to hear that. I'm not surprised. I knew it'd be a perfect fit. Well, I'm not going to keep you, man; keep up the good work. Tell Lauren I said hello, and you take good care of her, you hear me, son?" Dr. Davis insisted.

"Yes, sir, I will. Thanks for the call. Have a good night." Derek respected his mentor and couldn't understand how Lauren could have this man believing that she was anything other than the manipulative, sneaky, not so naïve woman that she showed herself to be.

Chapter 4

The next morning, Morgan walked with a pep in her step. Everybody at work noticed how chipper she seemed. When Renee and Stacy cornered her, asking about her mood, Morgan refused to admit that it had anything to do with Dr. McFine. Morgan woke to a sweet text message from Derek that read,

> "Good Morning, Ms. Barnes, thanks again for a
> great evening. I forgot how much I love to dance.
> Hope we can find some time later today to talk.
> Have a great day!"

Morgan couldn't wait to talk to Derek. Every time her phone rang, her palms would begin to sweat in anticipation that it was Dr. Patterson calling her. Finally, around noon, he called, but thanks to her damp hands, she almost dropped the phone.

"Hello?" Morgan answered.

"Hey, it's Derek. How are you?" he asked.

"Hi. I'm good," Morgan said, cheesing from ear to ear.

"Did I catch you at a bad time? I thought I'd try to reach you during lunch."

"Nope; now is perfect."

"Great. Well, I was wondering if you were free this evening? I know its last minute, I apologize, but I would really like to see you. I was hoping you would accompany me to one of my favorite spots in the city," Derek said.

"Really? Where is that?" Now Morgan was curious.

"The MLK Memorial. There's something about walking around that memorial at night that feels..." Derek began, searching for just the right word.

"Empowering?" Morgan offered.

"Yes, and uplifting," he added.

"You know, I don't think I've ever been there at night. I'd love to go. What time did you have in mind?"

"Is 9:00 too late?"

"No. Meet you there?"

"No way. I'll come to pick you up. 8:30-*ish*. Does that work?" Derek inquired.

"Yes. See you then."

For the remainder of the workday, Morgan was on cloud nine. She left work a few minutes early so she could go home to figure out what to wear on her date. When she arrived, she found a note on the dining room table from Mrs. Barnes: "Going to dinner and a movie with Mr. Bailey. Don't wait up. Love you."

Morgan laughed and said, "Ha, you aren't the only one with a date tonight, Momma." For a minute, she questioned whether hers was a date, but why wouldn't it be? The man asked her out and insisted on picking her up. This was definitely a date. Morgan scoured her closet for something cute to wear. She was going to be outside in the element, walking around. That required comfortable shoes. Comfortable shoes screamed jeans. Morgan decided on a pair of ripped, faded jeans with a fitted black t-shirt that said, "100% Original – No Added Preservatives."

Dr. Patterson was extremely punctual. He rang the doorbell at exactly 8:30 p.m. Morgan opened the door to find Derek standing on the porch with a dozen pink roses in hand.

"Just in case you killed the orchid from yesterday."

* * *

The MLK Memorial was truly a sight to see at night.

There was something about the way the memorial was lit that made the Stone of Hope seem even more grandiose. As Morgan and Derek walked along the Tidal Basin admiring the thirty-foot high granite statue of Dr. King and reading his fourteen quotes etched in stone, they couldn't help but notice the diversity among the visitors. Tourists from all over the world eagerly posed in front of the giant statue, with their arms crossed just like King, cheesing from ear to ear as family members snapped photos. This great man who only lived thirty-nine years on this earth made such an international impact on this world. Morgan and Derek couldn't help but reflect on their own lives and assess whether they were truly walking in their purpose. They both agreed that there was more they could be doing in the community. Morgan shared how she enjoyed working with the young girls in her youth program and the upcoming church bake-off that she was planning. Derek was thoroughly impressed. *This woman is the total package.*

From time to time, someone would interrupt their conversation to ask if one of them could take their photo. After the third request, Derek, in turn, asked an older lady to take a photo of him and his friend. He gently grabbed Morgan around the shoulder and they both smiled for the camera. Morgan immediately asked to see the photo and disapproved of it. Derek didn't see anything wrong with it, but Morgan insisted that they take another one. She didn't trust that he would delete it so she did it herself before handing the phone back to him. The poor lady had no clue when she asked Derek to take her photo, that he and his friend would monopolize nearly ten minutes of her time to take their photos. Exactly eight minutes and thirty-three seconds and twenty photos later, Morgan finally found one that she liked. They both thanked the lady for her patience and Derek discreetly apologized for the picture-taking consuming so much time.

Morgan couldn't get over how their conversation flowed so effortlessly. She was a woman of few words, and she hated talking about herself, but around Derek, without trying, she spoke freely. Derek, who seemed to have been smitten since their first 'hello,' was captivated by how down to earth Morgan was. It was like she was either unaware of how her beauty and presence commanded attention, or she just didn't care. Either way, the fact that they shared so much in common— God, travel, food, Mrs. Barnes, community engagement, being D.C. natives to politics—made Derek not want this date to end. The two of them sat on a black metal bench talking for what seemed like an hour. Derek looked at his watch. "Oh wow, it's going on midnight. Where did the time go? I didn't mean to keep you out this late."

Morgan checked her phone as if she didn't believe the time either. "Are you serious? Wow, I guess there is some truth to the saying time flies when you are having fun." Before she could think about what she was about to say, she blurted out, "I almost wish tonight didn't have to end."

Derek stood to his feet and extended his hand to Morgan, "The lady has spoken. Where to next?"

Morgan graciously accepted his hand and asked, "You hungry?"

"I can eat."

"How about Gourmet Rapido?"

"Where is it?"

"Negro, you've never been to Gourmet Rapido? I'm about to revoke your D.C. card. It's a local gas station uptown that serves the best empanadas and fries in the city," Morgan joked.

"Aww. Got it. Let's go." And just like that, with their hands interlocked like perfect puzzle pieces, Derek led Morgan back to his car and headed uptown.

* * *

Derek agreed that he must have been living under a rock for all these years for not knowing about Gourmet Rapido. His BBQ chicken sandwich and fries were on point. He also enjoyed tasting Morgan's chicken empanada. While driving her home, Derek's phone rang. Given the time, he looked at the phone perplexed, "Excuse me for a sec," Derek said to Morgan, who nodded in agreement. "Hello? Oh, hi, Mrs. Davis. Is everything okay? Wait—what?" Derek pulled the car over to the nearest empty parking space on the dimly lit street. "When? What happened? Okay. Yes, I will cancel the rest of my appointments for the week and will be down there tomorrow. Mrs. Davis, I am so sorry. I really appreciate your calling me. My deepest condolences." Derek was in shock.

"Is everything ok?" Morgan asked. Looking at his face, she answered her own question, "Okay, obviously everything is not okay. What happened? Is there anything I can do?"

"My mentor passed away tonight. That was his wife. He told her that if anything happened to him, to call me and I would know what to do," Derek said.

"Oh no, I am so sorry to hear that. Had he been sick?" Morgan asked.

"Not that I know of. I just talked to him yesterday, and he sounded fine. Mrs. Davis said that he just dropped dead while getting up in the middle of the night to use the bathroom. She was hysterical on the phone. I didn't know how to console her. They don't have any children," Derek said, eyes filled with tears.

Morgan felt for Derek. She could tell that he really loved and cared for this man. She took Derek's hand and squeezed it softly. "Do you want to pray?" she asked.

Derek's eyes lit up as if the thought never crossed his mind, but in that moment, it was exactly what he needed and said, "Yes! Yes, please."

At 2:05 a.m., on the main thoroughfare, Morgan and Derek sat in his car, praying that Dr. Davis would rest in peace and that God would be with his family during this difficult time. After they prayed, a calming sensation came over Derek, and he thanked Morgan for suggesting it. When they finally pulled up to Morgan's house, Derek jumped out of his car, came around and opened Morgan's door, then extended his arm and walked her to the front door. Morgan was about to thank him for a nice evening, but he beat her to it.

"I had a really good time tonight, Morgan."

Looking up at him, Morgan replied, "Me too. Thanks for the invite."

"I wish the evening ended differently, but honestly, I am grateful that you were with me when I received the news. God was definitely looking out for me."

"I'm glad I was able to help. It wasn't much. It's all that I could think to do in the moment."

"It was exactly what I needed." Derek looked at his watch – 2:25 a.m. "Okay, I better go. I've kept you out way too long, Ms. Barnes." He leaned in and kissed Morgan softly on the cheek. Her cheek tingled. As he turned to walk to his car, he turned back and said, "I gotta head to Atlanta for the next week or so. I'll call you tomorrow."

* * *

While Derek was out of town, Morgan hit up spin class on Thursday evening. The class let out at 9:30 p.m., but leave it to Renee and Stacy to lollygag for another hour or so. As they wiped down their bikes, Stacy turned to Renee and asked, "So did you tell her?"

Renee gave Stacy the side-eye.

"Tell me what?" Morgan inquired out of concern and annoyance that her two best friends were keeping something from her. She was getting even more annoyed because no one was saying anything. "Tell me what? Somebody better say something!"

"Courtney is expecting... again," Stacy blurted out.

Morgan stared at Stacy, processing the words that just floated off of her tongue and landed smack dab in her face. Stacy wasn't sure if Morgan knew who she was talking about, so she clarified, "Justin. Your ex. He and his wife, Courtney, are expecting again."

Renee looked at Stacy and smacked her lips, "Stace, she knows who you are talking about. Let the chile digest the news. Geez."

Morgan wasn't sure how she felt. She couldn't remember the last time she thought about Justin. It was well over a year. She assumed he was going on about his life with his wife, so the idea of more kids seemed plausible. *Do I care?* She asked herself. She contemplated for thirty seconds. *No, not really.* She could see clearly that Justin was not a part of her future. And while the jury was still out on Derek, this past week of talking with this man had Morgan feeling like a seventh-grader with a schoolgirl crush. She couldn't wait to see him again and anxiously awaited his return. She never experienced this, whatever this was, with Justin. Grabbing her gym bag, Morgan turned to her friends and said, "Good for them."

The girls got kicked out of the spin class and chatted it up in the parking lot until 10:40 p.m. On her way home, Morgan pulled to a 7-11 to grab a bottle of water. As she got out of her car, she was overcome by the potent smell of skunk. She quickly looked over in the direction where the smell was originating and saw a group of young boys smoking weed by a dumpster. Morgan quickly dashed into the store to avoid the smoke from getting in her hair. As she waited at the counter for the attendant to finish helping the person in front of her, she peered through the storefront window and observed the group of boys again. Morgan's eyes were drawn to one boy in particular whose back was toward her. All of the other boys were goofing around acting silly while he just stood there observing the others. He seemed out of place. Just as the boy turned his head slightly toward Morgan, she immediately left the bottled water on the container and dashed outside.

"Tra'maine! What are you doing out here at this hour?"

The boys looked up at Morgan and then back at Tra'maine like, "Who is this woman?"

Turning toward Morgan, Tra'maine whispered, "Uh. Nothing." He looked back over his shoulder at his friends, who were mocking him at this point.

"Tra'maine, get in the car," Morgan could not believe this boy whom she placed with a loving family was out here smoking.

Tra'maine parted his lips as if to say something, but Morgan gave him the "do you want me to embarrass you in front of your friends" look, and he reluctantly got in the car after saying goodbye to his friends.

On the way to take him home, Morgan interrogated

Tra'maine. "What were you doing? Were you smoking? Does your father know you were hanging out with those boys? Why aren't you in bed? It's after 10:00 p.m. on a school night."

When Morgan pulled up to the house, it was pitch black. The porch light was out, as well as all the lights inside the house. *Was Mr. Stevenson even home?* she wondered. Using his key, Tra'maine unlocked the door and went inside. She followed behind and fumbled for the light switch to the right of the door. The house smelled musty, but unlike last time, she didn't smell spoiled milk. On the dining room table lay an open pizza box with two slices of pepperoni pizza. Morgan instructed Tra'maine to get his dad. After about ten minutes, Mr. Stevenson appeared in the living room draggy and sleepy.

"Uh, Hi, Ms. Barnes. What are you doing here so late?"

"Mr. Stevenson, I just brought Tra'maine home. Were you aware that he was hanging out with kids smoking at the 7-11?"

"Say what?" Mr. Stevenson looked at Tra'maine in disbelief. "No. I....I ordered him a pizza and then laid down. I guess he snuck out after that." Tra'maine darted to his room and closed the door.

"Mr. Stevenson, Tra'maine is at a very impressionable age. And without proper supervision, he can easily get caught up with the wrong people. I'm glad that you are seeing to it that he eats and all, but you have to engage him and keep an eye out for him. You should know where he is always and who he is with. Is this news to you? I thought you were aware of the responsibility of fostering a child. Do I need to revisit this arrangement?"

"No. No. Absolutely not. We, uh, typically eat dinner together, and I help him with his homework, but my head was throbbing this evening, so I went to lie down early. I'ma talk to him. He can't be sneaking out this house. It's not safe."

It was late, and Morgan didn't want to belabor the issue. This was the second time that Morgan counseled Mr. Stevenson. In her gut, it was only a matter of time before she would have to find another home for Tra'maine. For the time being, he was fed and home safely. Hopefully, Mr. Stevenson would take this warning seriously.

* * *

When Derek returned from Atlanta, he took Morgan to a fancy restaurant on Capitol Hill. Dinner was scrumptious; she had the swordfish with double-baked mashed potatoes, and Derek ordered lambchops with risotto. Morgan felt like she was dreaming. With candle lights flickering, here she sat across from this man who genuinely seemed interested in learning all about her. He was confident, but not arrogant, sincere and not pretentious. Despite his charming looks, he was a down to earth guy that for whatever reason, put Morgan at ease. As they exited the restaurant, Derek took her hand and began to caress it slowly as they walked to his car. He was a true gentleman, always remembering to walk on the outside and open her car door. Everything was perfect until he went to turn the ignition, and the car wouldn't start. He left the lights on and the battery died. Instead of calling AAA, he decided that the best thing to do would be to walk to his condo which was only a "couple" of blocks away.

"You have got to be kidding me," Morgan blurted out as the pain in her foot from walking crept up to her ankle.

"Trust me—my place is five minutes away. If we wait for AAA, who knows how long that will be. Cabs don't normally come around this part of town." He pulled out his phone to check Uber. "Uber is twelve minutes away. Walking is our best option. Really." He extended his elbow, and Morgan interlocked her arm in his, and he escorted her down the dimly lit street. The sky was radiant with infinite stars and nearly a full moon, while crickets sang harmoniously to a tune of their own. She tried her best to play off the pain she was experiencing, but when her stride turned to a turtle's pace, he knew immediately what the issue was. "Take your shoes off," he said.

"Excuse me?"

"Take your shoes off. I'll carry you."

"Excuse me?" She froze in mid-step. While the average woman fantasized about a man sweeping them off their feet, the idea of this man picking her up was terrifying. Yes, she changed her eating habits over the past few months and even lost a few inches, but the scale hadn't budged. More importantly, she knew that although her awesome Spanx could nip and tuck her rolls, no piggyback ride could hide how much she really weighed.

"Your feet hurt. I get it. Please don't fight me on this," Derek pleaded. "It's my fault we are in this predicament."

As she imagined an ambulance abruptly stopping before them to rescue this man from a broken back due to his chivalrousness, she reluctantly took off her shoes one at a time as the ball of her left foot then right foot kissed the concrete sidewalk. *Thank you, Jesus.* Morgan's toes began to wiggle in reprieve. He graciously waited as she took them off, smiling when he noticed the sigh of relief on her face, and scooped Morgan up in his arms.

Mrs. Barnes always said you have to have faith, but more importantly, you have to ask God for what you want. Morgan never specifically asked for a man to be this chivalrous, and she wasn't sure what she did to deserve it, but... *Hallelujah!*

She placed her arms around his neck and breathed in his fresh yet earthy scent. With his hands strategically placed on her lower back and upper thigh, Derek crossed the street and said, "Here we are."

Are you kidding me? Five hundred feet? Really? He put Morgan down gently and opened the door to an obscure building that she would never have thought were condos. "*This* is where you live?" Morgan asked. Mrs. Barnes always said she lacked tact.

"Yeah, I live on the top floor. I own the building. Don't' let the outside fool you. I renovated the entire building, and besides, this neighborhood is in transition. It will be thriving in a couple years, just wait and see. Everyone thought I was crazy for buying this building four years ago, but its property value has doubled since then. My tenants are mostly graduate students and young professionals. Everyone pays on time for the most part." As Morgan listened to him talk, she couldn't help but wonder how on point this man was. He was not only a doctor, but he was also business-savvy and down for his people. *Yessss, my brother.*

He wasn't lying about renovating the building. On entering his condo, Morgan was taken aback by the high ceilings and loft-like feel, with exposed brick walls. Did she just leave D.C. and enter Manhattan? Hardwood floors. Stainless steel appliances. Double-sided fireplace. She quickly noticed that everything on the first floor was white, clean, and crisp. *Okay, this brother is OCD,* she thought. *He has to be!* While there was beautiful artwork on the walls, she noticed that there were no family photos. As Derek went into the kitchen to make coffee, Morgan sat down on his plush, overly comfortable couch, which absorbed her body like none other. Having left her shoes by the front door, Morgan's bare feet melted in the thick throw rug beneath her. When he came back, he handed Morgan a mug.

"Oh, I'm sorry, I don't drink coffee," she said politely.

"I know. I made you hot chocolate," he said, smirking, "with marshmallows."

"Oh! Excuse me. Why thank you, Dr. Patterson." Morgan thought to herself, *Are you kidding me? What grown man has hot chocolate, with marshmallows in his kitchen? This is ridiculous. Where's the camera because I'm sure I'm being fooled.*

"So, I noticed that there aren't any family photos up. Why is that?" Morgan's nerves were setting in. She couldn't hold her tongue when that happened. *Nice segue, Morgan. Great job!*

"I really don't have any family. My dad died before I was born. He was driving drunk and lost control of the car. So it was just me and my mom and she died ten years ago. I have a picture of her upstairs."

"I'm sorry to hear that." Quickly changing the subject, Morgan said, "This hot chocolate is delicious. What's your secret?"

"I use two kinds of chocolate."

"Really? So does my mom. She didn't happen to tell you that I love hot chocolate, did she?"

"You know, doctor-client confidentiality precludes me from discussing that with you, but I'm glad you like it. You mind if I turn on some music?"

Morgan shrugged while thinking about what else her mother told this man. This woman didn't play fair.

"What are you in the mood for?" he asked. Morgan

walked with him over to his vintage record player and scanned a vast collection of albums on the adjacent bookcase. Her hands slid across some of the greats— Stevie Wonder, Teddy Pendergrass, The Temptations.

"My dad would have loved your collection. He was a music connoisseur who appreciated vinyl." Just then, she saw it - Donny Hathaway's *Extension of a Man.* "I love Donny. This was his last studio album. "A Song for You" is my all-time favorite, but from this album, I think my favorite is "Someday We'll All Be Free.""

"Aww, Donny. He's definitely a legend. My fav on that album is "Love, Love, Love." He took the album out of the cover and placed it on the record player. Adjusting the needle, he gestured with his hand, "May I have this dance?" Morgan accepted, but she cut her eyes. This man thought he was slick. First, the hot chocolate, and now Donny Hathaway? Morgan refused to be seduced.

With his hands resting on her waist, they began moving side to side to Donny's harmonious voice. Morgan closed her eyes and rested her head on Derek's shoulder. *This is nice. I could do this all day,* she thought to herself. There was something about Donny's voice that could take you from your current state and transport you to a place where you lived every word he sang. Just then, Derek spun her around. They laughed at Morgan's reaction to being caught off guard.

"I think we can hand dance to this piece," he said. He took her hand and began moving with the standard six steps known as D.C. hand dance. Morgan moved in sync. After years of watching her parents hand dance at every social function, Morgan begged her dad to teach her about seven years ago. At this moment, she was so grateful he did. Her father always said that the right man would not only be able to keep up with her on the dance floor, but he would be able to lead her while doing so.

The song ended while they were still holding hands. She looked at their hands and then at him. The nervous bug was itching its way up through her mouth. She just kept telling herself, *Morgan, don't say anything stupid.* She wanted to release her hand and run toward the door. She was so outside of her comfort zone. She had kissed more than a few tadpoles in her life, but there was this energy between them that she had never experienced before with anyone. A part of her felt like they had known each other for ages, as though their spirits were well acquainted. Yet her mind, which she could never control, was spiraling into an abyss of nerves and insecurities. Derek pulled her in close. He released her hand and brushed a curly strand of hair from her face. Looking deeply into her eyes, he smiled a cheesy smile like a little kid who was just given cotton candy. His smile was unexpected, and Morgan burst out laughing.

"Are you nervous?" she asked shockingly.

"Ah. I guess I am," Derek said, shaking his head.

"Why are you nervous?" Morgan was relieved that she wasn't the only nervous one, but for the life of her, she couldn't understand why this fine man was nervous too.

"Umm… it's been a minute," he admitted bashfully.

"It's been a minute since what exactly?" She knew with each question she asked, she was killing the moment for him to kiss her. Part of her wanted to keep the questions flying, yet another part wanted her to shut up immediately.

"Since I've genuinely liked someone. Trust me; it's been a minute. I feel like we've connected beyond physical chemistry, and I don't know, I just want to go about this the right way."

In that moment, Morgan's guards retreated. She didn't know if he was using reverse psychology, or what, but just like that, her nerves went away. "Well, there's definitely no reason for you to be nervous. And I appreciate your candor." Morgan inched closer to him and slid her arms around his neck. Whispering in his ear, she said, "And I think you may be right about there being a connection." With that, their eyes met, and he leaned in and kissed her softly.

The kiss started off slow and innocent, but it eventually elevated to PG-13. There was no denying that they were attracted to one another. She couldn't speak for him, but she never kissed anyone that she connected with on this level. It felt good. After standing for what seemed like an eternity, they made their way over to the couch. In the heat of the moment, clothes started to fly. With his shirt off and her bra exposed, he began to kiss his way down her neck. As his lips tickled her skin, he slid his hand up her thigh.

In a flash, Morgan was back in her dorm room during her senior year of college, and Terrence's hands moved up her dress. She pushed Derek off her as hard as she could. "Stop. Stop. No," she blurted out. Confused and startled, Derek raised his hands in surrender. Morgan quickly realized what just happened and felt humiliated. "Ah, where's your bathroom?" she said.

"Down the hall. First door on the right."

Deep breath, Morgan, she said to herself while looking at herself in the bathroom mirror. *Tonight was so perfect. Why did I have to go and ruin it?* She kept replaying what Derek said earlier in the night, "I genuinely like someone... we've connected...I want to go about this the right way...." This definitely was not the right way with her completely freaking out. She didn't know what to say to make this right. She gathered her composure and what was left of her dignity. She redid her high ponytail, wiped the tears forming in her eyes, and headed back to the living room.

The room looked different—brighter. Derek had turned the lights up, and the pillows were placed back on the couch in their original position. He was fully dressed.

"I'm sorry. I don't know what to say." Morgan was at a loss for words.

"It's okay. It's been a long night. I called you an Uber. It should be here any minute."

Morgan completely ruined the night. The man was shipping her off like parents send their unruly teenager off to boarding school. "Oh, okay. Thanks." She grabbed her shoes and quickly put them on. Just then, his phone rang, and she knew it was the Uber driver downstairs. They walked down the steps and to the Uber car in silence. He opened the car door for her, and said, "Morgan, I had a really good time tonight. I hope we can do it again sometime. Please call or text me and let me know you made it home safely."

Relieved, she admitted, "Me, too. Tonight was wonderful, and I look forward to the next." *Wishful thinking Morgan. You just completely scared this man away. Way to go!* With that, Morgan leaned in and kissed him on the cheek. He closed the car door behind her and stood in the street and watched as the Uber drove off.

Chapter 5

Morgan woke up exhausted and irritated. She tossed and turned all night, rehashing how she single-handedly ruined her "perfect" date. Dinner was impeccable. The conversation flowed seamlessly. There was just the right balance of serious discussion with light-hearted humor. Derek understood her quick wit, and his jokes were funny. This man was hot. The thought of his beautiful pearly white smile, which rose just slightly higher on the right side, popped in her head. He could have gone out with any woman, but he chose her. Morgan hadn't pulled out her list of ideal qualities in a mate in a while, but she knew that Derek exuded most, if not all, of the qualities she was looking for in a man. He was a gentleman, and not just sometimes. He carried her to his doorstep for heaven's sake. As a matter of fact, that act in and of itself gave him double points on her Richter scale of a good catch. Morgan was solid as a rock, and he picked her up with ease, making her feel light as a feather. He was an excellent dancer and knew how to lead. Their bodies moved in sync when they danced. It was like their souls moved in unison to the melody of the music. He was genuinely nervous about kissing her, which Morgan found hard to believe because this eligible bachelor who could have anybody was sure to have a long body count. This grown man kissed his fair share of women, yet he stood nervously in front of Morgan, the one person who had only kissed a handful of tadpoles, and who stood equally nervous in front of him. It was like they were standing on an even playing field. What did he say again? Shaking her head, she recalled him saying that he genuinely liked her. She thought, *How could this be? Why?*

After last night's fumble, Morgan was sure he wouldn't like her anymore. She completely jumped off the cliff with no parachute. How did such a lovely evening end in disaster? Morgan closed her eyes and recalled their first kiss. It was sweet. Up until that moment, as he inched in closer to her, with Morgan's arms around his neck, her eyes invited him to plant one on her, but she couldn't breathe. Right there in his hands, Morgan was stuck in fear. But something happened. He leaned in, grabbed the sides of her face, and gently laid his lips on hers. He kissed her, and she kissed him back. She remembered slowly exhaling as they began to kiss. The physical attraction she felt for this man took over. The excitement from it all was almost too much. She began running her fingers through Derek's closely shaven hair as she eased her tongue in his mouth. Before she knew it, she was unbuttoning his shirt and kissing his neck and shoulders.

OMG!

In an instant, Morgan realized that last night, she jumped Derek! She initiated the make-out session that ended horribly. She led Derek to second base in less than sixty seconds and then cried wolf. He must think she's either a whore or a tease. Or maybe both. He said he wanted to go about this the right way, and he had. It was Morgan who was the problem. And to be honest, she knew she had a problem, but she didn't think she needed to bring it up so soon. And if she had just stayed in the moment and embraced his gentle kiss as any normal female would have done, everything would have been fine right now, and she wouldn't have to have this dreaded conversation so soon.

Morgan reluctantly got dressed and headed to the kitchen for breakfast. Mrs. Barnes was reading the Metro section of *The Washington Post*.

"Morning, Sweet pea. You know what your mayor has gone and done now?" She looked up and quickly assessed Morgan's mood. Morgan loved her mother because she knew her so well. She'd never pressure Morgan into talking when she obviously didn't want to be bothered. She gave Morgan the space she needed and always reminded her that her door was open if she ever wanted to talk. Morgan grabbed the plate of eggs and bacon Mrs. Barnes prepared for her and placed them between two slices of burnt toast, just the way she liked it. Morgan downed some orange juice and put her breakfast sandwich in a paper towel.

"Thanks, Momma, for breakfast. I'm late this morning, so I'll eat it on the go."

"Sure thing, baby. Have a good day at work. I love you."

"I love you, too, Momma."

"Oh, and Morgan, Mr. Pickney and I are going to dinner this evening. Don't wait up," she said with a chuckle.

Morgan gave her mom the parental eye of "I'm watching you," smirked, then headed out the door for work.

* * *

At work, Renee anxiously approached Morgan's desk. Morgan texted her while on the Metro, "911. No more Doc. Don't tell Stacy."

"Girl. What happened?"

Morgan rolled her eyes. "I happened. That's what."

Renee and Morgan had been friends for nearly ten years. She was the one person, outside of her school counselor, who knew what happened homecoming weekend her senior year in college. It wasn't something that she intended to tell Renee, but one day, Renee came to Morgan distraught. About seven years ago, Renee had a case where a ten-year-old girl reported that her foster parent inappropriately fondled her. The news made Renee hysterical. Once she was able to remove the girl from the home and place her with a different family, she calmed down. She came to Morgan's desk and apologized for her agitated behavior and shared that she had been molested as a child by her uncle. The thought of an innocent girl having to endure what she experienced as a child, for nearly three years, sent her over the edge. Renee's ability to talk about her experience so freely and matter-of-factly baffled Morgan. And at the same time, it gave Morgan the courage to blurt out loud, "I was raped." Even to the school counselor, Morgan had never used those words exactly. It sounded weird rolling off her tongue but was liberating at the same time. That night they stayed at work late, talking about their ordeals, only to never discuss it again with anyone. There wasn't a need. They shared a bond. They knew each other's stories and they knew each other's strength. And after ten years of friendship, they also knew each other's crazy.

"What?" Renee asked.

"We went to La Rosch. After dinner we got into his car so he could take me home, except it wouldn't start. Apparently, he left his lights on and the battery died. So he suggested we walk to his place which was nearby instead of waiting around for AAA or an Uber."

"What? Are you serious? I've never heard of that line before. And you went?" Renee asked with surprise in her tone of voice.

"Well, I didn't really think I had a choice. I mean, I got the sense that he was a good guy, so yes, I went. But along the way, my feet were hurting like crazy, so he picked me up and carried me to his place." Morgan purposely left out the part about it only being like five hundred feet.

"He what? Stop lying!" Renee couldn't contain her laughter. "Okay, I ain't mad at him. Go on."

"So we went inside, and he went into the kitchen where I thought he was making coffee, and I was looking around."

"Wait. You don't drink coffee."

"I know, but girl, he came out with hot chocolate, and it was good. I mean really good. So we started listening to music, and he asked me to dance. Then he kissed me, and, before I knew it, we were on the couch. His shirt was off, and his hand started up my skirt, and I snapped. I had a flashback, and I screamed, 'Stop!'"

"Pause. Rewind. He forced himself on you?" Morgan loved Renee. She was always so protective of her.

"No, that's just it. He was and has always been a true gentleman, since day one when I met him. I jumped him. I escalated the whole thing. I unbuttoned his shirt. I pulled him over to the couch. And then I just snapped on the poor man."

Renee laughed. "So now we see what happens when you go without for too long."

"It's not funny. It was a beautiful evening. An epic date, and I ruined it. I can never see him again."

"So why do you think you had a flashback? Did this ever happen with Justin? I mean, you two were getting busy."

"No, never," Morgan said in disbelief.

"Was there something about Derek that reminded you of the guy from college?" Renee was determined to get to the root cause of the problem.

"No. Nothing at all, thank you, Jesus. Girl, I don't know. I think for once in my life, I let my guard down."

"What do you mean? You were having sex with Justin. Wasn't your guard down then?" Renee asked.

"I guess not. I mean, with Justin, I knew when it was about to happen, and I could mentally prepare."

"Mentally prepare?"

"Yeah, like, 'it will be over in like ten minutes. You got this, girl. What's on schedule for tomorrow?' You know stuff like that to keep my mind busy."

Renee's mouth dropped open. "Morgan, are you serious right now?"

Morgan was confused by Renee's reaction. "Yeah. Why wouldn't I be?"

"You realize that, although you were physically having sex with Justin, you weren't the least bit intimate with him? You sound like a robot who went through the motions but completely detached from the power source. That's not good."

"I mean, after senior year, I vowed never to have sex. And, more importantly, never to allow myself to not be in control of the situation. Even though I caved in on the not having sex part, at least I was in control with Justin. I said when, where, and how."

"Did Justin know about the rape?"

"No. I was embarrassed to tell him. And honestly, as long as his needs were being met, I don't think he was interested in getting to know that vulnerable side of me."

"Morgan, I hate to say it, but I am so glad he cheated on you. If not, who knows where'd you be right now? You would have settled for Door Number One—Mr.

Okie Doke, when all along your prize was waiting for you behind Door Number Two—Mr. Doctor Oh So Fine."

Morgan burst out laughing.

"Honestly, Morgan, it sounds like you had your first intimate encounter since college. Your guards were down, and you were in a vulnerable state. If that's the case, I can see how that would bring up memories. So... how'd the night end?"

"I excused myself to the bathroom, and when I returned, he had an Uber waiting outside to take me home. I mean, he couldn't usher me out any faster if my life depended on it."

"And what did he say?"

"That he had a good evening and wanted to see me again. But girl, you and I both know that was just something to say. I mean, there is no way I can confront him. I just need to accept the fact that it wasn't meant to be."

"Morgan. Shut up," Renee said. "You freaked out. Big time. Okay. It's not the end of the world. You owe him an explanation for sure, but the good news is that he wants to see you."

"You don't understand. I imagined having to tell my story one day to someone, but not this soon. I mean, we are still getting to know one another. I don't want to give him a reason to run in the opposite direction."

"Well, technically, you've already done that, and he hasn't run," Renee explained as she cocked her head to the side and squinted. She was right; they both knew it. "Morgan, this is a part of you. In order for him to get to know you, you should let him in. I mean, I agree it's not ideal to have to tell him this early on. But look at the bright side, you are ripping the band-aid off, so you are getting the pain out of the way."

Just then, Morgan's cell phone buzzed. She looked at it and then quickly up at Renee who was leaning beside her desk. They both eyed the phone lying on Morgan's desk. Renee grabbed it before Morgan had a chance.

"Well looky here. It's Derek." She read the text out loud, "Morning, Ms. Barnes. I hope you made it home safely last night. You didn't text me. Sad face emoji. Nonetheless, I hope you have a great day!"

"Oh, no. He did say text him to let him know I got home safely. I completely forgot."

"See. He still wants to talk to you, Morgan. This plane has not come in for a landing just yet."

"But I don't know what to say to him. I'll have to think about how to respond. Maybe something will come to me by lunch," Morgan said flustered.

"Lunch? That sounds like a great idea." Renee began typing a response to Derek.

"Renee. Stop. Don't do it. Please," Morgan begged.

"Hey, Doc. I apologize for not letting you know I arrived home safely. Can I make it up to you? Lunch at noon. My treat." Renee read the drafted text aloud, then quickly hit the Send button.

"Lunch? Today? How do you know I don't have field visits?" Morgan said with an attitude. At this point, Morgan was regretting having told Renee about last night. She thought she would at least have a couple of days to avoid Derek before having to extend an explanation for her weird behavior.

"Do you have field visits?" Renee asked sarcastically.

"Well, no, but what if I did? You can't just go making dates for me." Morgan rolled her eyes and snatched her phone from Renee's hands.

The phone buzzed again. Morgan quickly skimmed the text to herself, 'No, but lunch at noon, my treat sounds good to me.'

"What he say?"

"He said no," Morgan mumbled.

"He said, no? Girl, let me see." Renee snatched the phone from Morgan's hand to read the text. "Did you read this? Can you read? He said no, meaning no, you can't make it up to him, but yes, he would like to do lunch, but he's treating."

Morgan grabbed the phone back and reread the text. This time she actually saw the words on the phone instead of the ones running around in her head. She cracked up to herself. What would she do without Renee? "Roti?" Morgan looked up, asking Renee for approval. At that very moment, Morgan trusted Renee's brain over her own. She texted Derek, "Roti? Foggy Bottom?"

Within five seconds, he texted back: "Sounds good. See you at noon."

"You see. Crisis averted, thanks to me." Renee was a very confident woman.

"Yes, but…" Morgan suddenly looked down at what she was wearing. She wasn't the most fashionable. As a matter of fact, Renee and Stacy often got on her about dressing like an old woman. Morgan liked her clothes loose. Rarely did she wear colors other than black, gray, and brown. Morgan was so depressed this morning that she didn't think twice about what she was wearing, and now she regretted it. She wore a long-sleeve, shapeless black shirt with a pair of wide-legged black slacks and her orthopedic, super comfortable black flats. She was dressed like she was headed to a funeral.

Renee followed Morgan's eyes and quickly assessed her situation. "No sweat. Between me and Stacy, we got you. Come on." She grabbed Morgan's hand and led her down the hall to Stacy's cubicle. As they approached, they could clearly hear Ella Mae singing her heart out. Even though they all worked in a large open area, Stacy had no shame about blasting her music loud. In her defense, she thought she was lightening up the mood in the office.

"Morning, ladies! What y'all doing?" Stacy asked.

"Somebody has a hot lunch date with Dr. Too Fine," Renee blurted out.

"Oooh. Do tell! Wait. That's what you're wearing?" Morgan loved the fact that Stacy always got right to the point. Morgan didn't have to tell her the problem. It was obvious. Thank goodness they wore the same shoe size and she kept a box of shoes under her desk.

"Well, I didn't know when I got dressed this morning that we would be meeting for lunch," Morgan said defensively.

"That's why I tell you to always dress to impress. You never know when you'll meet your Mr. Right, and we all know men are visual."

Stacy looked at Morgan's outfit and shook her head. Then she looked at Renee, and without speaking, they came up with a game plan. Stacy started to go through her shoebox. She pulled out a pair of four-inch fuchsia platforms. For the life of Morgan, she didn't see how those shoes would ever be appropriate for their line of work, but she kept her comment to herself. Stacy took the vibrant, colorful scarf from around her neck and commanded Morgan to "put this on." Morgan followed her instructions. The scarf matched the shoes perfectly.

"What am I supposed to do with these shoes? You know I can barely walk in two-inch heels."

"Girl, suck it up. I told you that you need to learn to walk in heels. Wear your flats on the Metro and change before you cross the street," Renee suggested.

Stacy continued to look at Morgan with disapproval.

"You need a waistline. Well, you have one. One that I would die for as a matter of fact, but for whatever reason, you prefer to hide it and look like you weigh two hundred pounds."

"How's this?" Renee pulled a skinny black patent leather belt from the loops of her pants. Morgan put it on and buckled it as tight as it would go. She took a step back to give them both a good vantage point.

"Ehh. Accessories?" Stacy took off her silver bangle bracelets and hoop earrings and handed them to Morgan. "So now you look great and I look like a bama. Great! What are friends for?"

Renee and Morgan laughed, but she knew Stacy was right. Only true friends would have helped her out this way. For two people who value fashion and appearance, to give up their statement pieces for her was a gesture of love. Now Morgan knew that within fifteen minutes, Stacy would have completely changed her outfit, including complimentary accessories. This act of kindness did not go unnoticed.

"You can carry my black tote," Renee offered. Renee loved big bags, so Morgan knew the heels would fit perfectly in the tote.

"Thanks, ladies. I don't know what I would do without you both," Morgan said graciously.

"Oh, I know. You'd continue to be a big dateless bama," Stacy said, louder than Morgan would have preferred.

Maurice and Cordell, who sat on opposite sides of Stacy, looked up at her and assessed her outfit.

The girls chatted for another minute before Morgan headed back to her desk, where she tried to script out her conversation with Derek.

* * *

Morgan snuck out of the office early to reach the restaurant before Derek. That way she was guaranteed not to run into him while wearing her flats. She arrived at Roti and sat at a booth in the corner. She pulled out the heels from Renee's black tote and slipped them on. She quickly imagined her slow strut back to the Metro in the awful heels. Morgan was sure that after she spilled the beans to Derek, she would be left with no escort to guide her across the brick sidewalk back to the Metro escalators. She took a deep breath. She still didn't know what she was going to say to Derek or how she would approach the conversation. Exhaling, she prayed, "God, please put the words on my lips." Morgan pulled out her compact and checked her lips. She loved MAC Lipglass. It was like the superglue of lip gloss because it lasted forever. As she sat in the booth, her nerves started to unravel. She could feel herself perspiring between her thighs. Her mind started to drift, *I guess skinny chicks with thigh gaps don't have this problem. Thigh gaps. Where did this concept come from, and why suddenly is it such a phenomenon?* Morgan was so into her own world that it wasn't until Derek cleared his throat that she looked up and realized he was standing beside her. *Oh, shoot! How long has he been standing there?* Morgan nervously blushed just as she got up to stand. She slightly lost her balance as she realized that she was standing four inches taller than when she originally sat down. As a true gentleman, Derek grabbed her arms to balance her.

"Hi," Morgan said, shaking her head. She felt like she was one big walking disaster. The warmth of his hands on either side of her arms permeated her body.

"Well, hello," he said, smiling that beautiful smile. "I

hope I haven't kept you waiting too long."

"No, not at all." Morgan looked around to find a clock, and it read 12:02 p.m. *Right on time, doc,* she thought to herself.

"Good. You hungry? I know I am." Derek led Morgan to the line to order and stepped aside so she could go in front.

Morgan ordered the usual—falafel, salad with red pepper dressing, side of eggplant and roasted veggies. As the server fixed her plate, she reminded herself to check her teeth throughout the meal. It would be her luck to get a big ole piece of broccoli stuck in her two front teeth. *Come to think of it, having food lodged in my teeth might be a good distraction for the conversation I'm about to have.*

The cashier grabbed her plate and asked, "Is this it?"

Before she could say "no," Derek chimed in. "These two are together."

Morgan looked over at him, and he smirked, "My treat, remember?"

They settled back into the booth. Morgan asked Derek if they could bless the food. He agreed and asked if she would like to do the honors. She respectfully declined. Morgan was curious to hear him bless the food. If he came out the mouth with some ole, 'rub a dub dub, bless this grub, yeah, God,' she would know she was better off without this fine specimen of a man. He took her hands into his, which once again immediately warmed her freezing, anemic fingertips. They bowed their heads, and he began to pray.

"Dear Heavenly Father, we come before you today to thank you for this day. We thank you for waking us up this morning, for giving us traveling mercy, for new friendships, and for the food we are about to receive. We ask that you bless the cooks who prepared this meal and that it be nourishing to our bodies. We ask you this in Jesus' name, Amen."

"Amen," Morgan affirmed. "Nicely done," she added.

"Why, thank you. My mom taught me well. So how is your day going so far?"

"It's going well. I can't complain. And you? Do you normally have time to step away for lunch?"

"If I don't have any surgeries, yes, I do. My assistants do a good job of blocking out a lunch hour for me between appointments. I normally just head up to the cafeteria. I have to confess; I get a little cranky when I am hungry."

"Good to know. Thanks for the heads up. I guess in full disclosure, so do I."

They both laughed. *Okay, Morgan, so far so good,* she thought. They sat in silence for a few minutes as they consumed their food. His eyes were on her while he chewed his food. It started to make Morgan nervous. She finally broke the silence. "So, I know what you must be thinking. What in the world happened last night? I want to apologize. I owe you an explanation, and I just want to say that you didn't do anything wrong. It was all me." Morgan just jumbled multiple sentences into one. "It's just that…"

Derek interrupted, "Morgan. Stop, please. That's not what I was thinking. Actually, I was thinking you chew with your mouth closed. That is so refreshing," he said, shaking his head.

"What?"

"You don't know how many women chew with their mouths open. Either that or they smack their lips while chewing. It's a pet peeve of mine. Sorry."

"Uh, thank you? I have never been complimented for

my chewing etiquette. This is definitely a first," Morgan said jokingly.

"Well, I wasn't going to say anything, but then you completely took my pensiveness the wrong way, so I had to come clean and, well, I'm not a good liar," he admitted. *Great, Morgan, you did it again. You just completely took the conversation left when it was going oh, so right.*

"Morgan, I want to apologize for last night. I overstepped the boundaries I created for myself and I'm sorry. I've been celibate for two years now, and somehow those lips of yours just put me in a trance. Now that I am aware of the power that those lips possess, I will act accordingly, if that's okay with you?" Derek began to blush from his confession.

Morgan smiled and nodded in agreement.

"But seriously, I like you, and I apologize if I made you feel uncomfortable in any way. That wasn't my intent. I realize that we all have baggage, and someday, you can tell me all about yours, but not today. I am a patient man, and I get the sense that, like me, it takes you a while to develop trust. Let's continue to get to know one another. So enough about last night. Why don't we enjoy lunch and keep the conversation light for now?"

"Okay."

This man just let me off the hook. Morgan felt a big weight being lifted off her shoulders. *Did this man just say he has been celibate for two years?* Morgan made a note to herself to definitely revisit this conversation at a later date.

"So, tell me something good."

"Good?" Morgan asked.

"Yeah, I just confessed my annoyance for loud chewing. How about you? What are some of your pet peeves?"

"Well, none are as interesting as that, I must say,"

Morgan said. "Umm, I'd have to say it annoys me when people say they are going to do something and don't follow through. I get that things come up, but at least acknowledge that you agreed to do whatever, and offer an explanation as to why you couldn't follow through, you know?"

"Yeah, unfortunately, that's a lot of people. I think most people are well-intended; they are just overwhelmed with life. Being a person of your word is an old school character trait that has gotten lost in this technological world. What else?"

"Uhh… I hate corny dudes."

"Corny? How so?"

"Maybe corny is not the right word. It annoys the heck out of me when people think they are funny when they aren't. And it seems like they are always cracking jokes and expecting you to laugh. I refuse. I will just give them the 'you've got to be kidding me' glare." Morgan imitated her special glare.

"Ouch. Have you ever thought that maybe some guys are intimidated by your reserved disposition? They probably think that the only way to break through your guard is to make you laugh."

"Well, maybe if they were actually funny, it would work. Wait. 'Reserved disposition?' What is that supposed to mean? Are you calling me a prude?"

"No, not at all. You are not like most women today. Loud. Bold. Aggressive. Reserved was the first word that came to mind, but I meant old school, classic. You are a lady. And you are looking to be treated as such. It's a rare but attractive quality. It's re…"

"Refreshing." Morgan finished his sentence.

"Yes, it is."

"Watch out now. I am starting to sound like a glass

of lemonade on a hot summer day," Morgan said sarcastically.

"And who can resist that?" Derek said. They made eye contact, and Morgan blushed again and quickly looked away. This man said the sweetest things so effortlessly. And her spirit told her that he was being genuine. How is this possible?

Changing the subject, Morgan asked, "What time is your next appointment?"

He looked at his watch, stunned, and said, "Oh, wow. It happened again. Time seems to stop when I'm with you. I actually have an appointment in ten minutes. When can I see you again?"

"Not sure. Why what's up? Maybe tomorrow?" Morgan inquired.

Derek nodded. "I'd like to see you again, Ms. Barnes," said Derek.

"Can I get back to you this evening? I need to check with my mother to see if she needs me to do anything." Morgan realized in that moment that her life was so mundane. It was all about routine. She never gave her evenings any thought because she always did the same thing. How embarrassing. Of course, she would never share that with Derek or anyone else for that matter. Somewhere along her life, she gave up on the idea of planning. If she were honest with herself, she would have said it was around the time her father died. His death definitely wasn't expected. For the life of her, she never imagined growing old without her two best role models, friends, and confidants by her side. They were the ones who pushed her, challenged her to dream big, and dusted her off when she'd fallen down.

"Oh, most definitely. You are a good daughter. It's apparent how much you love your mom."

"With all my heart."

They got up from the table, and Derek extended his arm, which Morgan graciously accepted. Despite his 1:00 p.m. appointment, he kept a turtle's pace while escorting her to the Metro. She was sure he recalled last night's walk to his place from the restaurant. *Who am I fooling? This man knows that I can't walk a lick in heels.* When they reached the escalators of the Metro, Morgan turned to him to thank him, but he gestured for her to get on the escalator. She stepped on, and he stood on the next step behind her. They were extremely close, but not touching. He rested his hands on her shoulders. When they reached the bottom of the escalator, he again extended his arm and he walked Morgan up to the Metro gate. Releasing his arm, she fumbled for her fare card in Renee's big ole tote as he said, "Morgan, thank you for lunch. I had a really good time."

With fare card in hand, Morgan said, "Me, too. Thank you for lunch and good conversation." She gave him a tight embrace, half out of mere attraction and half out of complete appreciation for not making her reveal her secret today. He reciprocated the hug, squeezing her tightly. As each loosened their grip, Morgan looked around him to spot the train approaching.

Just then, he planted a quick kiss on her cheek and said, "Thanks again." As she passed through the Metro gates, Derek said, "Text me and let me know you got to work safely, please."

"Will do."

"You've said that before," he reminded her.

"I will. I promise." Morgan smiled, then dashed for the escalators and on to the train that was stationed on the track. She immediately switched out her shoes as soon as she sat down. What was she thinking running for a train in these things anyway? She could have broken her neck or ankle. Thank goodness she didn't. *Good looking out,* God, she said to herself.

Chapter 6

After a long, stressful week at work, Derek surprised Morgan with a trip to Six Flags. She mentioned in passing her love for rollercoasters and hadn't thought any more about it until he pulled into the parking lot of the amusement park. Morgan was super excited. Once parked, Derek opened her car door and she jumped out, grabbed his hands, and started skipping toward the entrance gate. Morgan hadn't been to an amusement park in years. Each visit brought back fond memories of going to the park with her parents as a child. Her father was a die-hard rollercoaster fanatic. As soon as Morgan was tall enough to ride, he broke her in. Mrs. Barnes, on the other hand, was scared to death of rollercoasters. She was not going to put her fate in the hands of man. She proudly claimed the duty of watching everyone's bags as Mr. Barnes and Morgan went from one rollercoaster to another. The feeling Morgan experienced on that first ride, Smurf Mountain at Kings Dominion, was like no other.

As Derek and Morgan entered the park, their nostrils took in the delicious aroma of funnel cake. Morgan looked at Derek and said, "You know funnel cake is on the to-do list today, right?"

Derek smiled and said, "Of course. Where to first?"

They stopped in front of a map of the amusement park. After skimming it carefully for a few seconds, Morgan turned to Derek, pointed to the map, and said, "Let's start here." She pointed to the Superman rollercoaster.

Derek took a deep breath and said reluctantly, "Lead

the way."

As they approached the line for this rollercoaster that stood two hundred and five feet high with a two-hundred-foot drop, Derek tried his best to settle his nerves. Standing in what seemed to be a ridiculously long line, Derek decided to focus on something other than the gigantic metal contraption in front of him that could reduce him to a pulp. He turned toward Morgan so that his back was to the ride. He noticed the huge grin on her face. "You look happy," he said.

Morgan drew closer to Derek, wrapping her arms around his waist, engulfing his signature scent that she had become so fond of, and said, "I am. Thank you so much for this. Best surprise I've had in a really long time."

Derek embraced Morgan, resting his chin on the top of her head. He looked down and saw two little boys standing in line behind Morgan. They looked like they were no older than ten and just barely met the height requirements. Similar to him and Morgan, one boy, short and pudgy, was super excited to be in line, and the other, lanky and freckle-faced, looked extremely nervous. To the nervous boy, Derek asked, "Hey, are you okay?"

The little boy tried to hide his nervousness by changing from a slumped to erect posture. "Yeah, I'm fine. I've been on this ride a ton of times."

The other little boy interrupted, "No, you haven't. Stop lying. I dared you to ride the Superman."

Derek asked, "What do you get for doing the dare?"

The little boy with freckles went to respond, but the pudgy little boy beat him to it. "Im'a let him ride my brother's BX bike."

"BX bike, huh? Sweet."

Morgan admired the ease at which Derek talked to the young boys. The two of them continued to chat it up with the boys as the line inched closer to their turn. By the time Morgan and Derek reached the top of the stairs and could see the rollercoaster cars fill up with anxious patrons, Derek's disposition seemed to change. He became oddly quiet. Morgan pulled on his t-shirt and said, "Front or back of the line?"

Derek was in his own world. He saw Morgan's lips moving but didn't seem to understand the question, "Huh?"

Morgan smirked, "Do you like to be pulled or pushed?"

Realizing his options, Derek reluctantly asked, "Can we do the middle?" He wasn't sure how he found himself in this current predicament. *Lord, help me to keep it together and not pee my pants. I don't know if I can recover from that. Come to think of it, please just let me survive this ride.*

Morgan, eager to please, said, "Sure."

As the Superman car pulled into the station, the gate doors opened for them to get into the car. Derek's heart dropped to the floor. Morgan immediately got into the car and put on her seatbelt. Derek stood there looking down at her. The people behind him almost pushed him forward. Morgan looked up at him, and with her gorgeous face and sweet smile said, "You okay? Come on; I got you." With that, she reached out her hand and Derek took it. He then proceeded to put on his seat belt and lock it as tight as he could. As the worker went by to pull down the lap strap, Derek asked him to pull it down some more as there was still too much give. The worker obliged. Holding on to the lap strap for dear life, Morgan put her hand on top of his. By this point, she could sense he was nervous, and she wanted to do her best to keep him calm.

At a rapid speed, the car instantly pulled out of the

station. As it turned the first corner and sped its way up the steep slope, Morgan turned to Derek and said, "Derek, I just want to say that I am so appreciative of you surprising me and bringing me here. Thank you."

Derek could not concentrate on anything then, except preparing his eulogy. So as not to be completely rude, without looking at Morgan, Derek whispered, "Can we talk about this later?" And with that, the two-hundred-foot-drop that he was still not prepared for happened. Derek screamed at the top of his lungs. Once he realized that he was still alive after the drop, he still could not contain himself. The twists, turns, and drops that followed at a speed of seventy-three miles per hour kept him slightly popping out of his seat and he found himself screaming uncontrollably for the entire duration of the ride.

As the car pulled back into the station, Derek realized that he was alive and well, though the adrenaline continued pumping profusely through his veins, overwhelming him with excitement. Seeing the line of anxious people ready to take their turn at the rollercoaster, he hollered, "Whoa! Yeah!" and gave one guy waiting in line a high five. Morgan chuckled. Derek may have approached the Superman rollercoaster with fear, but he left it victoriously, having tackled it like a pro. He was so proud of himself. He took Morgan's hand as they walked down the path toward Gotham City.

"So what's next?" he asked.

"Batwing?" Morgan asked.

"Let's do it!" Derek said confidently.

After several more thrilling rollercoaster rides, and having gotten his screaming under control, it was funnel cake time. Approaching the window, Derek politely asked the young girl for one funnel cake with extra powdered sugar. He remembered that Morgan liked herself some extra powder.

Confused, Morgan turned to him and asked, "One?"

"Uh, yeah. I thought we could share one, no?" Derek looked perplexed.

"Uh, sir, I like you and all, but uh, I needs my own funnel cake. No offense," Morgan said with a straight face.

"Well, all right. Excuse me. Can you please make that two funnel cakes, extra powder?" he asked the cashier.

They found some shade under a wooden table with a huge bright red umbrella attached to it. Spreading out some of the napkins Morgan secured, they began to eat their funnel cakes over the napkins.

"So, I just want you to know that I conquered my fear of rollercoasters today. All thanks to you," Derek admitted.

"Fear? Like, you never rode a rollercoaster before today. Dude, I peeped how nervous you seemed once we got strapped in on the Superman, but I had no idea it was a real phobia. I am so sorry!" she exclaimed.

"For what?" he asked.

"Derek, if I knew you were afraid of rollercoasters, I wouldn't have suggested that we start with the biggest one here at the park."

"Well, I brought you here to ride to your heart's content, so who was I to tell you to put a pause on riding rollercoasters? And besides, because I tackled the biggest ride here, I realized I could ride any of them. It was a blessing in disguise. So, thank you!" Derek said.

"I guess it was. Girlie screams and all," Morgan said, no longer able to hold back the laughter.

"Girlie screams? Really?" Derek grabbed Morgan close and started tickling her. Just then, his phone buzzed.

Derek opened his text messages and said with disgust, "WTF!"

Concerned, Morgan asked, "What's wrong?" Derek's phone buzzed again.

"Ah, come on, man," Derek shook his head. "I'm sorry. My assistant just sent me a very inappropriate text message. And apparently she sent it in error."

"How inappropriate?" Morgan asked. Derek handed her his phone. It was a nude photo of his assistant, Lauren, posed strategically on a bed with some Red Bottom shoes on. Morgan started laughing.

"What's so funny?" Derek asked.

"She sent that in error, like you came to this park eager to ride coasters." Morgan was hip to the games young girls played, or rather women played. She wasn't surprised that someone would try such tactics with Dr. Patterson. He was a catch. But she also didn't like the fact that this woman worked in such close proximity to Derek. "So, what are you gonna do about this?"

"Nip it in the bud asap," Derek assured Morgan. "This is so not cool. I am her boss. And I am spoken for."

"You are?" Morgan said, surprised and flirting at the same time, "My bad. I didn't know."

"Well, in my mind, I'm spoken for because there is someone I'm interested in, and it ain't her," Derek clarified.

"Well, someone is interested in you, too, and likes the sound of you being spoken for," Morgan said, pointing to herself in case Derek wasn't sure who she was referring to.

As the two of them sat at the table talking about everything from loose assistants to kids and life, Morgan spotted a cute little boy about five years old holding an ice cream cone with two melting scoops of ice cream that were about to topple over. In awe of the little boy's cuteness, Morgan tapped Derek and pointed to him.

"That poor little guy's ice cream cone is a goner."

Derek followed her fingers and saw the catastrophe in action. Just when the ice cream fell to the ground, the boy dropped the cone and ran to his mother, crying. In that second, Derek's heart fell to the pit of his stomach for the second time in one day.

Morgan, still admiring the little boy, said, "He's a cutie pie. He looks like a young version of you. I'm sure you pulled all the little girls at that age, huh?"

Derek noticed the resemblance before Morgan said anything. He also noticed that the little boy ran in the arms of a woman he had been with a few years back. He couldn't believe what was happening.

"Morgan, I know that little boy's mother."

"Oh, you do? Well, you should definitely go speak to her. We can say hi when we get up," Morgan said.

"No, I mean, I knooowww that woman." Derek didn't want the thought in his head to be true, but he also didn't want to lie to Morgan.

"How is that possible? That little boy is like five years old?" Morgan asked perplexed.

"I know. I don't know. I need to go talk to her."

"Of course. I'll be right here."

Derek slowly got up from the bench and walked toward the woman. She was about five foot two, shapely with a rather high behind, and a head full of long blond tresses. As Derek approached, Morgan saw the woman's reaction. She didn't look happy to see him.

"Hey, Tasha?" Derek said.

Tasha looked up. Blinded by the sun, she shielded her eyes with her hands and cocked her head to the side so she could make out who was standing before her.

"Hey...."

"Looks like little man dropped his ice cream cone," Derek said, stating the obvious. He didn't know what to say.

"Yeah, it appears so." Tasha wasn't going to make this an easy conversation.

"So, what's his name?" Derek asked.

"Why?" Tasha asked with an attitude.

"You know why Tasha. What's his name? What is he, like, five?" Derek wanted answers.

"His name is Deitrick."

"Deitrick?" Derek tried to take it in.

"And he's five," Tasha said, rolling her eyes.

"So, he is..." before Derek could finish the sentence, Tasha cut him off.

"Look, we are good. We don't need anything. And this ain't the time nor place to be having this conversation."

Derek stood there for a second dumbfounded. Within less than thirty seconds, he learned that he was the father of a five-year-old son. How did this happen?

"Tasha, look, I don't know how this happened, but I'm not that dude. You not gonna just tell me that I fathered a child and expect me to be ghost. I've already lost out on five years of this boy's life. Who knows what you've told him about me? I can't control what I didn't know. But now that I know, you best believe I'm going to be in Deitrick's life. Now I give you that this isn't the time or place, but I will be calling you tomorrow to discuss." Derek said authoritatively. "Is your number still the same?" he asked.

Tasha nodded.

"And you still stay at the same spot?" Derek asked.

"No, we moved, I bought a house a couple years ago," Tasha said.

"Oh, nice. Congratulations. Address please," Derek already opened up her contact info in his phone.

He quickly took down the address and told her he'd call her around 1:00 p.m. He was serious about meeting and figuring things out. Before he left, he turned to Deitrick and said, "Hey, little man, I'm sorry about your ice cream cone. You want another one?" The boy nodded. Derek came back with a big ole vanilla ice cream cone, three scoops high and handed it to the little boy who received it with a big grin.

"Now, you gotta eat it fast before it melts, okay?" Derek said.

"Okay," Deitrick said, grinning from ear to ear.

As Derek turned around to walk back to Morgan, he realized that his whole life had changed since he left her only a few minutes ago. As he approached her, it seemed like the weight of the world was on his shoulders. Morgan knew that this date stemmed from her needing a stress reliever from work, but somehow it seemed to have caused more stress for Derek than the two of them could have imagined.

"You ready to go?" Morgan asked, rubbing his shoulder.

"I'm so sorry. This isn't how I planned the day to go. I just." Derek struggled to find the right words to say.

"Have a lot to think about," Morgan completed his sentence. "I get it. I can't begin to imagine what's going through your head right now. It's fine. I had an amazing day! And you overcame your fear of rollercoasters to be able to ride with the best of them. And who knew such a burly guy could sing soprano." Morgan laughed, trying to lighten the mood.

Derek laughed, "You got jokes. Thanks, Mo, for understanding. We gotta do this again. I can't believe

I've been missing out on rollercoasters all these years." He grabbed her hand, and they walked through the amusement park back to his car. On the car ride home, he couldn't stop thinking about Deitrick.

"I grew up without a father. I said I would never be a deadbeat dad. But here we are. Deitrick has been without a father for five years," Derek said with disappointment.

"Derek. You didn't know. You can't beat yourself up." Morgan tried to console him. But she, too, was curious how this happened. "So, you and his mom dated?"

"No, that's the thing. We weren't together. I met her at a bar one night. We exchanged info. Hung out a few times. And that was that," Derek said.

"Oh," Morgan said with disappointment. She didn't mean to sound that way, it just kinda came out.

Pulling up to her house, Derek said, "Morgan, you gotta understand. Back in the day, I was living the life. A single doctor in the DMV. Worked hard. Played harder. You know how it is in this area for an educated, employed black man. I may have gotten caught up in the lifestyle for a few years too many. But trust me, it's completely out of my system." Derek tried to reassure Morgan that he was still the man she thought he was prior to their Six Flags date.

"Derek. I get it. No need to explain."

Derek parked the car and walked around to open Morgan's door. He extended his arm, and she graciously accepted it as they ascended the steps to her front door. While so much had changed in just a matter of hours, so much remained the same. There was still this sense of comfort and connectedness between the two of them. Morgan couldn't deny that. But at the same time, she knew that a child was now involved, and she couldn't be selfish about what she wanted out of Derek. She needed to give him the space he needed to figure things out. Morgan turned to Derek.

"Thank you again for an amazing day. I had fun." And with that, she leaned in and kissed Derek on the cheek. "Be sure to text me and let me know you got home, okay?"

"Yes, ma'am. I had fun, too. Have a good night."

As Morgan showered and got ready for bed, her phone buzzed. She picked up her phone and saw a text message from Derek. It read:

"Morgan, thanks again for a great day. I conquered my fear of rollercoasters! We have so many more amusement parks we have to hit up now—you've created a rollercoaster junkie LOL. And thanks for being there for me today and for being so understanding. I don't know what's going to happen and I'm not sure I've fully processed things, but I want you to know that this news doesn't change how I feel about you. Just wanted to make sure you knew that. Have a good night. Sweet dreams. P.S. I made it home safely."

Morgan read the text message like two more times, paying close attention to the phrase, "this news doesn't change how I feel about you." Morgan did her little happy dance in her head because, despite her efforts to remain guarded, she was falling for this guy.

* * *

The sun couldn't rise fast enough for Derek to call

Tasha to set a time to meet later in the day. He realized that he told her 1:00 p.m. Unfortunately, he was only able to hold off until the clock on his phone changed to 8:59 a.m. before calling. To his surprise, Tasha answered and agreed to meet him at 11:00 a.m. at the nearby Denny's. The two-hour wait dragged on forever. He arrived at Denny's an hour early and took a seat at the corner booth facing the front door. In his mind, he anticipated that Tasha would be on the defensive and reluctant to be straightforward. Her reaction at Six Flags didn't give him any reason to think anything differently. As he tried to predict the conversation, he realized he knew very little about her. He concluded that's what he got for sleeping with a stranger.

Tasha walked up to the table around 11:15 a.m. in jeans, a white t-shirt, and a jean jacket. Her hair was pulled up in a high bun with her baby hair slicked down.

"You made it," Derek said with relief. *It's about time.*

"I said I would. Sorry I'm late. My mom was late coming by to watch Deitrick." As she took her seat, the waitress who had been checking on Derek for the past hour came by to take their drink orders. She was planning to give them some time to look over the menu, but Tasha already knew what she wanted – the Grand Slam with scrambled eggs with cheese and a double side of bacon.

Derek couldn't wait any longer. "Tasha, is Deitrick mine?"

"Yeah."

"I'ma need a DNA test," he said.

"Okay."

"Okay?" Derek was starting to get annoyed at the ease of this conversation and Tasha's one-word answers. "Tasha, why are we here? You had no intention of letting me know that I fathered a son?"

"Derek, it's a long story. I mean, you know we weren't together," Tasha began.

"I know."

"Well, what you don't know is that I had a man. And when he would piss me off, I would call you. So, when I came up pregnant, I thought it was his. I wanted it to be his. He was super excited. He proposed. We went to the justice of the peace. It was everything I ever wanted."

"So you never thought to do a DNA test?"

"No. Like I said, I wanted it to be his. You and me were only together a few times. What were the odds?"

"Obviously, not in your favor," Derek mumbled under his breath. He realized that he needed to be open to what Tasha had to say in order to get all the information he needed. "So, how do you know he's mine?"

"About a year and a half ago, I found out my husband cheated on me with my best friend."

"Oh, wow. Sorry to hear that," Derek said.

"Apparently, she was able to get him in bed by telling him that I cheated on him before we got married. Long story short, he asked for a DNA test, and it came back negative. You were the only other person I was with, so I knew Deitrick was yours."

"For four years, this dude raised my son as if he was his own?" Derek asked for clarification.

"Yeah," Tasha said, nodding.

"When you got the test results, why didn't you tell me then? My number hasn't changed." Derek still didn't understand. In his mind, there wasn't any acceptable scenario that would make it okay not to tell someone that he fathered a kid.

"What was I supposed to say? We weren't together. I didn't even know your last name. And some four years later, I'm just supposed to call you up and be like, oh yeah, we got a kid? Nah. I just couldn't bring myself to do that. I'm not that chick." Tasha said, shaking her head in an emphatic no, affirming that she made the right decision.

"Not only did you have some man thinking Deitrick was his, but you denied me the opportunity to step up and be the man that I am and have a relationship with my own flesh and blood. There's nothing right about that. And I don't know what 'that chick' means, but if you are referring to being independent and not having to rely on a man to raise your child, let me tell you, it took the two of us to make that kid. I'll be damned if it don't take the TWO of us to raise him into the man that he will become."

"Wait a minute. If you thought the baby was your husband's, then why did you name him after me?" Derek asked.

"I didn't. I named him after my husband and my dad – Deonté and Cedric," Tasha explained.

"Oh. Got it. Well, if Deitrick is mine, I want joint custody. There is not enough time in the world to make up for the past five years, and I don't want to miss another minute."

After another thirty minutes, Derek was able to leave Denny's feeling good about his conversation with Tasha. She agreed to drop off Deitrick's saliva swab to Derek's office in the morning. Being a doctor had its perks. Derek picked up the swab kit that morning from work and sprung it on Tasha right before he got up to leave. Tasha also agreed to have Derek over for dinner to introduce him to Deitrick. Derek was determined to do right by his son. He canceled all his appointments for the next afternoon, except for Mrs. Barnes, so he could visit the courthouse to file paperwork for joint custody. Anything that he did moving forward regarding his son would be documented.

* * *

As Mrs. Barnes patiently waited in the doctor's office to be seen by Dr. Patterson, she was slightly irritated by the assistant who took her vitals. For some reason, the older, slender, fair-skinned assistant could not seem to do anything right that morning. She mixed up the patient files when she came into the room to see Mrs. Barnes, calling her Ms. Humphreys instead. Once Mrs. Barnes clarified who she was, and the assistant retrieved the correct file, she attempted to take her blood pressure. She concluded that Mrs. Barnes' pressure was high, at 140 over 90. However, Mrs. Barnes always had exceptional blood pressure. She demanded that the assistant take it again. When she did, the assistant apologized and confirmed that her pressure was 120 over 80. During this time, Mrs. Barnes couldn't help but wonder – *where is Dr. Patterson's thirsty thot assistant, Lauren?*

When Dr. Patterson walked into the room, Mrs. Barnes could immediately see that his mind was preoccupied. She had never seen him like this and wanted to be a sounding board for him, if possible. But, first things first, Mrs. Barnes had to know.

"Where is Lauren? This new girl has got to go. Come telling me I have high blood pressure. Dr. Patterson, you know that my pressure is always in a good range."

"That it is. You have exceptional blood pressure, Mrs. Barnes, for as long as I've been treating you. Between you and me, I suspended Lauren."

Secretly, Mrs. Barnes hoped he fired the girl. Her little fast self wouldn't know a good thing if it hit her in the face. Now in curiosity mode, Mrs. Barnes asked,

"Why?"

"Mrs. Barnes, I'm surprised Morgan didn't tell you. Lauren sent me a very inappropriate text message. Now, in her defense, it was sent in error. Nonetheless, I had to take some type of disciplinary action. That type of behavior cannot be tolerated."

"Hold up, baby, let me get this straight. Your little assistant, who you've already checked about groping you, sent you a nudie picture of herself and you just sent her home for two weeks? I mean, geez, what does the child have to do to get fired...fall on your john?" Mrs. Barnes couldn't hide her disapproval for his decision.

"Mrs. Barnes, it's complicated," Derek tried to explain. "Lauren came highly referred by my mentor, Dr. Davis, who asked me to look out for her since she was like a daughter figure to him."

"Well, his daughter is a hussy who can jeopardize your career and practice. What does your mentor have to say about that?"

"I couldn't bring myself to tell him when I spoke to him last. And then he died a few weeks ago. I feel obligated to keep my promise to look after her. Dr. Davis was good people."

"Dr. Patterson, you kept your promise to your mentor. You gave Lauren a job and multiple opportunities for her to grow and develop in her profession. You turned your cheek and gave her a second chance after she fondled you inappropriately. Don't be confused. Dr. Davis was good people. Lauren is not. She is a rotten apple and will spoil the bunch. Hear the words coming out of my mouth."

He acknowledged her warning with a nod. Mrs. Barnes made a good point, but Derek was confident that his verbal reprimand and two-week suspension without pay would get Lauren to see that her actions were unacceptable and had to end. Derek always appreciated Mrs. Barnes' candor. She never sugarcoated anything. It was for this reason that he wanted to get her opinion on his other dilemma.

"Mrs. Barnes, can I ask you your opinion on another matter?" Derek asked.

"Of course, sweetie, anything."

"I just found out that I have a five-year-old son."

Mrs. Barnes tried to contain herself, but her mouth opened and dropped all at once.

"I know. Apparently, my son's mother thought that he was her ex's and therefore didn't get a DNA test. Long story short, four years later when she did decide to have the test done, she determined that the baby wasn't her ex's, and, by the process of elimination, it only left me. What do you think I should do?"

"Baby, that's a lot. Well first, you need to get tested and see if he is yours. Second, you want to go down to the courthouse and file paperwork. If he is your son, you want joint custody, so child support isn't needed. You want him to have your last name. And then, you need to figure out the best way to start to establish a relationship with the boy and his mother – though it sounds like his mother isn't working with a full deck, 'cause any woman who denies a man to be a father just doesn't make any sense. I'm sorry, but it doesn't."

Derek seemed relieved by Mrs. Barnes' advice. He was going to the courthouse later that day to begin filing the necessary paperwork. What he hadn't thought about was Deitrick's last name. What was it? Of course, he wanted his son to carry his name. He wondered if Tasha would put up a fight. There was so much to contemplate. In that moment, Morgan's beautiful smiling face popped in his head and he stood before Mrs. Barnes looking perplexed.

Mrs. Barnes immediately noticed and asked, "Doc, what's wrong?"

"Morgan," Derek blurted out.

"What about her?" Mrs. Barnes asked.

"Mrs. Barnes, I really, really like your daughter and I can definitely see a future with her, but I can't expect her to be okay with this situation. I don't even know if I would be if the tables were reversed."

"Well, for starters, you are talking about wanting a relationship with your son. Any woman who can't respect that and support that is not the woman for you. My daughter included. Second, it's safe to say that this situation is rather unusual. It's not like you conceived a child while dating Morgan. That would be a different story. One that she is all too familiar with," Mrs. Barnes said, shaking her head.

"Oh, wow, are you serious?"

"Unfortunately, yes. Derek, I think you need to wrap your head around all of this, determine what it is that you need and want, and communicate that to Morgan. Obviously, you two are still getting to know one another, but communication is key. That and giving yourselves time to adjust and figure out what works for you. That's all I got, Doc."

"I really appreciate it, Mrs. Barnes. You always give me a lot of food for thought. Have you talked to Morgan about your condition and the Do Not Resuscitate order yet?" Derek asked.

"Uh, no. Not yet. It's on my to-do list," Mrs. Barnes confessed.

"Mrs. Barnes. You know you've put me in a very awkward situation. I don't like keeping things from

Morgan, and, well, communication is so key to any successful relationship as you just so eloquently told me. Obviously, because of my job, I must keep this from her. But making her aware of your situation would be so much better for us all, including you."

"I know, baby, I know. I promise I will talk to her," Mrs. Barnes said.

* * *

As Mrs. Barnes left the doctor's office, her cell phone rang. It was Morgan. Mrs. Barnes thought Morgan's ears must have been burning from her conversation with Dr. Patterson.

"Hey, Suga. How are you?" Mrs. Barnes asked.

Morgan called her mom on her lunch break, and, after dialing the house phone and getting no answer, she decided to try her on her cell. "Hey, Momma. Good. Where are you?"

"Leaving the eye doctor," Mrs. Barnes said nonchalantly. As soon as the words left her lips, she knew that this was an opportunity to have the discussion with Morgan, but she concluded that it wasn't the right time. After all, these talks should be done face-to-face.

"Momma, have you met Derek's assistant? Young. Thick. Wears a wig or tracks. Not sure which," Morgan asked.

"Lauren. Yes, I met the heifer," Mrs. Barnes said.

"So does Derek and this chick have history?" Although Morgan's gut believed Derek, she wanted to better assess the situation and needed more details. Why not start with asking the one person who would tell it like it was?

"If by 'history,' you mean, 'Have they been intimate?' No, honey. It's not like that. Well, not on Derek's part.

This little girl has a thing for Doc and has tried to push up on him. But that's it," Mrs. Barnes said, trying to reassure Morgan.

"Well, she sent him a photo of her naked and said she sent it by accident." At the same time, both Morgan and her mother said, "It wasn't an accident."

"Dr. Patterson suspended her. Not sure for how long, though," Mrs. Barnes shared.

"I just don't like her being that close to him, Momma," Morgan confessed.

"Well, baby, what better time to practice trusting him than now? You have no control over what other people do or don't do. All you have control over is your actions and how you allow other people to treat you. I know after the whole Justin thing, you may be extra sensitive, but you can't put Derek under the microscope just because your last boyfriend stepped out on you. That's not fair. Continue to collect information and observe his actions. When his words and actions stop lining up, that's when you give him the side-eye. But sweetie, from where I sit, all I see is a man whose actions and words indicate that he is extremely smitten with my baby."

Morgan knew her mom was right. Just then, Morgan got an incoming call from Derek.

"Momma, hold on for a second, please," she said as she clicked over.

"Hello?" Morgan answered with excitement in her voice.

"Hey good looking, how's your day going?" Derek asked with some base in his voice.

Morgan being the sarcastic person she was, responded with, "Such the charmer, it's so much better now that you've called." They both started laughing. "No, seriously, it's good. How 'bout yours?"

"All jokes aside, it really is better now that I get to hear your voice. I was calling to see if I could see you this evening. Like after dinner. Is nine too late?" Derek asked.

"Sure," Morgan said.

"Bet. I'll come through at nine."

Morgan clicked back over and realized that her mom had put her on hold. Five minutes later, Mrs. Barnes clicked over apologizing.

"Baby, I'm sorry. Walter was calling to invite me to go listen to some jazz tonight. You and I didn't have plans, did we?"

"Nope," Morgan said, chuckling to herself.

"Good…because I already told him I would love to go."

"Momma! Really? Geez, just kick your own flesh and blood to the curb, why don't you?" Morgan said half-jokingly.

"Girl, you'll be ok. What were we talking about?" After a few seconds, Mrs. Barnes remembered, "Lauren. The assistant. Morgan, I've told Doc that I think he should get rid of her. She is more drama than she is worth, but he said he feels like he owes it to his mentor to look out for her. So he keeps giving her second and third chances. I hope it doesn't backfire on him," Mrs. Barnes said.

"Well, for her sake, I hope not. All I know is she has one more time to come after my man, and I'll…"

"Your man? Oh, so you two made it official?" Mrs. Barnes asked.

Morgan wasn't sure. They conversed about being spoken for, but she didn't know if that equated to them being in a full-blown relationship. She realized in that moment, with everything that was going on in Derek's life, this probably wasn't the best time to have "the talk."

So Morgan changed the subject.

"Hey, Momma, I gotta go. Have fun with Mr. Jenkins."

* * *

Derek arrived ten minutes early. When Morgan answered the door, she was greeted with a large slice of red velvet cake—her favorite. She took the cake and embraced Derek in a long, tight hug. Derek held on longer than usual, embracing the sense of peace and comfort that he grew so fond of when he was around Morgan.

"Why, thank you. But it would be impolite for me to eat this in front of you. Did you get yourself a slice?" Morgan asked, knowing that they were supposed to share.

Derek laughed. "Aww... man, I thought the only thing that was unsharable was funnel cake. I didn't know it applied to all fried and baked goods. My bad."

As Derek took a seat on the couch, Morgan went to get two spoons and two bottled waters. When she returned, she found Derek sitting, hunched over with his hands in his face, as if he were deep in thought.

"You okay?" Morgan asked.

"Honestly? No. But I know I will be." He patted the couch, signaling Morgan to sit beside him.

Morgan sat and opened the plastic container holding the cake and said, "I know what you need." She scooped a nice size chunk of cake on the spoon and fed it to him. Derek savored the bite and reciprocated the gesture.

Savoring her first bite of cake, Morgan asked, "What's on your mind, Doc?"

"I don't know where to begin," he confessed.

"Start anywhere. You said you wanted to see me

tonight. How come? What's up?"

"I've been thinking about you all day, and I knew that seeing you would make me feel at peace."

After swallowing another bite of cake, Morgan said, "Oh, you've been thinking about me. Good thoughts, I hope."

"Of course. Nothing but good thoughts."

As the cake dwindled down, the spoon size that Morgan was feeding Derek started to decrease significantly, but he didn't seem to mind. Morgan knew that if the tables were reversed, she definitely would have called him out, but that was her inner fat girl talking.

"Babe, I like you…," Derek shared.

Morgan interrupted, "I like you, too."

"A lot. And I want to court you. And only you."

Again, Morgan couldn't keep her mouth shut. "You do?"

"Yes, but I don't think it's fair of me to ask you that, given my current circumstance."

In the moment, Morgan almost forgot about the situation.

Derek continued. "I've always wanted a family. And I've always wanted to go about it the right way. Never in a million years would I have thought that I'd simultaneously find the woman of my dreams and find out that I have a five-year-old son."

"So, you are sure he is yours?" Morgan asked.

"I am waiting for the results, but I'm 99.8% sure. And Morgan, with that being the case, I plan to file for joint custody," Derek said, sitting back to see Morgan's reaction.

"As you should. If he is your son, you should be the one to raise him. His mother can't teach him how to be a man," Morgan said.

Derek was relieved by Morgan's response. He smiled because she just reinforced what Mrs. Barnes told him earlier in the day. He leaned forward, gently placed his hand on her cheek, and drew her in for a soft kiss on the lips.

"So, you aren't mad?"

"Mad? No, what is there to be mad about? It's not of your doing. Well, I mean it is, but you know what I mean. I'm a little unsure what this all means for us, though," Morgan said.

"It means that you and I are together, and I am the father of a five-year-old. Is that okay with you? I don't want to force this on you, but I do want us to get to know him together. That'll mean we'll be an instant family. Are you good with that?"

"Wow. Hold your horses, Derek. Let's take one thing at a time. I think it's important that you bond with your son. I mean he hasn't known you at all. If you want to introduce me as your lady, cool. I will embrace him and love him because he is yours, but I don't want to confuse the poor boy or throw too much at him all at once, you know. As for us, yes, I want us to be together exclusively." Morgan was adamant that this was the right approach.

Relieved, Derek said, "Good. I mean, that makes sense. You make a good point. I just know how all this is gonna end up and I guess I was projecting what I know on you."

At this point, Morgan's legs rested across Derek's knees. He was rubbing her feet and she would wince when it started to tickle.

"Oh, you know how it's gonna end? Do I need to call you 'Mr. Cleo?'" Morgan asked.

"I don't want to scare you, and it may be too early to say it out loud. But I know that I've found the woman I want to spend the rest of my life with. So why not have Deitrick get to know his future bonus mom. I mean, he is gonna be the big brother to our kids," Derek started to ramble.

At the mention of kids, Morgan sat up, removing her legs from Derek's lap.

"What's wrong?" Derek asked. "Too much, too soon, huh? I'm sorry…"

Morgan blurted out, "I can't have kids."

"How do you know?" Derek asked, inquisitively.

"Well, I don't know if I can or can't, but there is a chance I can't. And with you talking about our future kids, I thought you should know. I mean, I understand if it's a deal breaker." Morgan went on to explain how she contracted chlamydia and what the doctor told her. As she told her story, Derek slowly grabbed one leg at a time and placed them back on his lap and resumed rubbing her feet.

When Morgan was finished telling her story, Derek paused and said, "Morgan, I am so sorry that you endured that. That dude was an idiot. But then again, if it weren't for his shenanigans, I probably wouldn't be sitting here with you now, so I have to say *thank you*. When I said that I've found the one, it didn't come with any stipulations. I want you, Morgan Elizabeth Barnes. I am falling in love with you. Whether or not we can conceive a child together down the line is something that I will leave in the Lord's hands to decide. This news doesn't make me want you any less."

Tears started to form in the corner of Morgan's eyes. "It doesn't?" she asked.

"Not at all." Derek pulled Morgan in close and kissed her passionately.

In true Morgan fashion, she pulled away and asked,

"So just to clarify, we're an item?"

Derek laughed. "Yes."

"So, I can refer to you as my man?"

"You betta."

"And I'm your girl?"

"No."

Morgan looked confused and disappointed all at once.

"You are my lady. My woman." Derek clarified and kissed away the lines in her forehead from frowning.

Morgan closed her eyes and took a deep breath. *This is really happening. This man beyond my wildest dreams is all mine.* This felt right; her heart was full. The two of them cuddled on the couch for the next hour watching the news and then *Late Night with Jimmy Fallon* before Derek headed home.

Chapter 7

While shooting the breeze with Stacy at work, Morgan received a disturbing phone call from Tra'maine's school. During football practice, Assistant Coach Roberts noticed shirtless Tra'maine had a severe bruise under his rib cage. The bruise appeared to have come from internal bleeding. When pressed about what happened, Tra'maine lied. Since he knew it wasn't caused by football practice, the coach knew instantly that the boy was lying because it took him too long to respond. Tra'maine tried to explain that he got into a fight with some kid from around the way and pleaded with Coach to not tell anyone because he didn't want to get in trouble with his father. In the weeks to follow, the bruise was followed by an elbow fracture, and like the rib cage before, Tra'maine had trouble explaining. After talking with the head coach and sharing his concerns, Coach Roberts informed the school counselor, who was now contacting Morgan.

Morgan was surprised to get the phone call about Tra'maine and was hopeful that there was a reasonable explanation. She prided herself on placing Tra'maine with a loving and caring family. That afternoon, Morgan conducted an unscheduled site visit, and she was saddened by what she saw. The house was a mess. Trash was everywhere. The refrigerator was bare. And the most alarming factor was Mr. Stevenson. He was a shell of the man she met a few months prior. His face was sunken in from lack of eating. He reeked of alcohol and he was extremely irritable. He refused to let Morgan talk to Tra'maine, so she spoke to him at school the next day. Tra'maine was a smart kid. He was also extremely loyal. Although his dad was physically assaulting him, he knew his dad was hurting from the loss of his mom and blamed himself for provoking the man. No matter what question Morgan asked, Tra'maine would not confess that his father laid a hand on him. Morgan knew in her gut the real deal, and as a precaution, decided to report it. Child protective services arrived that evening and removed Tra'maine from the house.

* * *

It was just another Saturday morning with Morgan out and about, running errands. She was off her routine of waking up by 8:00 a.m. and heading to the smoothie spot, All Natural Smoothies, to get her favorite morning beverage. The night before, Derek invited her to a Paint and Sip event, which she really enjoyed. Morgan took up studio art in college, but after comparing her finished works with classmates', she decided that maybe she wasn't gifted in that area and dropped the class. During her date with Derek, she realized that she found painting to be therapeutic. It didn't matter whether she was good at it or not. Of course, Derek thought her painting of the moonlight image of The Washington Monument and Lincoln Memorial Reflecting Pool was a masterpiece. In comparison to his abstract painting of blues, grays, and white specks, it really was. He couldn't stop praising her artistic abilities. Afterward they bar hopped until they ended up dancing at an Ethiopian spot with great music.

The next morning, Morgan managed to leave her house three hours later than usual and still decided to hit up All Natural Smoothies. There was something about the Strawberry, Raspberry, Blueberry, Pineapple Juice, and Blackberry smoothie that always got her Saturday mornings off to a good start. As she approached the door, a couple was exiting the smoothie bar with a stroller, while the woman swaddled a baby to her chest. As Morgan held the door, she realized it was Justin, Courtney, and their newborn and toddler. She and Justin made eye contact at the same time.

"Hey…" Justin said, seeming a bit uneasy.

"Hey, how are you?" Turning to Courtney, Morgan said, "Hi, you must be Courtney. It's nice to meet you."

The woman frowned and immediately turned to Justin and said, "Courtney? Who is Courtney?"

Morgan was confused. She looked the woman over. The woman was wearing a wedding band and appeared to be the mother of the baby and child in the stroller. As Morgan observed the woman's reaction, she realized that she had seen her before, but couldn't pinpoint where.

Justin appeared to be at a loss for words. Morgan decided to try to fix whatever drama her sincere greeting caused. "I'm sorry, I thought your name was Courtney. My bad. You are Justin's wife, no?"

Still looking at Justin, his wife answered, "Yes, but my name is Morghan, with an *h*," adding emphasis to the *h*.

"Huh?" Morgan burst out laughing, "Are you serious?" By this point, Morgan was now looking Justin dead in the eye while Morghan with an *h* was staring at Morgan.

"Yeah, is something funny?" Morghan asked with an attitude.

It was in this moment that Morgan realized where she knew this woman from. On at least a handful of occasions, Morgan saw this woman leaving Justin's condo complex, sometimes coming out the front door, other times, getting off the elevator and at least one time on the same floor as his condo. Morgan never thought anything of it because she assumed she was just a woman that lived in his building. But now, Morgan's blood was boiling. How dare this bama blindside her for a second time.

"So, you are just gonna stand there, speechless? Really?" Morgan asked Justin.

"I mean, what do you want me to say?" Justin responded, looking as pathetic as the day he told Morgan that "Courtney" was pregnant.

"So, let me get this straight. Your ex, who's now your wife, has the same name as me?" Morgan asked.

"Justin, who is this chick?" Morghan inquired.

Before he could respond, Morgan chimed in, "I'm Morgan, his ex-girlfriend, whom he cheated on with you. He told me your name was Courtney. Probably because he realized that would have set off alarms to know that I shared the same name as his ex, I mean wife. You know what I mean," Morgan's mind was running a thousand scenarios through her head at once. Turning to Morghan, she asked, "So, let me ask you a question."

Morghan didn't seem surprised by the news at all. She acknowledged Morgan's question with a nod.

"Did you and Justin live in the same building on Randolph Street?"

"No," Morghan replied.

In that split second, Morgan realized that God answered her prayer. She wanted answers for so long, and here they were just spewing out like a faucet. But none of this made her feel any better.

"So let me get this straight," Morgan said, taking a deep breath. "You knew of me and still you two were messing with each other the entire time that he and I were supposedly together?"

Morghan's nod was more like a get-to-the-point nod.
"Wow. So you were okay with being the other woman
that entire time?" Morgan didn't understand.

Morghan cackled. "I was never the other woman.
You were. Justin will never leave me, us." She looked
down at the sleeping toddler in the stroller and caressed
the swaddling baby. "So what if we took a break here or
there? Who cares? In the end, he made it official," she
grabbed Justin by the waist and hugged him.

Morgan couldn't believe what she was hearing. Was
Morghan right? Had she been the other woman? How
did she not know any of this was going on right in front
of her? Disgusted, she said, "You two are so deserving of
one another. Have a great life." With that, she proceeded
into the smoothie shop. Before the door closed, Morgan
paused, hesitated, turned around and said, "Oh, by the
way, you might want to get tested for chlamydia. That
was your husband's gift to me, and well, we know how
generous he can be." Morgan laughed, "Y'all take care
now." Then she turned and walked over to the counter.
In her periphery, Morghan appeared to be interrogating
Justin outside the smoothie shop.

All these thoughts started to invade Morgan's brain.
She decided to text her girls the highly important code
"911" and ask who was free to meet up for lunch to help
her make sense of all this morning's drama.

* * *

Despite the short notice, the girls met up at BJ's,
which was close to where Renee lived as well as the
errands Morgan had to run. Per usual, Stacy arrived first
and secured a half moon-shaped booth in the middle
of the restaurant. While she waited, she decided to take
full advantage of the happy hour special: two-for-the-

price-of-one margaritas. As Morgan was parking her car, Renee pulled up, so they walked in together. As they approached the table, they noticed two empty glasses.

"What took y'all so long?" Stacy asked, holding up the two empty glasses as if it was their fault that she finished off two drinks.

"Sorry. I had to stop past the credit union before they closed," Morgan said.

Renee and Stacy looked at each other and in unison said to Morgan, "Get a debit card!" Then they all laughed.

Concerned for her friend and anxious to unpack the 911 text message, Renee asked, "So what's going on? What's so urgent?"

"I ran into Justin," Morgan started.

"Okay, and?" Stacy asked.

"and Morghan," Morgan continued.

"*Who?*" Renee asked in confusion.

"Exactly," Morgan said, shaking her head. "Apparently, you know Courtney, right, his wife? Her name is really Morghan."

"Shut the front door!" Stacy blurted out.

"I know." By this point, Morgan was able to laugh at the absurdity of the whole situation. "Oh, it gets better. So I'm looking at this chick and thinking she looks familiar. But I couldn't pinpoint where I knew her from. After a minute of seeing her, it hit me. I saw this woman on multiple occasions leaving Justin's condo building."

"No...." Stacy said in anticipation of what Morgan was about to say.

"Yup. So I just straight up asked her. I'm like, so did the two of you live in the same building? And she was like 'no,' and then she proceeded to tell me that I was the other chick because I guess they technically never broke up or something. I kinda zoned out after that."

Renee and Stacy were speechless and completely confused. "So, she knew about you?" Renee asked for clarification.

"She knew of me. And apparently, she knew my name cause she wasn't surprised when I told her my name was Morgan. But she didn't blink an eye when she told me that I was the other woman. Can you believe that? Me? The other woman? How is that possible?"

"Wait. How is what possible?" Renee asked.

"How is it that I was the other woman? How did I not know?" Morgan asked.

"Morgan, don't spiral back down that rabbit hole. Please. You've come too far. You didn't know because Justin was a great, consistent liar. Now about this other woman business. Don't drink the Kool-Aid," Renee said.

"Yeah, girl, the two of them sound like a hot mess. There's some serious interdependency going on, along with straight-up immaturity." Leave it to good ole Stacy to break out her psychology degree.

"I just felt like an idiot all over again. And I stood there before this man and his picture-perfect family. By the way, his son looks just like Justin with his curly black hair," Morgan shared.

"Morgan, you prayed for answers, did you not?" Renee asked.

"Yes," Morgan said. She knew where Renee was going with this line of questioning.

"So you can't be mad when God gives you the answers you've been looking for. No one said that you'd like the answers. It's just that now that you have the information, you can completely close the chapter without any coulda's, woulda's, shoulda's. From everything you said, it sounds like the two of them were never done, and you happened to come along when he was on a time-out. He likely realized what a good thing he had in you and didn't know how to break things off. Maybe a part of him didn't want to. The moral of the story is that Justin was a season in your life. And now, you are on to bigger and better things, right?" Renee always kept it real with Morgan and helped her to see positivity in every situation.

Picking up on Renee's segue into the good doctor, Stacy asked, "How is Dr. McFine?"

Morgan laughed. "Good. He's coming over later for dinner," Morgan added, blushing. "He's still waiting for the test results, but he's pretty sure the little boy is his."

"How do you feel about that?" Renee asked.

"Which part?" Morgan asked for clarification.

"All of it," Renee said.

"I mean, if the boy is his, Derek is going to step up and do his part, as he should. But I would be lying if I didn't say a part of me feels like I'm being cursed. Here I am, possibly sterile, and all the men that I encounter just so happen to procreate or father random children while dealing with me. It's like a sick joke I can do without."

Renee and Stacy looked at each other again. This time, they made eye contact, and their eyes nonverbally said, "who should handle this one?" Stacy deferred to Renee.

"Morgan, the doctor said you might be sterile. God didn't tell you that. Don't go around here claiming mess that man puts on you. If you are meant to have kids, you will," Renee said.

"And if you want to adopt, you can have my two 'cause they are on my last nerve. And the good thing is that they are potty trained," Stacy said to lighten the mood.

Renee rolled her eyes. She couldn't stand being

interrupted. "As I was saying, don't get me wrong. It's not cool that babies and children have popped up in your last two relationships, but at least for Derek—cause we are done talking about What's His Face forever—you have the advantage of getting to know the kid from day one, which is ideal. I mean, he's not a newborn, but he might as well be since Derek is just now coming on the scene. You know what I mean?"

"Yeah, you're right," Morgan said. She left the restaurant feeling restored. Her girls always had a way of helping her get off the ledge of despair and overanalyzing. By putting things into perspective, Morgan saw that Justin was an idiot, and his actions and lies were no reflection of her. Secondly, there was no need to worry about her reproductive organs for now. Besides, the tables turned, and Derek and Deitrick were a package deal, and that was okay.

* * *

It was eight o'clock on Saturday evening, and the doorbell rang. Mrs. Barnes, who was already coming down the stairs, yelled toward the kitchen, "I got it."

Always on time, Morgan thought to herself. Her heart fluttered at the thought of opening the door to Derek for the very first time. This time around, not only did she know he was coming, but she invited him. Morgan heard him and her mom talking. The sound of their voices got louder as they approached the dining room where Morgan was placing the last dish on the table.

"Hello, Ms. Barnes, how are you?" Derek walked over to Morgan and embraced her with a hug and kiss on the cheek.

"Good. Thank you. I hope you are hungry."

"I intentionally skipped lunch because I knew this

was a home-cooked meal that I wanted to make room for."

"Oh no, Momma, we better start eating soon because Dr. Patterson is about to turn into Dr. Jekel if he gets too hungry," Morgan said chuckling.

Derek handed Morgan two bottles. "The cider is for you, and the Syrah is for Mrs. Barnes."

"Oh, thank you, baby. You know wine is good for the heart," she winked. "Okay, let's hold hands so we can pray and get this man some food," Mrs. Barnes demanded.

Seated at the head of the table with Derek and Morgan on either side of her, Mrs. Barnes clutched both Morgan and Derek's hands tight. Derek and Morgan locked fingertips as they struggled to reach each other over the crowded table that smelled of delectable goodness. Mrs. Barnes kept the prayer short and sweet, released their hands and said, "Okay, let's eat." She handed Derek the balsamic green beans followed by the stuffed Cornish hen. As he fixed his plate, Morgan grabbed a fresh hot homemade roll. Hot and moist on the inside and slightly crunchy on the outside, the rolls required no butter.

"Oh, Mrs. Barnes, you outdid yourself this evening. This food is delicious," Derek said between chews.

"Excuse me? *Mrs.* Barnes? You think my mother fixed this meal?" Morgan snapped her neck to look at Derek and said half insultingly and half-amused that he thought she was as good a cook as her mom.

"You fixed this? I just assumed your mom did since she cooked last time. Babe, you can cook!"

Morgan said, "Yes, I can cook. You think this woman here would raise a daughter and not teach her how to cook? That ain't happening."

Laughing, Mrs. Barnes added, "You got that right,"

"Well, I do stand corrected. Morgan, everything is amazing. I had no idea you could throw down like this."

"Why, thank you. My momma taught me everything she knows. I just put a little healthier spin on my dishes. But I'm glad you are enjoying everything. I hope you saved room for dessert."

"Dessert?" Derek had just grabbed two additional rolls.

"Yup. Chocolate molten cake, with ice cream."

"What? Get out of here. Are you serious? I didn't know my invite was to Le Restaurante de Morgan."

Morgan laughed, then excused herself to the kitchen to put the molten cakes in the oven. When she returned, Mrs. Barnes and Derek's discussion quickly ended. Her mom looked disturbed.

Intuitively, Morgan asked, "Momma, is everything okay?"

"Yeah, baby. I just got a headache all of a sudden. I'm going to excuse myself and head to my room for the night. I'ma give you two young folks some privacy."

When she got up from the table, Derek stood, and she embraced him in a hug. Returning the favor, he kissed her on her cheek. She did the same to him. Then Mrs. Barnes walked around the table and gave Morgan a big old hug that she cherished as an adult and planted a soft kiss on her cheek.

After that, Derek and Morgan proceeded to the kitchen, where Morgan grabbed some potholders to remove the ramekins from the oven.

"So, this is where the magic happens?" Derek asked as he looked around the kitchen and took stock. It wasn't a fancy kitchen.

She shared with Derek that when she bought the house, she envisioned remodeling the kitchen with state-of-the-art appliances. She planned to knock out a wall to open it up to the dining area and place an island in the middle of the floor with extra countertop and seating. But one year after buying the house, Morgan experienced a winter from hell. When the pipes burst, water flooded the basement, and her dream kitchen floated away in an instant.

"Do you want ice cream with your dessert?"

"Please." Derek sounded like an excited five-year-old who was eager to devour his dessert. In the moment, she saw Deitrick with his larger-than-life ice cream cone.

As Morgan scooped the ice cream from the carton, she felt his presence behind her; specifically, his hand grazing her hip and the tip of his nose brushing the back of her neck. "Thank you, Morgan, for dinner. It was delicious. You are amazing," he whispered in her ear.

Morgan's ear tingled from his warm breath. To try to lighten the mood, she said sarcastically, "Shouldn't you be thanking my mom for that great meal? I mean, that is who you thought cooked for you," she said with a roll of her eyes. With both hands on her hips, Derek slowly turned her around to face him. Now Morgan's back was against the kitchen counter.

He rested his forehead on hers and said, "Morgan, I'm sorry. I didn't mean any disrespect. I know your mom likes to cook, and, well, the food was freaking awesome. I mean, we've never talked about cooking, or that you enjoy cooking. I made an assumption. I'm sorry." He pouted his lips and gave Morgan a short peck on the lips. His lips were so soft. He slowly inched his face away from hers and began to stare deeply into her eyes as if he was searching for something.

Morgan broke the silence. "Well, for the record, if I invite you to dinner, it's because I intend to cook for you.

I would never ask my mother to cook for my company. That's just wrong," Morgan shook her head gently from side to side.

Derek considered the statement she made, then nodded in agreement. Morgan wanted to kiss him, so she leaned forward and quickly pecked him on the lips as he did her a couple of minutes before. He placed his hands on either side of her on the edge of the counter and tilted his head to one side as his lips touched hers. Slowly they began to kiss. *I could do this all day*, she thought to herself. Goosebumps began to creep up her neck. She wrapped her arms around his neck. He reciprocated by embracing her waist. She could feel her heartbeat begin to flutter. She felt her hands moving up the back of his neck to his hairline when she reminded herself of how she attacked him at his place. *Calm down, Morgan.* She talked herself down from Attack of the Celibate Woman Part II. Regrettably, Morgan pulled her lips away.

"Hey, your dessert is getting cold."

They looked over at the bowl where the ice cream had melted. Morgan's face frowned with a look of disgust.

Derek politely said, "Babe, trust and believe, I'm going to tear that dessert up. Where's my spoon?"

She handed him a spoon, and he quickly consumed the ice cream. With the edge of the spoon, he cut into the cake, which, to her surprise, oozed with chocolate. He took a bite and his eyes lit up like a Christmas tree. He began to moan with each chew. Nodding his head up and down, he started motioning to the bowl.

"This is….good!" he said with conviction.

Morgan laughed.

After a few more bites, he said, "I'm sorry, Morgan. I know the polite thing to do would be to share my cake with you, but umm, I can't do that. My mother taught me better, but I just can't get enough of this." And with that, he ate the last bite.

In that moment, Morgan felt satisfied. Her dinner was a success. Mrs. Barnes always said that the way to a man's heart was through his stomach, and from the look of gratification on Derek's face, she succeeded. Humbly, she said, "Glad you liked it."

"Liked it? I loved it. Are you going to eat yours?"

"Help yourself."

As Derek consumed the second molten cake, Morgan began to wash dishes. She was a neat cook. She believed in washing as she cooked so that by the end of dinner, there were limited dishes to wash. Upon finishing, Derek placed the bowl and spoon in the sink and grabbed the dishtowel that rested on the oven door handle and began to dry the dishes. With excitement in his voice, he said, "I want to cook for you."

"You don't have to do that."

"No, I want to. My specialty is breakfast, though."

"Oh." In that moment, the thought of Morgan spending the night at his place and waking up to breakfast in bed was outshined by the image of her spending the night and freaking out again during a passionate make-out session.

Derek must have read her mind., "Morgan, there's no pressure. We can eat breakfast any time of the day."

"Yeah, but we need some serious ground rules. We've committed to this celibacy thing, and I can't have you all over this," Morgan motioned her hands over her body. She was trying to convince herself as much as she was Derek. "Look, I'm not trying to tease you. I know you are a grown man with needs."

"Morgan, my needs are being met. You just fed me like a king. I'm not looking for something easy. Trust me, if that's all I wanted, I wouldn't be here. I told you before I am a patient man. I stand by that. Shoot, babe, I told you this is it for me. You are it for me. I mean that. I love you."

Morgan looked up at him and, staring in his eyes, words came out of her mouth, effortlessly, "I love you, too."

Derek clarified, "But I do want to cook breakfast for you. So, whether it's served in the morning, at lunch, dinner or late at night, my infamous French toast awaits. You just let me know what works for you." He smiled and kissed Morgan on her forehead. She buried her head in his chest. This man was too good to be true.

"You have a second bedroom, don't you?" Morgan began plotting the logistics of their next date.

"Yup. I have an in-law suite. I don't have family, so it's never been used. But it's dying to host a house guest," Derek grinned.

"Hmm. Then breakfast it is. Next Saturday?"

"Next Saturday."

Chapter 8

Morgan hated testifying in family court. Out of all the rooms in the courthouse, the one that Morgan always appeared before was the small, dark, and uninviting one. It was always packed with hundreds of kids, parents, and other family members who, for one sad reason or another, found themselves having to plead with a judge for yet another chance. Today was no different. Morgan was called to testify in the custody hearing of Tra'maine Edwards. Two months passed since he was removed from the Stevenson household. Morgan could only imagine that Mrs. Stevenson was turning over in her grave at this current situation that her husband found himself in.

Today's hearing was Mr. Stevenson's chance to regain custody of Tra'maine. Mr. Stevenson sat on the stand before Judge Nathaniel Clarke, clean-shaven with a fresh haircut. He testified that he got help. He was going to AA meetings twice a week. He even picked up a part-time job at the nearby Home Depot and there was now plenty of food in the fridge.

When Morgan took the stand to testify, she could feel Mr. Stevenson's eyes burning straight through her. The family law attorney didn't waste any time asking Morgan the hard questions, and she was obligated to share what she knew. The facts were that on two of three unscheduled site visits since Tra'maine was removed from the house, Mr. Stevenson had been drinking. Mr. Stevenson burst out, "That's a lie! Objection, Your Honor!" The judge scolded him and asked Morgan to proceed. In the first instance, the bottle of bourbon was left on the kitchen counter, the top was off, and Morgan could smell it on Mr. Stevenson's breath. During the third visit, Morgan spotted a glass half full, hidden beside the couch, as if Mr. Stevenson put it there intentionally before answering the door. Given this information, Morgan was still very concerned for Tra'maine's well-being and she could not recommend sending him home. The judge agreed.

On exiting the courtroom, Mr. Stevenson grabbed Morgan's hand from behind. Morgan immediately snatched it back, turned to him and commanded, "Don't touch me!"

"I'm sorry, Ms. Barnes. It's just—I've changed. What do I have to do to show you that I've changed? I was in a dark place. I was mourning the loss of my wife. Can't you understand that? I miss my boy. I need my boy."

"Mr. Stevenson, I am sorry for your loss. I truly am. But at the end of the day, my responsibility is to ensure the welfare and safety of Tra'maine. Until you get your drinking and anger under control for a considerable amount of time, I can't in good conscience recommend that he return home. I'm sorry." As she turned down the hall, she could hear him yelling at her.

"Do you know how it feels to lose someone you love? I'd hate for you to have to experience that!"

Morgan paused to take in what he just said. *Was that a threat?*

* * *

Friday night could not arrive fast enough. The week seemed to drag on day by day. However, nothing could dampen Morgan's mood. The toilet in the first-floor bathroom of her house overflowed again. No problem. She got assigned seven additional cases because of the laziness of some of her coworkers who just sat on the cases. No worries. All she could think about all week was what to wear on her overnight visit and how not to freak out. After trying on clothes for five nights straight, Morgan decided on an oversized tank top and some boy shorts. It exposed her bra on the sides but covered up her love handles. The thought of wearing something a little skimpier crossed her mind, but she kept having visions of her previous freak-out moment with Derek. Morgan didn't want to give the impression that she was ready for something more than she was. Besides, she didn't want to tempt Derek or appear as a tease since they agreed to remain celibate. At the end of the day, Morgan just wanted and needed to be comfortable.

Morgan contemplated what to tell Mrs. Barnes. She was grown. She didn't owe her mother an explanation, but she felt compelled to give one. The perfect opportunity presented itself when on Wednesday at dinner Mrs. Barnes asked Morgan what was planned for the weekend.

Nonchalantly Morgan said, "I'm hanging out with Derek on Friday. I may be out late. It may just make sense to stay at his house."

Mrs. Barnes smirked and said, "Okay, baby, have fun." And that was it. No interrogation. No slick comment or joke. It was a relief. Morgan was relieved. She wasn't sure what her mom was going to say, but it definitely wasn't that.

Friday evening came, and, as Morgan expected, the nerves set in early. As she drove to his house, she anticipated what would be waiting for her on the other side of the door. She imagined candles lit throughout the house, with a sweet hint of lavender aroma filling her nostrils upon entry of his home. Derek opening the door shirtless with his chest glistening with baby oil.

She quickly snapped out of her daze when she went to parallel park across the street from his crib. As she got out of the car, she remembered Derek carrying her across the street the first time he invited her over. Morgan gushed as she ascended the stairs. Taking a deep breath, she hit the intercom button for the penthouse. After a buzzing sound, the door unlocked. It was then that she remembered that the building didn't have an elevator as she looked for one and was only greeted by a stairwell.

As Morgan took her last step on the stairs, she looked up and saw Derek at his door, smiling, waiting for her. This gave her no time to catch her breath, so she just took a deep one and exhaled slowly.

"Hey, beautiful," he said.

"Hey," Morgan replied.

He ushered her inside. Morgan noticed he was wearing pajama pants and a fitted black tank top to her disappointment. Upon entering, she also noticed the entryway was bright. She quickly scanned the first floor and realized that nearly every light was on. *OMG, I have scared this man to pieces. He will never attempt to make out with me again. There is no element of romance here,* she said to herself. Her fantasy of being seduced by candlelight by a baby oiled glistening man quickly faded.

"Can I get you something to drink?" he asked. "I hope you are hungry. Dinner is ready."

"You cooked?" Morgan asked with surprise.

"Uh, no," he clarified, "Take out. There's this really good Mediterranean spot around the corner. I got us falafel, rice, and mixed vegetables. I hope that's okay. When we went to Roti, I remembered you mentioning that you liked falafel."

"I do! Sounds delicious." *How did he remember that?* Morgan thought to herself. Obviously, while she was sweating bullets at Roti, worried about how to tell this great man why she freaked out on him the night before, he was paying attention to what she was actually saying. *Look at God,* Morgan said to herself with a subtle chuckle.

"What's so funny?" Derek asked as he placed the last dish of food on the table and sat down across from her.

Caught off guard, "Huh? Oh, nothing." Morgan quickly grabbed his hand and offered to bless the food. Heads bowed and eyes closed, Morgan thanked God for the food they were about to receive, the hands that prepared the meal, and for the wonderful company she was in.

Derek was right. The food was really good. Authentic. Throughout the course of dinner, Morgan learned more about Dr. Patterson. As a child, he wanted to be Mr. T. His fascination with the actor got him interested in lifting weights. Ultimately, all the weightlifting helped him develop the solid, ripped body that sat across from her.

Thanks, Mr. T…. oh, how I pity a fool, Morgan thought. She couldn't get over how their conversations were so effortless. She was surprised. She never, ever opened up to anyone this quickly or easily. Even her mother had to pry with crowbars from time to time to get information out of her. But not Derek. Around him, she was an open book. Well, almost. There was still the topic of senior year homecoming that Morgan couldn't bring herself to initiate.

After they cleared the table and washed dishes, Derek and Morgan headed over to his couch, which sat in front of a seventy-two-inch television.

"Is there something in particular you want to watch? I have a couple movies under the console if you are interested. Or, I can pull up Netflix," Derek said.

If anyone ever questioned Derek's age, his extensive

DVD movie collection would be a dead giveaway. Morgan made her way over to the console, plopped herself down on the hardwood floors and began skimming the alphabetized movie collection. *Yup, this man was OCD*, she thought. As her eyes glanced over the movies, Morgan stopped with excitement and said, *Coming to America!* Oh yeah! This is a classic!" Moving down the row of DVDs, she noticed *The Notebook* and said, "You have got to be kidding me? What grown man has *The Notebook*?" It just came out of her mouth before she could even think about what she was saying.

"You didn't like it?" He asked.

"Yes, I liked it, but that doesn't mean that I'd expect a guy to own it. Come on, is this a joke. This is a chick flick. Either this is your 'get the draws' move, or it was a gift."

Laughing, he said, "Really? It has to be one or the other, huh? A grown man can't just appreciate a good love story? Geez…"

"No. Not at all," Morgan said. "So, which is it? Signature move or a gift?" She wasn't sure if she should be concerned, but she wanted to know.

"Dang, woman. If you must know, a friend left it and never came back for it. You happy now?" Derek said.

"More like relieved. A friend, huh?" Morgan said, laughing loudly.

"What?" Derek asked, dumbfounded.

"You guys trip me out categorizing every female you've ever entertained as your 'friend.'"

"What's wrong with that?"

"Besides the fact that you are lumping all of your relationships into one big ole bucket—your one true love, long-term girlfriends, one-night stands and all the thots in between. Doesn't seem fair to the women who really meant something to you." Morgan wasn't sure why she went off on this tangent. She really didn't want to have a conversation about his past relationships. Given his age, occupation and fineness, she knew his smash list was ridiculous. And she definitely didn't want to have him flip the table and ask her about her pathetic relationship history. *Morgan, shut up,* she kept telling herself.

"Well, that's an interesting point. I guess I never really looked at it from that perspective. I'd like to think that at the end of the day, I was friends with everyone I dealt with or at least cool with them. But I wouldn't want to discredit the two," he said, holding up two fingers, "women who were near and dear to me."

"Good." Trying to lighten the mood, Morgan changed the subject, "So can we watch *Coming to America*?"

"Of course!" Derek got up from the couch and made his way over to the DVD player. Morgan got up from the floor and headed over to the couch, where she intentionally sat down right beside the imprint he left behind. Before coming back to the couch, Derek turned the living room lights off and dimmed the lights in the dining room. When he made his way back to the couch, he didn't exactly sit in the same spot, but he got comfortable, extended his arm and pulled Morgan into him. There she sat, nestled in his arm, resting her head on his chest. *Dang, this feels good.*

Before they got too engrossed in the movie, Derek turned to Morgan and said, "And for the record, until now, I hadn't come close to finding my one true love."

* * *

After the movie ended, with the living room light still dimly lit, Morgan decided to engage Derek in real talk. She was so comfortable resting on his chest that her nerves about having this conversation subsided. Well that, and all the laughing from the movie. She sat up and turned to Derek and asked, "Can we talk?"

"Sure, what's up?" He, too, sat up and repositioned himself to face Morgan, who was now sitting crossed-legged on the couch.

"I owe you an explanation about that night," Morgan began.

"Babe, no, you don't. I mean if you want to tell me, okay, but you don't *owe* me anything," Derek said.

"I know, but I want to.... I just need to get it out, okay?"

"Okay," Derek said, nodding.

"When I was in college, my friends nicknamed me Second Sacker."

"That's a baseball reference, right?" Derek asked.

"Yeah. They teased me because freshman year I dated this guy on the baseball team, and he ended up dumping me because I wouldn't go past second base," Morgan said with annoyance.

"You had boundaries. There's nothing wrong with that." Derek tried to reassure her.

Morgan nodded in agreement. "Homecoming weekend, my senior year. Me and some friends had a little pre-party in my room with some Boone Farms. You remember that?"

"The real cheap stuff. Oh, I remember. It was like the right of passage for all college students."

"Well, we drank before we headed to this homecoming party. Two of my four friends got really wasted and ended up not even making it to the party. Shortly after we got there, this guy walked up to me and introduced himself. His name was Terrance. He was the friend of this guy in my Econ class and was visiting for the weekend. He was from Detroit and was majoring in engineering. He was the oldest of three children, two of whom were girls, and he played lacrosse," Morgan recited the facts as if they were tattooed on her brain. "He seemed cool. You know, we talked and danced and by the end of the night, he offered to walk me home. My friends bailed. When we got back to my room…" Morgan paused. Derek put his hand on top of hers, which rested on her foot. Morgan took a deep breath and continued. "I invited him in." As she talked, Derek could tell that she was reliving the events of that October night. There was a glaze over her eyes and her body stiffened. He didn't know how to respond but chose to continue to rub her hand gently.

"Things were cool at first. We started kissing and it led to us making out. I didn't think anything of it because, well, technically we were still at first base. Clothes started to come off, and I was still fine, 'cause we were at second base," Morgan paused, "and then in an instant, we weren't. He reached down under my skirt and tried to pull my panties off, and I told him to stop. I kept telling him that I was a virgin and didn't want to do this." A single tear ran down Morgan's cheek and Derek leaned in and wiped it dry with his thumb. "I tried to get from under him, but he was so heavy. I couldn't move. I started to hit him as hard as I could. With one hand, he pinned my arms above my head. I tried to scream for help, but he stuffed something in my mouth. He forced himself on me. I just laid there crying, as it felt like he was ripping me apart." Morgan blinked, having come out from retelling the nightmare. After a long pause, she said, "You know what the crazy part is?"

Derek was obviously disturbed, more like angry and fuming inside, but he tried to keep his composure. "No, what?"

"The whole time, I kept wondering if I led him on.

What grown woman invites a guy back to her room after midnight, with the intention of just making out? Why was I so naïve to think that he would be okay with that?" Morgan said.

"Baby, you can't blame yourself. No means no. No matter the circumstance. I'm so sorry that happened to you." Derek pulled Morgan in, cradling her and embracing her gingerly. "You said this dude had sisters? WTF? Did you file a report?"

"No. I didn't want anybody to know. I didn't want to be the talk on campus. I just wanted it to all go away."

"So, you've carried all of that by yourself, all these years?" Derek asked.

"I eventually told a counselor at school because it was starting to affect my grades. I couldn't sleep. I started missing classes and I had to graduate. The counseling helped. I stopped blaming myself mostly, but I didn't tell anyone after that until a few years ago when I confided in Renee."

"So, Mrs. Barnes doesn't know?" Derek asked with surprise.

"No. Although I feel like my mom has eyes in the back of her head, so I wouldn't be surprised if she figured it out. But no, I didn't tell her. Until today, only two people knew."

"Wow. Morgan, I am honored that you feel comfortable to confide in me. Your secret is safe with me. But I want you to know that I never, ever want you to feel uneasy about anything, and I am truly sorry about that night. I…"

With both hands on either side of Derek's face, Morgan interrupted, "Stop. You have nothing to apologize for. I am not used to putting my guard down when it comes to guys, and well, I feel rather at ease with you. In that moment, I had a flashback, and well, I freaked out big time," Morgan admitted.

"Babe, I just... I don't want to hurt you," Derek confessed.

Looking deep into his eyes, she replied, "Then don't."

"You know where this joker lives now?"

"I believe in Texas. Why? You gonna go get him?" Morgan was flattered by his desire to defend her honor.

"The thought crossed my mind."

"Well, that's awfully nice of you, but I didn't tell you so you could be my knight in shining armor. I told you so you could understand why I flipped out and to understand better where I'm coming from."

"I know." Derek kissed Morgan on her forehead. "But so that you know, I will hurt any man who attempts to hurt you in any way. Straight up."

They laid on the couch, cuddling for a while, dozing off to sleep here and there in between light conversation. Finally, around 3:00 a.m., they straightened up a bit, plumped the couch pillows and took their glasses to the sink before heading upstairs. As Morgan ascended the stairs, butterflies began to form in her belly. She began to take long extended breaths and repeated to herself, *Calm down, Morgan. You can do this, girl! Get it together.*

Derek showed Morgan where the bathroom was and the fresh towel and washcloth he placed on the towel rack before heading to the guest bedroom. Turning on the light, Morgan noticed how spacious the room was. The room was cozy with a natural color palette. The king-size bed was a little intimidating as it seemed larger than life.

"So, this is where you will be sleeping. I hope it meets your standards. The bed is pretty firm. You are the first person to break it in," Derek said with a smirk.

"Oh, I don't know. You might have to call the coast

guards to come find me in that sea you call a bed,"
Morgan said sarcastically.

He laughed. "Well, I hope you get some sleep. I'm
down the hall if you need anything. Are you an early
riser? I'm trying to figure out what time to get up to start
breakfast."

Looking at her watch at the time, "Uh, 10:30 a.m.? Is
that okay?" Morgan asked.

"Sure. Get some rest, Morgan. See you in the
morning." Derek lightly grabbed her shoulder, leaned in,
and kissed her. In that moment, Morgan wanted him to
embrace her tenderly in a hug and kiss her passionately,
but she knew that her crazy alter ego might resurface
and cry foul again. So, after he left the room, she closed
the door behind him and got dressed for bed. Morgan
contemplated whether to leave the door cracked open, in
case he wanted to sneak in the room and join her in this
massive bed. Then again, she knew that scenario wouldn't
end well, so she kept the door closed. By then, Derek had
consistently demonstrated that he was a true gentleman
and wasn't out for a quick lay. More importantly, she
knew that she wasn't ready, even if her mind fantasized
about taking things further with Derek.

* * *

Morgan was in a deep sleep in this heavenly bed,
when she started dreaming about floating pigs. In that
instance, she woke up to the good ole smell of fried
bacon. She grabbed her phone to see what time it
was—10:04 a.m.—and nonchalantly checked to see if
the bedroom door was a jarred. Maybe he got up this
morning and poked his head in to get a glimpse of her
sleeping. She could tell from the reflection in her cell
phone that she looked a hot mess. Morgan intentionally

left her headscarf at home because she didn't want to look like Aunt Jemima, so her hair was all over her head. She looked down at the pillow that comforted her head all night long and saw stains of drool. She quickly looked at the door again. Just as she left it, tightly shut. *Good.*

When getting out of bed, Morgan forgot how huge the bed was. She hurled herself to the floor. She forgot to pack a robe, so she gingerly opened the bedroom door and peeped outside to see if he was in the hall. Coast was clear. *Dah, Morgan, the man is downstairs fixing you breakfast!* Then she quickly tiptoed to the bathroom in her oversized tank top.

After making herself presentable, changing into a pair of leggings and a tank top, and doing something with her hair, Morgan neatly straightened up the guest bedroom before heading downstairs. She could hear Mrs. Barnes now: "Girl, don't go making yourself at home too quickly." As she headed downstairs, Morgan noticed a large photo of a beautiful young woman. She must have been in her mid-twenties. She was brown-skinned with red undertones and high cheekbones. Her hair was long and wavy, and she smiled from ear to ear. This must be Derek's mom. No wonder he was so fine.

Downstairs Morgan could feel the bass of the trap music coming from the kitchen. The music was so loud that Derek couldn't hear Morgan approach and was startled.

"Good Morning," Morgan said with a smile. *This man may be a doctor, but he likes his trap music just like any other brother,* she said to herself.

"Hey, good morning." Finding the remote to his Bose system, he turned down the volume and switched the station to R&B. "How'd you sleep?"

"Like a baby. That was until I started dreaming of

pigs," Morgan joked while trying to spot the bacon.

Derek must have read her mind because he slid a plate of hot crispy bacon her way. Out of habit, she took two slices then sat down in the nearby stool at the oversized quartz countertop.

"Well, I hope you are hungry. Let's take this in the dining room," Derek said. Morgan followed his lead as he walked toward two large sliding wood doors. She didn't notice them before, but the double doors were an Asian motif.

Behind the sliding doors was a massive table with food galore. There was homemade hash browns, shrimp and grits, waffles and French toast, scrambled eggs with cheese, biscuits with honey butter, and yes, more bacon. To say Morgan was impressed was an understatement. Derek had even gone a step further and set the table with paper plates and paper napkins folded underneath the utensils. Morgan turned to Derek and said, "Well, doc, you've definitely outdone yourself."

"Why, thank you; however, I'd save the accolades until after you've tasted the food." Derek pulled out Morgan's chair, sat down beside her and started to pass her the dishes. As they blessed the food and began to eat, Derek's phone rang.

"Hello? Yeah. I did, but I can change it. What time? Okay. Alright. Bye."

Morgan, who was chewing until her heart was content, looked up and asked, "Everything okay?"

"Yeah. Umm, we didn't have any set plans today, did we?" Derek asked.

"No. Why? You need to end our date early?"

"No, not at all. That was Tasha, and apparently, her mom was supposed to watch Deitrick, but she's not feeling well. So, I told her we'd watch him," Derek replied.

"I didn't hear anything about 'we' during that two-second phone call. You sure she is gonna be okay with me being around her son?" Morgan asked with concern. "You mean my son? Babe, we are a package deal. She will be fine with it. It's not up for debate."

* * *

The morning flew by, and as the afternoon approached, Derek's nerves started to get the best of him. It started with what to wear. He tried on the same polo shirt in two different colors, salmon and a light gray. He asked Morgan which one she liked better. For her, it was an easy choice because charcoal and all things gray were her favorite colors, but she quickly reminded him that Deitrick wouldn't care what he wore. After stating the obvious, she suggested he wear the gray one. Then Derek couldn't decide where they should go that afternoon. The calm, collected, mature man that Morgan had come to know was melting before her. She understood and decided to take charge to help him out. She suggested they go to the trampoline park. What kid doesn't like to jump around? Afterward, they could grab a bite to eat. Derek thought that was an ingenious idea.

As Derek and Morgan approached Tasha's house, it dawned on her that she didn't know what Deitrick actually knew about Derek being his father. She didn't want to make Derek feel any worse or more nervous, but she also didn't want to put her foot in her mouth accidently. So without hesitation, she asked, "So, does Deitrick know you are his dad?"

Having pulled up in front of the house, Derek stopped the car and looked at Morgan, dumbfounded. He shook his head, "I don't know. I should ask, right?" he asked rhetorically as he dialed Tasha's number. "Hey, umm, so did you tell him I'm his dad, or…. oh. Okay, so how should I play this? Really, Tasha? Alright, we are outside," Derek said.

Morgan was staring at him with anticipation. "So?"

"She told him this afternoon that he was going to meet his real dad, and Deitrick got upset and said he didn't have a dad, not anymore anyway," Derek said with hurt in his eyes.

"So why'd you say 'Really Tasha?'" Morgan knew Derek had a lot on his mind, but it seemed to her that he was leaving out critical information.

"Oh, she was just like, he will get over it. He's ready to be picked up."

"Oh, wow." Even Morgan was surprised by Tasha's nonchalant response.

"Exactly. You ready?" Derek asked.

"Almost," Morgan said before taking his hand and bowing her head to pray. Derek followed suit.

"Dear Heavenly Father, we come before you today to say thank you. Thank you for allowing Derek to find out that he has a son. Thank you for blessing this world with Deitrick. Thank you for this opportunity to foster a lifelong relationship with this little boy. God, we ask that you put a hedge of protection around him as he continues to grow up. God, please be with us, but especially Derek today as he meets his son for the first time. Please remove all anxiety from him. Give him the confidence he needs to know that you have already equipped him for this day. That you have placed everything in him that he needs to raise a young, black boy in this world. God, please help Deitrick to be open to this new relationship and help us all start off on the right path. God, we thank you in advance for what you are about to do in all our lives. We ask you these things in Jesus' name, Amen."

Derek looked up and smiled his big, pearly white grin. "Amen. Thank you, babe. You are the best. I needed that." He leaned in and kissed Morgan softly on the lips. "You ready now?"

"Yup, let's go."

They weren't sure how long Tasha was waiting at the door, but as soon as they approached the front door, she opened the screen door and invited them both in. To Morgan's surprise, Tasha didn't give any sense of attitude or stankness toward her after Derek introduced her as his lady. If anything, Tasha was most appreciative that they could help out on such short notice. Tasha called for Deitrick. He slowly walked toward his mother's voice, stopping only to peak his head from behind the corner into the living room where Derek and Morgan sat on a small loveseat. He wore a Wakanda Forever t-shirt and a Black Panther mask over his face.

To lighten the mood, Morgan said, "Oh my, I think Black Panther is amongst us."

Derek decided to play along, "Well, how do we know it's Black Panther and not Killmonger?" Deitrick giggled, still slightly hiding behind the corner.

Tasha was not in the mood for any of Deitrick's games. "Boy, stop playing and come on. I got things to do," she yelled.

Deitrick came hopping around the room with his Black Panther superhero action figure in his hand. Still giggling, he responded to Derek, "I'm not Killmonger. I'm Black Panther. See, my mask has purple in it. Not yellow."

Derek rose and bowed before the King of Wakanda and said, "Oh, I see. Well, King T'Challa, it is a pleasure to meet your acquaintance, I am..." Derek, who was playing along just fine, suddenly froze. What was he supposed to tell this five-year-old little boy to call him? Tasha and Morgan both understood his dilemma; however, Morgan didn't think it was her place to interrupt.

After what felt like a significant pause, Tasha said, "Deitrick, come over here and say 'hi' to your father."

Deitrick walked up and grabbed his mother's legs from behind. Peeking around Tasha's chubby, short legs, Deitrick whispered, "Hi."

"And this is your Dad's girlfriend, Ms. Morgan," Tasha added to finish out the introductions.

"Hi," Deitrick said again, this time talking directly into the back of his mother's legs.

"Hi, Deitrick. It's nice to meet you. We are going to the trampoline park. You want to come?" Morgan asked.

The mere mention of trampoline park encouraged Deitrick come from behind his mom. His eyes lit up as soon as Morgan extended the invite, and he nodded with excitement.

"Good. I may need your help," Morgan continued.

"Help?" Deitrick asked.

"Yes, I told your Dad that I could jump higher than him, but he doesn't believe me. I need you to be the judge and let me know who jumps higher."

"I can jump high," Deitrick exclaimed and began to jump on his tippy toes.

"Well, let's get going so we can show your Dad who can jump the highest," Morgan stood and grabbed Deitrick's hand. Although there was a chance that she could never have her own kids, it was quite evident that God gave her a motherly instinct, which she was most grateful for at that very moment.

Derek stood awkwardly and followed Tasha to the car to grab his son's car seat. He made a mental note that he needed to pick one up for his own car.

* * *

Overall, the day turned out to be a true success. God truly answered their prayers. It took a little while for Deitrick to warm up to Derek. It was apparent that he was used to being around females, so Derek was beyond ecstatic to have Morgan there with him. Deitrick shared that he had never been to a trampoline park and that his friends at school talked about it all the time. Not only did he have a blast at the park, but he also won the jumping contest. He jumped a zillion, cabillion times higher than Morgan and Derek combined. Morgan faked some tears, saying it wasn't a fair contest because they were competing against Black Panther.

After the park, the three grabbed dinner at a nearby Red Robin. They all shared a stack of onion rings, and Derek and Morgan gave Deitrick free rein to talk as much as he wanted. It was the perfect way for all three to get to know each other better. Derek and Morgan learned that he was in kindergarten. His teacher was Mrs. Henry, and she was nice. His favorite color was blue, the same as his best friend Preston. His favorite food was mac and cheese. He owned five goldfish, but they all died and went to heaven. And he wanted to go fishing so he could catch some fish to put in his now empty fish tank. Derek explained that if he caught any fish, they would likely be too big to fit in his tank, but he promised Deitrick that they would go fishing one day soon.

By the time they reached Tasha's house that night, around 9:30 p.m., Deitrick was knocked out in his car seat. Derek carried him into the house and placed him gently on his bed. Derek took a minute to examine his son's room. It was a small room with a racecar-shaped bed set against the wall. By his pillow was a stuffed brown bear. Derek wondered who gave it to him and if it had sentimental value. The walls were painted sky blue.

Along his bed were hand-drawn sketches drawn with crayons. Derek chuckled to himself because if Tasha was anything like his mother, she wore his tail out for drawing on the walls. Next to the narrow closet was a bin of toys. Of course, there were more toys outside of the bin, than inside, but they consisted of action figures, robots and Hot Wheels cars. There was a half-built Lego house on a mini rocking chair that was scooted to the middle of the room. Derek looked around and took it all in. This was his son's world. A world that he had not been a part of, but after spending the day with him, he could easily see himself fitting right in. And by the looks of Deitrick's interests, he definitely took after his father.

After leaving Deitrick's room, Derek took a minute to explain to Tasha that he promised to take his son fishing and that he wanted a set schedule to see him. He suggested that they start with every other weekend and work up to every weekend. He emphasized that it would give Tasha a break, which she agreed she desperately needed. When Derek approached the car where Morgan waited patiently, he found her jamming to Guy's, *I Like*, which played on the radio.

As soon as Derek settled into the driver's seat, Morgan turned down the radio, "You good?" she asked with concern.

"Oh, don't stop singing 'cause of me. Do your thang, Mo!" Derek said jokingly.

"I'm serious," she said.

"Yeah, I'm good." Derek grabbed her hand and looked deeply into her eyes, "Thanks to you, I'm good. Never been better. Thank you, Morgan Elizabeth Barnes. I love you."

"Babe, I didn't do anything. I love you, too." Morgan was always so modest. "Deitrick is a good kid. Tasha did right by him. And he reminds me so much of you."

"I know, right? Yeah, I see it too. Babe, you did a lot. You were by my side. You lightened the mood. You helped to warm him up to us. You came up with a great activity that we all could enjoy. You will make a great mother," Derek said. In that moment, Morgan looked down, and Derek gingerly grabbed her chin to face him, "You will make a great mother, Morgan. Deitrick can't have too many moms, and me and the Lord have been talking."

"Oh, y'all have, huh? What He say?" Morgan asked while giving Derek the side-eye.

"That's for me and the good Lord to know. But seriously, thank you for everything." Then Derek leaned in and kissed her. "Now, let's get you home. It's been a super long day. Oh, before I forget, there's an awards banquet coming up at work, and I'd like for you to do me the honor of being my smokin' hot date," Derek said with his picture-perfect smile.

"Awards banquet? Are you getting an award?" Morgan asked.

"Uh, I might be the honoree for the evening," Derek bashfully admitted.

"What? Baby, that's awesome. You know I would love to go. I'ma have to work on the smokin' hot part, though."

"Nah, you definitely got that in the bag," Derek said bluntly.

It only took about twenty minutes to get to Morgan's house. They held hands the entire way and quietly listened to the radio. Both were contemplating the day's events. Derek was planning the next outing, while Morgan thought about what Derek said to her—'you will make a good mother.' Would she have the opportunity?

Day one with Deitrick went well, but could she have the same bond with him that Tasha had? Obviously not, but something similar and uniquely their own?

As Derek pulled onto Morgan's street, they were blinded by flashing lights from several police cars. Morgan was first to notice the caution tape wrapped around the front of her house. She immediately jumped out of the car as Derek stopped the car in the middle of the street and ran inside. She was stopped by several officers who made her identify herself. She told them she was the owner of the home. Derek found the nearest parking space and came in shortly after Morgan. There were multiple police officers, some in uniform and some in regular clothes canvassing her living room. She anxiously searched the first floor of the house for Mrs. Barnes. Morgan exhaled when she found her mother in the kitchen talking to a detective.

"Momma, are you okay? What happened?" Morgan interrupted the detective.

"Oh, baby, I'm okay. I was sitting in here drinking some tea and watching TV when I heard a pop, pop, pop and car speeding down the street. I didn't think anything of it until this gentleman came knocking on my door and told me that the bullets went through the window."

The detective turned to Morgan, extended his hand and introduced himself, "Hi. I am Detective Sanchez."

"Hi. Morgan Barnes, homeowner. Why wasn't I called?" Morgan immediately asked the detective.

"Well, it happened about twenty minutes ago, and I've been taking your mother's statement. Since she was a witness, we thought it was imperative to question her while the event was still fresh in her mind," the detective said.

By this time, Derek came in, hugged Mrs. Barnes

and stood off to the side, observing the conversation. He could tell that Morgan was irritated, so he walked up behind her and squeezed her shoulders. She slowly began to loosen up.

Morgan took a deep breath. "So Detective Sanchez, do you have any leads as to why my house was targeted?"

"Unfortunately, not at the moment. Your mom was telling me about the attempted carjacking back in December. We know that there has been an increase in gang activity in the neighborhood over the past couple months. It's likely a random act of violence, but we will definitely investigate it. And we will be keeping a patrol car outside for the next forty-eight hours. After that, I'll add this street to the nightly patrol watch."

"Momma, you sure you're okay?" Morgan asked again.

"Yes, sweetie. I'm fine," Mrs. Barnes said.

* * *

After the police left, Derek took the liberty of cleaning up the glass in the living room. He offered to spend the night, but Mrs. Barnes and Morgan insisted that they were fine, and he should go home to get some rest. That night, Morgan slept in bed with her mom. She kept thinking to herself, *How could such a wonderful day end on a sour note?*

Morgan's thoughts must have been written on the wall because out of the blue, Mrs. Barnes asked, "Isn't He awesome?"

"Huh?" Morgan asked with confusion as she was distracted in her own negative thoughts.

"God is so good," her mom stated.

Morgan agreed with a slow nod. "He sure is."

"Baby, we got to count our blessings. I wasn't hurt.

Heck, I wasn't even in the room when it happened," Mrs. Barnes said.

"True." Just then, Morgan realized she was so blown by the event itself that she never took the time to see the blessings.

"Baby, you have to get your two windows repaired. I know windows aren't cheap, but Walter can patch up the holes in the wall. The bullets just missed the flat-screen TV."

Morgan wasn't aware that there was a bullet in the wall. It made sense that a bullet coming through her window would have to land somewhere, but she didn't inspect the living room. She thought to herself, *Thank you, Jesus. You know I just bought that TV this past Thanksgiving during the Black Friday sale.* To Mrs. Barnes, Morgan said, "Dang, you're right, Momma. Thank you, Jesus."

"Baby, He has us covered. Never question that. I love you, sweetie. Sleep tight," and with that Mrs. Barnes kissed Morgan on the cheek and turned over and went to sleep.

* * *

At 12:04 a.m., Morgan was startled out of her sleep by the sound of her cell phone ringing. When she answered, it was Tra'maine's new foster mother on the other end, screaming that he never made it home from school. According to his friends, someone picked him up after football practice, and that was around 8:00 p.m. She checked his room and all of his clothes were missing. She had no idea where he could be. Morgan immediately jumped out of bed, got dressed, and drove directly to Mr. Stevenson's home. Despite his recent behavior, Morgan was convinced that Tra'maine's loyalty lay with his foster father. This was the only man he ever called dad, and he was desperate for a sense of family, even if it was abusive.

Approaching the porch, Morgan rang the doorbell and knocked on the door. Two minutes went by with no response. Morgan put her ear to the door to see if she could hear anything. Nothing. She began to ring the doorbell profusely and bang on the door. Again, no answer. She pulled out her cell phone and tried calling Mr. Stevenson. She could hear the phone ringing inside the house. Morgan walked over to the living room window, peering in to see if she could see anything. The window was dirty, and the house was dark, making it hard to see anything. *This is ridiculous,* she thought. Just then, she saw something or someone move in the living room.

"Mr. Stevenson, I know Tra'maine is here. You know that the court has temporarily appointed custody to another foster parent. This means that if I call the cops, they will arrest you for kidnapping. Mr. Stevenson, please do not make me call the cops." Morgan waved her phone in front of the living room window and motioned like she was about to call 911. She walked back to the front door and knocked again. No answer.

Morgan was reluctant to call the cops because she didn't want to see Mr. Stevenson go to jail. He was a decent man who was grieving the loss of his wife. He needed therapy, not jail, but he was tying her hands. As a social worker, her responsibility was to Tra'maine. Shaking her head, she called 911, "Hello, this is Morgan Barnes. I am a social worker for D.C. Child and Family Services, and I would like to report a kidnapping. Yes, it's a unique situation. The boy has returned to the foster home that the courts removed him from. I believe his foster father picked him up from school and brought him here. No one is answering the door, but I am pretty sure the boy and his father are here."

Slowly, the front door opened and there stood a crying Tra'maine with Mr. Stevenson's arm on his shoulder comforting him. "Ok. Wait a second; I see the boy now."

Talking to Mr. Stevenson through the screen door, Morgan said, "Mr. Stevenson, I need to take Tra'maine back to his foster home. You could be in a lot of trouble if you refuse to allow me to take him. Do you understand?"

Returning to the phone, Morgan responded, "Yes, I am talking to the father now."

Mr. Stevenson grabbed Tra'maine and hugged him. He nodded in response to Morgan's question. He understood the severity of the situation. He wanted to regain custody of Tra'maine and knew that this would hurt his chances of getting him back.

Father and son walked onto the porch to meet Morgan. Turning to Tra'maine, Morgan said, "I know this is hard for you, but your foster mom is worried sick about you."

"She's not my mom. My mom died."

"I know, and I am so sorry for your loss, but Tra'maine, your being here is going to make it harder for your dad to get custody of you. The police are on their way to arrest him. Do you want your dad to go to jail for kidnapping?"

"No."

"Look, Mr. Stevenson is in really big trouble." By this point, a patrol car pulled up in front of the house with its lights flashing. Morgan made eye contact with the officer who got out of the car and waived her hand to ask him to stand down. "I need for you to come with me. I promise to revisit the frequency of your visitations with your dad. Ok?"

Tra'maine stood on the porch, with his bookbag on his back, defeated. He looked up at Mr. Stevenson, who softly stated, "It's ok. Go with Ms. Barnes. I will see you soon."

Tra'maine retreated and began to walk with Morgan to her car, but he quickly turned and contemplated running back to his dad. Mr. Stevenson stood on the porch teary eyed and shook his head at Tra'maine. Only after he was in the car and Morgan pulled off, did the police officer return to his patrol car and leave the scene.

Chapter 9

It sparkled. Reflecting the white light from the Ikea chandelier in Morgan's bedroom, the necklace Derek gave her sparkled on her neck. The two-karat diamond pendulum hung so elegantly on her neck that Morgan had a hard time believing it was her own. She was wearing a black, fitted three-quarter-length strapless dress with a floor-length sheer black tulle train that tied around the waist with an enlarged black satin bow. She took a step back because this person in the mirror, this woman was beautiful—stunning. Morgan wore her hair straightened so it rested down her back.

Today was a super special occasion. Derek was being honored for Best Cardiac Surgeon of the Year and he asked Morgan and Mrs. Barnes to be his very special guests. He ordered a car service to come pick them up to take them to the Four Seasons hotel.

Mrs. Barnes yelled up the steps. "Morgan, you almost ready? I don't want to be late. The car should be here any minute now." Her mom always got a little anxious whenever they had somewhere to be by a certain time. Someone would have thought she was the honoree this evening.

"Yes, ma'am, I'm coming," Morgan said while looking down at the four-inch black t-strap platform heels that awaited her feet. She gently bent over to put them on and thought twice. *I should definitely wait until I get downstairs to put these suckers on.* As she approached the landing to the stairs, she noticed Mrs. Barnes peeping out the window. Her mother was wearing a lovely floor-length ruby-red

A-line wrap dress that her father bought her a few years ago for a holiday party. The neckline and sleeves were embellished with red sequin. She looked radiant.

"Momma, I see you. I don't appreciate you showing me up here," Morgan said as she approached her and hugged her from behind.

"Oh, this ole thing, child, please. It sheds like nobody's business," she said while picking up little pieces of sequin that fell off her dress and landed on to the couch where she previously sat. Mrs. Barnes turned around and smiled at Morgan. "Girl, you clean up nicely. Derek isn't going to know what to do with himself," Mrs. Barnes said with a chuckle. "Now, let me see you walk in those shoes."

Morgan obliged, slipped into the shoes, and did a short walk from the living room to the front door.

"Okay, honey. But I'ma need you to strut like you realize why God blessed you with those hips. Come on; give it to me," Mrs. Barnes instructed. Again, Morgan walked toward the living room but this time she did so feeling like she was Betty Boop, switching her hips from side to side.

"That's it. Get it, girl; get it," Mrs. Barnes said as she laughed and clapped her hands.

The doorbell rang, and Morgan practiced her new walk as she went to answer it. The driver was an older petite man who looked like he was a ballet dancer in his hay day. He escorted them to the car, one at a time.

On the way to the hotel, Mrs. Barnes grabbed Morgan's hand. Rubbing it softly, she said, "Morgan, do you know how proud I am of you?" Morgan nodded. "You are an amazing young woman whom I've watched blossom into your own. Over the past couple of months, I have seen you grow into your own. You have broken out of your shell, letting your light shine through. You are no longer held back by fear, but instead living life, enjoying all that God has blessed you with and stretching yourself. I am so glad God answered my prayer and brought a fine young man in your life. You deserve to be happy, to be loved, and just to have fun. Life is too short. You hear me? I love you Morgan Elizabeth Barnes." Mrs. Barnes squeezed her hand tighter.

"I know. I love you too, Momma," Morgan whispered.

The thought never crossed her mind until now, but she really never laughed as much or as hard as she had in the past several months of dating Dr. Patterson. Their connection was so simple, yet so real. She knew her mother's late-night conversations with God about her and her non-existent love life paid off. Mrs. Barnes didn't want her daughter to end up old and bitter like some of the old women at church. And God knew Morgan didn't want that either.

* * *

When they arrived at the Four Seasons, they immediately noticed a large sign in the front lobby with a photo of Dr. Patterson in his white lab coat, arms crossed with that pearly white signature smile. The sign stated, "Honoring Dr. Derek Patterson" in bold white letters across the bottom of the photo. Mrs. Barnes begged Morgan to take a selfie with her in front of the sign. Now where she learned what a selfie was, Morgan didn't have a clue, but she couldn't do anything but laugh at how excited and proud her mom was.

Once they checked in, they were escorted to a sparkly round table with shimmery gold linen, shiny gold flatware and a larger than life gold candelabra with lit, tall, skinny, white candles that bounced light off the tablecloth. It was beautiful. The table was center stage, with six ghost chairs instead of ten. The chairs were placed strategically in a half-moon so no one's back would be to the stage. The room was dimly lit, and a four-piece band played soft music in the background. As they took their seats, Morgan anxiously scanned the room for Derek. With roughly three hundred people in the room, it took her all of five seconds to spot him across the room talking to three older white gentlemen in tuxedoes. She presumed they were other doctors. *Dang, my baby is fine.* He must have felt her stare because, in that instance, he turned and made eye contact with her, smiled, winked, then turned back around to continue his conversation.

How did he know where I was? Morgan thought.

Mrs. Barnes tapped her on the shoulder. "You see him over there? Looking all dapper this evening."

Morgan nodded as she looked him up and down. He wore a slim fit, charcoal three-piece suit that showed off his broad shoulders and back. She could tell he just came from the barbershop because his haircut was on point. As she stared at Derek, out of her periphery, she felt someone staring at her. Off to the left of Derek, approximately fifty feet away, stood a stumpy brown-skinned woman with a long weave and eyes set on Morgan. Morgan turned to her mother and discreetly asked, "Momma, who is ole girl who is staring me down over there?"

Mrs. Barnes didn't have to look up to know who she was referring to. "Oh, that's Lauren, Dr. Patterson's assistant."

"Oh, that's her?" Morgan looked up again to get a better look and to express with her eyes, *Chick, stare all you want, the man is mine.* For a split second, Morgan began humming the Brandy and Monica song from the nineties. She quickly regrouped. Turning to Mrs. Barnes, she asked, "I thought he fired her?"

"No, just suspended for a few weeks. I believe she's been behaving herself," Mrs. Barnes shrugged.

At their table, an Asian man introduced himself. With his hand extended, he greeted them. "Good Evening; I am Dr. Kim. This is my wife, Rachel, and you are?"

Shaking his hand firmly, Morgan politely smiled and introduced herself. "Hi, I am Morgan, and this is my mother."

A warm hand rested on the small of her back, and a voice added, "John, this is my amazing lady that I can't stop bragging about." Derek leaned in and kissed Morgan on the cheek.

Morgan couldn't help herself; she turned toward him and embraced him in a lingering hug. Mindful to not get lipstick on his suit, she turned her head slightly and melted in his arms. It felt like many days passed since she last saw him. He delicately grabbed Morgan's chin, lifting it toward him, planting a sweet kiss on her lips and then turned to his other woman, Mrs. Barnes, and hugged her.

Dr. Kim must have felt inspired by all the affection because he gingerly rubbed his wife's hand. "Morgan, it is a pleasure to meet you. Derek has been smiling from ear to ear for weeks…months now, and it all finally makes sense." Morgan blushed.

A voice came over the speakers, asking everyone to take their seats as the program was about to begin. Derek sat down between Morgan and Mrs. Barnes. It would be her mother, the woman with a slew of men at her beck and call, to have dibs on Morgan's man, but since she was the very reason he was in her life, she couldn't be mad. Derek leaned into Morgan's ear and said, "Before the night gets too crazy, I have to tell you that you are stunning. I spotted you as soon as you walked in. You took my breath away. I am by far the luckiest man in the room, shoot, in the world. I love you." He kissed her again on the cheek, but this time slowly and it tingled.

Well, that explains why we made eye contact so quickly. Morgan rested her hand on his thigh and squeezed it gently. It was the only thing she could do to remain calm and try to divert her attention so she wouldn't tear up. *This man is so sweet, so handsome and all mine. What did I do to deserve him?*

Morgan floated through the program, replaying every word Derek said to her and the kiss that she still felt lingering on her cheek. During the course of the evening, she learned that the black lady seated at their table was Stacy Reynolds, Anchor for ABC-7 news who served as the mistress of ceremony. She also learned that Dr. Johnny Kim was the Chief of Surgery and presented Derek with Surgeon of the Year award. This was the third year in a row that Derek received the award. Morgan wasn't sure why he failed to mention that before. In his acceptance speech, he thanked Mrs. Barnes for keeping him on his toes, for keeping him honest, and for introducing him to the love of his life. Everyone in the room "awed." He said some other stuff, but that was the only thing Morgan latched on to. Standing up at the podium, Derek exuded confidence, poise, and happiness. He seemed genuinely happy to share this experience with Morgan and Mrs. Barnes. He received a standing ovation as he took his seat.

Mrs. Barnes grabbed him before Morgan could and whispered, "I am so proud of you."

Morgan followed suit and said, "Great speech, Dr. Patterson. Congratulations." She kissed him on the cheek, leaving an impression of her ruby red lipstick. She quickly reached for a napkin and attempted to wipe it off.

"It's okay, babe. You've marked your territory; I like it," Derek responded with a chuckle.

"Dude, where do you come up with this stuff, Mr. Smooth Talker?" Morgan said. They both laughed.

After the ceremony, the band picked it up a notch. A singer joined the quartet and sang a bunch of hits, including Franky Beverly and Maze and the Temptations. After a few dances, Derek asked if Morgan would mind if he excused himself to dance with Mrs. Barnes. She wanted to say, 'uh, yeah, I mind.' Instead, she said it was fine. Morgan was a little concerned for Derek because she knew her mother was the queen of the dance floor and she would hate for her to show up the honoree on his big day. However, it was perfect timing because Morgan needed to excuse herself to use the restroom anyway. As she made her way to the bathroom, she glanced over at Derek and Mrs. Barnes moving to Stevie Wonder's *For Once in My Life*. She couldn't make out who was leading who, her mother or Derek?

Derek couldn't wait for some alone time with Mrs. Barnes all evening. He knew that she would keep it one hundred with him. "So, what'd you think? On a scale of one to ten, how did I do up there?" Derek asked Mrs. Barnes inquisitively, like a child looking to a parent for approval.

As Mrs. Barnes spun around in step with the song, "Oh, I'd say," she paused, winked at him and said, "an eleven. Derek, your speech was truly moving. It was genuine and from the heart. Just like your approach to caring for your patients. I couldn't think of anyone else more deserving of this award. I am proud of you, and I know you made your mother proud."

At that affirmation, Derek hugged Mrs. Barnes tight and whispered in her ear, "Thank you."

Hugging him back, she said, "Any time, baby, any time. Now, what else is on your mind because I can see your thoughts racing a mile a minute." Mrs. Barnes could always sense when people needed someone to talk to and no matter what she was doing, she would always stop everything to offer her ear.

Nervously, Derek said, "You could sense it, huh?" Mrs. Barnes nodded. "Well, I wanted to ask you something, but couldn't make my mind up if now was the right time."

* * *

While Morgan stood at the bathroom counter admiring her fineness in the mirror, in walked Lauren. Morgan wasn't the least bit surprised. The way the girl was eyeing her down from across the room, she knew she needed to get an up-close and personal look at Morgan. *Well today, is definitely the day to get a look. I look hot!* Morgan thought to herself, as she pulled out her ruby red lipstick to reapply it. Again staring at Morgan, but this time her reflection in the mirror, Morgan made eye contact with Lauren through the mirror and said, "Hello."

Caught off guard, Lauren said, "Hi. I was admiring your dress. Where'd you get it?"

"Thank you. Some small boutique. I can't remember the name," Morgan lied.

"Oh. So, you are dating Dr. Patterson?" Lauren asked.

"I am." Morgan wasn't one for small talk. She paused and asked, "Is there a problem?"

"Well, he never mentioned you to me." Lauren said.

"And you are?" By this point, Morgan didn't know where this line of conversation was going.

"I'm his assistant, Lauren."

"So, you expect your boss to tell you, his assistant, about his romantic relationships?" Morgan asked sarcastically.

"Well, no, not under normal circumstances, but," Lauren started to say before Morgan interrupted.

"But what?" Morgan asked.

"But if you are sleeping with your boss, in which case I am, I'd expect him to tell me that he has a girlfriend," Lauren said matter of fact.

"Come again?" Morgan thought she heard what Lauren just said, but needed to hear it one more time for it to sink in.

"I've been sleeping with Derek. I mean, he tried to resist at first because, well, he didn't think it was appropriate in the workplace. But something happened when we returned to Atlanta for Dr. Davis' funeral. We were both so messed up about his sudden death that we found ourselves in each other's arms comforting one another. I swear, I didn't know he had a girlfriend."

Morgan stood there, listening to the words that just came out of this young girl's mouth. Images of Derek's reaction to the news of his mentor's death ran across Morgan's mind and him mentioning that he would be gone for a week. In that split second, Morgan couldn't remember where she and Derek's relationship was at that time. So many thoughts began running through her head like – *We just met, right? I know we weren't exclusive yet, so technically he didn't cheat. This would explain the nudie pic.* But something happened, all of her insecurities that she overcame since her past relationship started to bubble to the top. *Had Derek been playing her like Justin did? Has he been messing with her this whole time? I knew no grown man could remain celibate and I knew this was too good to be true.* Although internally she was spiraling out of control, the loudest thought ringing in her mind was, *Don't give this girl the satisfaction of reacting to this news.* So Morgan turned back to the mirror, wiped the corner of her lip, adjusted her strapless bra, and said, "Lauren, is it? Let me give you a little piece of advice. If you meant anything, and I mean, anything to Derek, he would have acknowledged you this evening in front of all of his colleagues during his eloquent, yet uplifting speech. But he didn't, did he? So obviously, whatever you think you have going on with this man, you are mistaken." Morgan put her lipstick back in her purse and headed for the bathroom door. She opened the door and turned to Lauren who was still at a loss for words, "And by the way, you are a cute girl, but thirst is not attractive on you."

Now on the other side of the bathroom door, Morgan's mind was racing a mile a minute and she didn't know what to do next. She didn't want to cry or make a scene. She thought about hitting up the bar or leaving altogether, but every scenario that she played in her head ended badly, so instead, she took her seat at the table and tried to breathe deeply and counted to ten.

* * *

By this time, the band moved on to Larry Graham's *One in a Million You.* With her left hand on Derek's shoulder and her right in his hand, Mrs. Barnes looked up at him and said, "Well, there's no time like the present. What's on your mind, Doc?"

Derek cleared his throat, took a deep breath, and said, "Well, I meant every word I said in my speech. I am so grateful that God brought you in my life. You have been a breath of fresh air and if it weren't for you, I would have never met Morgan." At that moment, he looked over at the head table and saw Morgan talking to Dr.

Lee's wife. Cheesing from ear to ear, Derek continued, "I can't remember what life was like before I met Morgan because it seems like my life started once I met her. And I can't imagine my life without her. Mrs. Barnes, I love your daughter with all my heart. There is nothing that I wouldn't do to make her happy, to protect her, and to provide for her." In this moment, Derek stopped dancing and looked down at Mrs. Barnes who wore a slight grin on her face. "Mrs. Barnes, I want to know if I have your permission to ask Morgan to marry me?"

Mrs. Barnes squeezed his shoulder tight. At that moment, she felt a little shortness of breath. She was overcome with joy, and although she suspected what it was he wanted to ask her, to hear it actually made her a little weak in the knees. "Of course, baby. You two are good for one another; you complement each other. Thank you for being so good to my Morgan. She is so deserving of a happily ever after. You can just go ahead and call me the Queen of Matchmaking. I know how to pick 'em." Mrs. Barnes chuckled. "But Doc, I think I need to go sit down for a while. All this excitement is making me a little light-headed." Derek inquired if Mrs. Barnes was okay, and she insisted that she was fine. Derek escorted Mrs. Barnes back to the table where Dr. Lee was boring Morgan about the latest invention in cardiac surgery. Derek politely interjected and extended his hand to Morgan. She grabbed it reluctantly, stood, and allowed him to escort her to the dance floor.

As they approached the dance floor, Derek made eye contact with the lead vocalist. The band reset and began to play John Legend's song, 'All of Me.' Derek immediately spun Morgan, catching her off guard and pulled her in close. Unaware of her facial expression, he whispered in Morgan's ear, "Baby, I still remember how

I felt that first night we met when you opened the door. I got goosebumps. By the end of that night, they turned to butterflies. And ever since that night, I have been on cloud nine. You are everything that I want and need in a partner, and then some. God has blessed me abundantly, and I am forever grateful. What I am trying to say," Derek pulled away slightly so he could make eye contact with Morgan, "is…," he was now able to see something was wrong, "What's wrong?"

"I had a very interesting conversation with your assistant in the restroom," Morgan replied.

"Which one?" Derek was confused.

"How many do you have?" Morgan said with an attitude and rolled her eyes, "Lauren."

Derek pulled completely away, ready to prepare for some non-sense. "What did she say?"

"Did you two hook up while you were in Atlanta for Dr. Davis' funeral?"

"What? No!"

"Don't lie to me, Derek. We'd just met. You had no obligation to me. I get that emotions can run high. I just—I just don't want to be lied to. I'm done with dudes playing me for a fool."

Derek was pissed. The fact that his deranged assistant lied on him got him heated; however, the fact that the woman that he came to know and love so dearly could so easily think the worst of him and believe this chick was beyond disappointing. He grabbed Morgan by both arms and said, "Morgan, really? After everything…"

Just then, there was a loud bang, and they heard glass shattering on the floor. They both looked in the direction of the noise to find Mrs. Barnes on the floor. When she fell, she pulled the tablecloth with her, and all of the china and glassware came tumbling to the floor. Derek and Morgan rushed over to her to find Dr. Lee kneeling beside her.

"Momma, can you hear me?! What's wrong?!" Morgan said, touching her mother's face, whose eyes were open but non-responsive.

Talking to Derek, Dr. Lee said, "Her pressure is extremely low. I believe she is going into cardiac arrest. We need to call for an ambulance and start CPR right away."

"She has Dilated Cardiomyopathy and a signed DNR. Call 911, but there's not much more we can do," Derek said. Dr. Lee immediately stood up and stepped away from Mrs. Barnes.

Confused, Morgan turned to Derek and yelled, "Do something! Why are you just standing there?!"

Derek tried to explain. "Your mom has a Do Not Resuscitate order. If her heart stops, she does not want CPR or advanced cardiac life support."

"Derek, what are you talking about? In this very moment, I'm asking you as the daughter of the only best friend I've known all my life and as the woman you want to spend the rest of your life with to let my mother live!" Frantic to help her mother, Morgan pushed Derek aside and began applying CPR to Mrs. Barnes. In this moment, she was glad that her job required her to take the training. With tears running down her face, she kept saying, "Momma, come back to me, please."

After five minutes of CPR, Mrs. Barnes blinked her eyes. "Momma, stay with me. An ambulance is here to take you to the hospital. Everything is going to be okay." As the medics wheeled the gurney to the ambulance, Derek stood on one side of Mrs. Barnes and Morgan on the other. Derek felt helpless in that instance. Mrs. Barnes tied his hands, and, to make matters even worse, apparently, she never had that conversation with Morgan that she promised she would. Once in the ambulance, the medic turned and asked who was riding with Mrs. Barnes. Derek and Morgan both said at the same time, "I am."

Morgan turned to Derek and said, "For what? You're not going to do anything to help her."

Derek responded, "Morgan, I'm her doctor. I want and need to be with her, too."

"What kind of doctor just stands there and watches their patient lie lifeless?" Morgan was beyond angry. The medic motioned for the two of them to hurry up and decide who was riding as they needed to go. Mrs. Barnes, who was coherent, laid still on the gurney and extended her hand toward Derek. He hopped in the ambulance and grabbed her hand. She was hooked up to a cardiac monitor that showed a low pulse and wore an oxygen mask on her face to help her breathe. During the ride to the hospital, Morgan rubbed her mother's other hand and kept saying, "Momma, I love you. I love you." She rested her forehead on her mom's shoulder. At one point, Mrs. Barnes pulled Morgan's hand to her oxygen mask and began to peck it on the mask as if she were kissing it. Morgan started to ball. Derek wanted badly to console Morgan, but he found himself in tears as well. Mrs. Barnes then took Derek's hand and began to peck it, as she did Morgan. She ended by placing Derek's hand on top of Morgan's. Morgan looked at Derek and snatched her hand away and grabbed Mrs. Barnes' hand again.

Turning to her mother, she pleaded, "Momma, don't go. Please don't go. I need you. I need you so much. You are my best friend. Who's gonna stay up and watch the Hallmark Channel with me? Who's gonna talk me down off the cliff and tell me everything is gonna be okay?

Who's gonna remind me that God's got me covered and not to worry? Morgan wiped the snot dripping from her nose with the back of her hand.

With what little energy Mrs. Barnes had left, she gently squeezed Morgan's hand, as if to say, 'Baby, you will be okay.' And just like that, she took her last breath and closed her eyes. The cardiac monitor immediately flatlined.

"No! No! No, Momma, no!" Morgan screamed. She immediately began CPR again, but it was too late. Her mother passed away at 10:42 p.m.

Derek wept, he closed his eyes and said a prayer asking God to look over Mrs. Barnes and to make sure his mom met her at the pearly gates.

By the time the ambulance arrived at the hospital, the staff was already notified of Mrs. Barnes' transition. There was a grief counselor waiting to speak to Morgan. Morgan was in a daze. How could this day, that started out as one of the most magical and special days of her life, end with such a nightmare? She tried to wake herself up because it seemed like a bad dream, only it felt so real.

Derek approached her in the waiting room and handed her some hot herbal tea. She accepted it as she was extremely cold and didn't realize it until that very instance. A chill went down her spine. She mumbled, "Thank you."

"Babe, I hate to have to ask, but there are some papers I need you to complete. Are you up for it now, or do you want to take them home with you? I can come by later and pick them up."

"Don't do that," Morgan said.

Confused, he asked, "Do what?"

"Don't call me Babe. I'm not your Babe. I'm not your anything. We?" she motioned to the two of them,

"We are done. We are so done. After tonight, I don't want to see you ever again."

Derek felt horrible about the situation. He tilted his head downward and shook it. What could he possibly say to right this wrong?

"Morgan, I asked, no, I begged your mom to tell you. HIPPA prohibited me from saying anything to you. I wanted to. I really did. You got to believe me."

"I get HIPAA, I do. I deal with it every day. But you stood there and watched my mother die right before your eyes without doing a thing. And you say you loved her? You say you love me? And you say you know that I am the woman God sent for you? How is that possible? God doesn't work like that. I needed you to do one thing. I asked you to do one thing. And you just stood there. Now I have to bury my mother. Me. All by myself. Do you get that?" Morgan stood up, grabbed the paperwork he placed in the chair beside him, and said, "I'll return these on my own," then walked off.

Chapter 10

God gave Morgan the grace she needed to get through the funeral. With only a week to plan, there was a lot to do, or so she thought. When she went to meet with the pastor, she learned that her mom had already provided him with a list of demands for her funeral service. Pastor Johnson handed Morgan the handwritten note Mrs. Barnes gave him. In the letter, her mom selected what songs she wanted to be sung and whom she wanted to sing them, the Scriptures to be read, and her suggestions for pallbearers. The letter also stated the outfit she wanted to be buried in could be found in the back of her closet, along with shoes. She did not want to wear pantyhose and there was no need to bury her with any jewelry. Mrs. Barnes also wanted Morgan to eulogize her and Dr. Patterson to give remarks. Additionally, in the letter, Mrs. Barnes provided Morgan with the point of contact at the cemetery where she was to be buried with Mr. Barnes. Finally, Mrs. Barnes instructed her where she could find all her important papers. In true Mrs. Barnes fashion, she had crossed every T and dotted every I. *How long had Momma been planning her death and burial?* Morgan thought to herself.

When it came to writing her mom's eulogy, Morgan was stuck. How was it possible that this person that she thought she knew so well could keep such a big secret from her? And why? Morgan sat in her living room on the couch trying to think what her mother would say if she were here. Morgan thought for sure she'd say something like this, *Baby, just speak from your heart. You know what to say.* And with that, she began to write.

'*My Momma loved life. She thanked God every morning for waking her up, and she promised Him that she would make the most of each day she was given. She was the wisest person I knew. There was no situation that my mother could not help someone get through, and not only that, but she could also see how God was using it for their good. She had this uncanny ability to put people at ease. It was like she had a direct connection with God, and everyone knew it. No matter what she faced, her faith never wavered. Jesus was tried and true in her book, and no matter who she talked to, they left knowing that as well.*'

As tears began to roll down her cheek, Morgan noticed something sparkling between the couch cushions. She picked up the sparkling object and brought it to her face to examine it. It was a ruby red sequin from her mother's banquet dress. Morgan laughed. She knew that it was a sign that Mrs. Barnes was with her. Morgan placed the sequin on top of the laptop keyboard and continued writing. When she got stuck, she would look down at the sequin piece and start talking to it. Before long, she completed her first draft.

* * *

The funeral was lovely. Sparing no expense for the funeral, Morgan put her event planning skills to work. She asked guests to wear vibrant colors. She filled the church with colorful floral arrangements comprised of some of Mrs. Barnes' favorite flowers—peonies, roses, carnations, lilies, gerbera daisies, and more. The way Morgan saw it, her mom would want people to celebrate her transition, not mourn it. If anyone unfamiliar with the event walked into the sanctuary, they would have thought it was Easter. Instead of asking the bereavement choir to sing, Morgan hired gospel artist, Charles Douglas and Group Nation, to perform. They were a little uneasy at first, given the occasion, but when Morgan expressed her desire for an out-of-this-world worship experience, they agreed.

Renee and Stacy contributed financially to help Morgan finance both the funeral and repast. There were some issues with Morgan being able to get her mother's life insurance right away. Stacy surprised Morgan because she handed her a check for five thousand dollars and insisted that she take it. Morgan knew Stacy struggled as a single mother and didn't dare ask where she got it from. On the day of the funeral, Renee and Stacy were tasked with keeping Derek away from Morgan. To do so, Renee assigned herself to Morgan and Stacy took Derek.

During the viewing, Morgan stood at the front of the sanctuary, off to the left side of the open casket, with her back to the casket. After viewing Mrs. Barnes' embalmed body at the funeral home, she finally understood what Pastor Johnson meant about the fact that we are a spirit. We have a soul that resides in a body. As she stood there assessing her mother's hair and makeup, she knew that the person before her wasn't her mom. It was only a shell. After thanking the mortician for making Mrs. Barnes look beautiful, Morgan vowed not to view the body again. She wanted to remember her mother living her best life.

Derek arrived just in time for the service. It was like Morgan felt his presence when he entered the church. She immediately looked up and saw him walking down the aisle. It wasn't like him not to be punctual. Morgan wondered what caused his delay. She refocused, reminding herself that he was the reason she was burying her mother today. Morgan immediately made eye contact with Renee who turned and whispered something to Stacy. Stacy quickly got up and excused herself all the way down the crowded sanctuary until she reached Derek.

"Hey," Stacy said.

"Hi. How's she doing?" Derek asked.

"She's hanging in there." Stacy noticed the flowers and cards in Derek's hand. "Is that for her?" she asked.

"Yeah," he replied.

"I'll take that for you." Stacy went to grab it from Derek.

"No. I'll give it to her. I need to talk to her," he insisted.

"Derek, now isn't the time to talk. She doesn't want to talk to you, and I don't think you want a scene at Mrs. Barnes' funeral. Do you?" Stacy asked.

"No," Derek said through his teeth as he lowered his head in defeat.

"Okay, so like I said, I'll take them and be sure to give them to her." Stacy reached and took the cards and flowers. "Please keep your distance. I beg of you."

"Okay. I'll just sit back here. Is this okay?" Derek asked, pointing to the second to last pew in the back of the church.

"Perfect," Stacy said. She turned to walk back up the aisle to Morgan and Renee when Derek said, "Oh, Stacy."

"Yeah?" she said.

"Did she need any more money? Let me know. I can write another check."

"No, she's good. Thank you. She really appreciated it." Stacy knew that the only way Morgan would accept his money was if she had no clue where the money came from. Stacy asked Derek to write her a check that she put in her account and then transferred the money to Morgan's account. She knew Derek meant well and just really wanted to contribute. Stacy thought money could do a lot less harm than showing up to Morgan's house wanting to talk.

Turning once again to head down the aisle, Stacy canvassed the crowd just in time to see Justin approach Morgan. She looked again but couldn't find Renee. "Darn it, Renee; now is not the time for a bathroom break," Stacy said under her breath. She was too far away to stop the encounter.

Justin approached Morgan and attempted to embrace her with a hug. Morgan put out her arm to stop him before he got too close.

"Hey, Morgan, I am so sorry for your loss. Mrs. Barnes was like a mother to me. I can't believe she is gone."

Morgan stood unphased by the sentiment.

"I just wanted you to know that if you need anything, and I mean anything, I am here for you. I still love you, you know."

That was it. Morgan couldn't take any more bull. She punched Justin in the face. It caught him completely off guard and he immediately grabbed his nose.

"Thanks for coming, Justin. Don't come back," Morgan turned, made eye contact with Stacy and walked over to her.

Stacy was cracking up, "Girl, you didn't just…?"

"I am so tired of these wack negroes. They need to stop playing with me. Today is not the day," Morgan said.

"I know," Stacy agreed.

"What he say?" Morgan couldn't bring herself to say Derek's name.

"He just asked how you were holding up," Stacy said.

Morgan tried not to look in Derek's direction, but couldn't help herself. They made eye contact, and

Morgan quickly looked away. *I can't believe I have to listen to this man give remarks.* Morgan rolled her eyes.

Renee finally returned, and Stacy brought her up to speed on all the drama she missed.

* * *

Charles Douglas and Group Nation did their thing. All two hundred and fifty attendees were on their feet for most of the service, praising, and worshipping. It was a beautiful sight, and Mrs. Barnes would have loved it. It reminded Morgan of her mother's weekend ritual of waking up early, playing her gospel music, and dancing around the house while doing chores.

When it came time for the eulogy, Morgan took a deep breath and walked up to the podium. Her nerves tried to get the best of her, but mostly because she didn't know where to look. Looking to her right meant looking at her mom's all-white casket. Looking up and straight ahead meant running the chance of looking at Derek. She settled on looking at Renee and Stacy, who sat directly in front of her, six rows back. Slowly, Morgan pulled out her four typed pages and began to read them. She was composed, poised, and confidant. No one was better suited to talk about Mrs. Barnes. She managed to get through the entire thing without shedding a tear. When she was finished, she looked up at the stain glass windows where the sun peaked in. Morgan smiled because God gave her the grace she needed to get through it and she knew her mother was proud.

Pastor Johnson followed and said a blessing. He then introduced Dr. Derek Patterson, who was to give remarks. Morgan braced herself and quickly put on her dark lensed sunglasses. As Derek took the podium, Morgan noticed that he wore her favorite color – a charcoal gray tailored suit that accentuated his broad shoulders and back. His fresh haircut was on point; his lines were sharp and defined. Morgan reminded herself that this man that stood before her was the man who just stood there and allowed her mother to die before her eyes and therefore was no longer attractive.

Derek took out a piece of paper from his inside jacket pocket. He cleared his throat and canvassed the audience before setting his eyes on Morgan. Without looking down at his paper, he began.

"I had the honor and privilege of serving as Mrs. Barnes' cardiologist for almost two years. In that time, I can honestly say that she helped me grow, as a man, as a doctor, and as a child of God. She loved on me as if I were her own. As a man who had been without family for so long, I didn't know how much I desperately needed that. No matter what she had going on in her life, the first thing she would say to me was, 'So Doc, how are you? What's going on?' I always looked forward to her appointments because I knew she would lift my spirits, give me food for thought, and have me dying laughing. Mrs. Barnes was hilarious. There were times I almost forgot I was in the examining room because I would be laughing so hard. I'd have to remind her that this was my place of work and we had to calm down." Derek laughed while he reminisced about the visits. "Mrs. Barnes always called a spade a spade. You never had to guess what she was thinking, and you knew not to ask for her opinion if you weren't ready for the truth. Man, she had a way of telling you about yourself, and consoling you at the same time, letting you know that in the end, you'd be okay."

"When I first met Mrs. Barnes, my life was at a standstill. I was just going through the motions of life but not really living. She helped me to find my way back and I am forever indebted. Without Mrs. Barnes, I would never have found my soulmate. The person I want to spend the rest of my life with. The person, who," Derek paused as he saw Morgan get up from the first pew and exit the sanctuary. He lowered his head in disappointment, "who, I would do anything to start over with." Derek looked out among the congregation and then to the door that Morgan disappeared behind. He took a second to regroup his thoughts. "Mrs. Barnes will truly be missed. She was truly one of a kind. A real class act. Although she is no longer physically with us, I am reassured that she is in heaven with the love of her life and my mom. I know together they will be a handful up there." The guests laughed, and he laughed along with them. "Thank you," Derek said. He stepped down from the podium and took his seat.

Morgan never returned to the sanctuary. Realizing that Derek's remarks were right before the benediction, she decided to head to the limo and wait it out there. *Did he really think that his remarks during the funeral would somehow win me back?*

After the recessional, Renee and Stacy hopped in the limo. Morgan texted them upon exiting the church.

"Girl, are you okay?" Renee asked.

"Yeah, I just couldn't take all that," Morgan said with disgust.

"And tell me again what this man did?" Stacy asked confused. "'Cause you can't be mad at him because Mrs. Barnes didn't tell you about her health condition. The man is a doctor for goodness sake. It's against the law."

Morgan didn't want to entertain that at the moment. "He just stood there and did nothing while my mother was dying."

"But didn't you say she had a DNR? That prohibited

him from doing anything, Morgan," Renee reminded her.

Assessing that there were no Team Morgan fans in the limo, she blurted out, "He slept with his assistant."

"He did *what?*" Stacy said, making eye contact with Renee. They both looked perplexed. Looking for clarification, Stacy asked, "He cheated on you?"

"No, not exactly. It was around the time that we met," Morgan replied.

"Say what? Morgan you aren't making any sense right now. How do you know?" Renee quickly responded before Stacy could ask.

"She told me."

"Wait a minute. The chick told you? What exactly did she say?" Stacy asked.

Morgan was starting to get annoyed. Renee and Stacy were her friends, but it seemed like they were interrogating her. "She came up to me in the bathroom at the banquet and said she didn't know Derek had a woman and that the two of them hooked up while in Atlanta for his mentor's funeral."

"Morgan, is this the same girl who sent those photos?" Renee recalled and asked.

"Yeah. Same one."

"And you didn't think it was odd that she just approached you out of the blue?" Stacy asked.

"No. Why does this girl still have a job? I mean, the photos were grounds to fire her. But no, he obviously wanted her around. And not to mention, what fine man do you know that is celibate, I mean really? It sounds good in theory, but come on."

"Devon Franklin was celibate before marrying Meagan Good," Renee chimed in.

"Hello. Can you say, fine? I mean double fine," Stacy

added.

"Besides him?" Morgan asked.

"Morgan, the fact is that they do exist. They may be far, few, and in between, but they do exist. The man that stood up there today is madly in love with you. I don't think he would jeopardize that for no jump-off. Not to mention that here you are taking the word of someone who has already shown you that they are thirsty and reckless. That's not fair to Derek. Not to mention, even if he did sleep with ole girl, that was BEFORE you two were exclusive. Aside from the whole HIPPA factor, he has kept it one hundred with you! Don't let your insecurities with Justin ruin what you have now with Derek," Renee said.

"Justin? What does he have to do with this?"

"Morgan, Justin lied to you. He betrayed you. He took advantage of your kindness, your naivete, your love, and used you for his own selfish gain. And all the while, you accepted his crap because you told yourself that he was the one. You prayed for God to send you the man he intended just for you, but now that the circumstances don't match what you envisioned in your head, you are acting like you are ready to throw it all away," Renee continued.

"Y'all are missing the point. I don't want to talk about this anymore. Today is supposed to be about my mom." Morgan quickly shut the conversation down, and the three of them rode in the back of the limo in silence until they reached the cemetery.

* * *

It was a Monday afternoon, and Derek just returned from lunch. His new patient Ms. Davenport was in examination room three. Looking down at the patient's intake form, he opened the door and said, "Good Afternoon Ms. Davenport, I am Dr. Patterson." But to his surprise, when he looked up, there sat Renee in the corner and Stacy on the examination table.

"Uh, hey, what's going on?" Derek asked.

"You tell us," Stacy said.

"Did Morgan send you guys here?"

"Absolutely not. And she can't find out that we were here," Renee said.

"Where's your assistant? What's her name, Lauren?" Stacy inquired.

"Gone," Derek said with a straight face.

"Gone, like suspended again, gone?" Renee wanted clarification.

"I fired her. She was crazy. Mrs. Barnes tried to warn me, but I didn't listen. I was trying to keep a promise to my mentor by giving her multiple chances, but she completely ruined my relationship with Morgan by lying and saying we slept together."

"She did." Stacy rolled her eyes.

"I never touched that girl." Derek paused. "I was going to propose that night." Derek shared. He proceeded to tell the girls all about that night and how he expected things to play out. Instead, it ended not only with the death of Mrs. Barnes but also the end of his relationship with Morgan. He was at a loss for what to do and how to get Morgan back.

Renee explained that, at the moment, the one thing Morgan needed the most was space. "Derek, you gotta know that Morgan was here before. She thought she found her happily ever after and was completely caught off guard and embarrassed to learn that her ex played her the entire time."

"But I'm not him."

"I know. Derek, she was truly happy with you. She was vulnerable and upbeat and full of life. We have never seen that side of her. She won't deny that. But for some reason, I don't know if she truly believes that God intends for her to get her fairytale ending. This all happened so suddenly. It's a lot to process. Most of what she is dealing with is grief. Morgan lost her mom, her best friend. It's going to take time and space. Trust that if you two are meant to be, then you will be eventually. But at this point, you have to give it to God because although you are well intended, all of your actions here of late are pushing Morgan further away."

* * *

Six weeks later, the house still felt eerie. Morgan couldn't bring herself to clean out her mother's room, so the door stayed shut. Every now and then, at the most opportune time of missing Mrs. Barnes, Morgan would randomly find a ruby red sequin lying around. Whether she was in the kitchen, washing dishes, or in the bathroom filing her nails, she could look down on the counter or carpet and find a sequin. It was like her mom was around the entire house. *How did she do that?* Morgan wondered.

Morgan's forty-first birthday was in one day, but she refused to celebrate or even acknowledge it. She started the year with so much excitement about making this her best year. Yet, somehow the year was hijacked with death and despair. She wasn't up for celebrating. Morgan opened the front door to check the mail and felt the warmth from the sun caress her face. She closed her eyes and let the feeling travel through her whole body. She took a deep breath and noticed the smell of fresh-cut grass. Any other time she hated the smell, but today, the smell of the grass coupled with the smell of laundry from her basement dryer, she couldn't get enough of the smell. She hadn't felt anything this good since the last time Derek touched her. Man, how she missed him. She missed his scent, his strong hands on the small of her back when they walked down the street together. She missed the way he tilted his head to the side just a little when he was listening to her intently. She wanted to talk to him more than anything. She wanted to be wrapped in his arms and feel his breath on the side of her neck, but her pride just wouldn't allow it. After what he did, there was never going to be any more moments like that with Derek. Morgan sighed heavily as she resigned herself to the horrible truth—there was no happily ever after for the two of them. Morgan said out loud to no one in particular, "I guess I'm going to have to get used to the sun."

As Morgan returned inside the house, checking the mail, bill, bill, junk mail, bill, advertisement, and then, she held up an envelope written in Mrs. Barnes' handwriting. Morgan ripped it open to find a birthday card. She immediately opened it to see the signatory, which was indeed from her mom. Now she knew God could work a miracle, but sending cards from beyond the grave was not one of them. She looked at the envelope – no return address. She checked the postage stamp and could barely make out 'Severn, MD.' Mr. Jenkins mailed this, Morgan concluded. It made sense. Mrs. Barnes knew she was dying, and she asked Mr. Jenkins to mail this card on her birthday. Her mother always seemed to be ten steps ahead.

The birthday card was one of Hallmark's finest. On the inside front cover was a personal inscription that warmed Morgan's heart.

My dearest Morgan, I can only imagine how you

are managing to cope on this birthday. I am truly sorry for not telling you about my condition. A small part of me wanted to, but a larger part of me was just so happy to see you finally living the life that I dreamt for you that I didn't want to mess that up. Morgan, ever since you were a kid, you wore worry like it was a turtleneck. Over the years, it became your second skin. I watched as you stood paralyzed to life. I know something happened in college, and I waited for you to confide in me, but you never did. I always prayed that you would find healing. Seeing you with Derek, he brought out a side of you that I always knew existed but never had the chance to meet. You shed that skin. You genuinely smiled from within. You let down your guard. You had fun and took chances. I am so glad that Derek is there for you and you are not alone. Knowing that you two have each other helped me prepare for the end. And please don't be mad at him for not telling you. He begged me to talk to you on multiple occasions, and, well, you know how stubborn I could be at times. You get it honest. Morgan, I am so proud of you, and I know that when the time is right, you will be an amazing mother to your own children. (Yes, I said children, as in multiple.) Happy 41st Birthday, Ms. Morgan Elizabeth Barnes. I may not physically be with you, but I will always be with you in spirit. I love you with all my heart.

Momma

Morgan was in tears, but she managed to re-read the card four more times. Later, she finally decided to go in her mom's room and look around. As soon as she opened the door, her mother's favorite fragrance, Donna Karen's Cashmere, filled Morgan's nostrils. She laid down on Mrs. Barnes' bed, curled up like a ball with her pillow, and wept until she fell asleep. She felt Momma's presence; however, she still missed her immensely.

That night, Morgan got some of the best sleep of her life. She awoke to the sound of the doorbell. She wasn't sure how long the person at the door had been pushing the doorbell and knocking, but whoever it was seemed persistent. When she looked through the peephole, she didn't recognize the young man. Although hesitant, she opened the door anyway.

"Hi. Can I help you?" Morgan asked with a yawn.

"Are you Ms. Morgan Barnes?" the young man asked.

"Who wants to know?" Morgan asked suspiciously.

"Hi. I am George, with Rhonda's Funnel Cakes. He motioned to the blue food truck parked in front of Morgan's house. "Someone has gifted Ms. Barnes our services for the day for her birthday."

Morgan looked at the truck, then back at the young man, "George, is that what you said your name is?" He nodded. "What services are you offering exactly?"

"Well, you can have as much funnel cake as you want all day. Oh, and we offer other stuff, but I was told funnel cake with extra powdered sugar was your favorite so I should keep them coming your way."

"Oh, is that right?" Morgan said sarcastically. "What time is it?" she said. She was thinking it was too early to eat funnel cake and was trying to rationalize the decision to indulge even if it was early.

"10:45 a.m. But it's never too early to eat funnel cake," George said, smiling.

"My man, I agree! Hook me up, please," Morgan said with an even bigger smile. It was her birthday and well, funnel cake made her happy.

Before George turned to go to the truck, he knelt to

pick something up from Morgan's porch. It was a white orchid. He handed it to her, "Uh, this was left on your porch. That's an orchid, right?" he asked.

"Yes," she said, receiving it and examining it all at the same time.

"It's beautiful," George replied.

"It's my favorite flower," Morgan said.

"Well, dang, your birthday is starting off with a bang. Two of your favorite things before noon."

Morgan digested his comment and nodded in agreement. She devoured the funnel cake. It was piping hot and covered in confectionary sugar. It was so good. Since she was home alone, she didn't see any harm in ordering up a second one. While she waited, she picked up the orchid that she placed on the coffee table in the living room. There was no card, just a tag that said *Happy Birthday – With Love.*

Just then, her cell phone rang.

"Hello?"

On the other end of the phone, she heard multiple voices saying, "Happy Birthday!!!" Renee and Stacy called her on three-way.

"Thank you," Morgan said.

"So what we doing today?" Renee asked.

"Nothing. Chillin', I guess." Morgan said with no enthusiasm.

"Booooo. Ma'am, we are turning up somewhere, somehow," Stacy demanded.

"Let's go to the park and have a picnic. Stacy, bring the kids," Morgan suggested.

"Say what? I said let's turn up and you over there talking about a picnic with these little rug rats of mine." Stacy never minced her words.

"Well, I got a food truck that I need to share with

others, or else you guys will have to roll me out of my house tomorrow," Morgan tried to explain.

"Food truck?" Renee was confused.

"He bought me a food truck for the day." She still couldn't bring herself to say his name.

"Derek bought you a food truck? You ain't even talking to that bama, and he went and bought you a food truck? Dang, what I gotta do to get someone to take me to someplace other than Ruby Tuesday?" Stacy said, dumbfounded.

"No. He didn't buy me a food truck. He paid for me to have a food truck for the day," Morgan clarified.

"What kind of food truck?" Renee asked.

Morgan paused, "Funnel cake."

Renee and Stacy both said at the same time, "Funnel cake?"

"Girl, I am on my way now!" Stacy said. "He is good. Original. Thoughtful. Definitely a keeper. If it's really over, say the word, 'cause I'll take him. I don't normally do leftovers. Okay, I'm lying. I definitely do leftovers, and in this case, I will gladly take him off your hands."

"Yup. Me too," Renee chimed in.

After some more back and forth, they all agreed to meet at a local park by the lake. Renee would bring the music and some extra chairs, and Stacy was in charge of the beverages. They agreed to send out mass text messages letting folks know to show up around 2:00 p.m. Before getting off the phone, Stacy asked if Morgan planned to invite Derek, especially since he was funding all the food. Morgan quickly shut that idea down. Instead, when she got off the phone, she texted, "Thank you! I love my orchid and I've been crushing funnel cake all morning. I miss you." She quickly deleted everything except, "Thank you!" before hitting Send.

Within seconds, as if he was waiting to hear from her, he wrote back. Morgan's heart stopped when her phone buzzed with his notification. "Np. I hope you have a great day. You deserve it. Happy Birthday, Mo." She read his text and then read it again. Morgan started to respond and decided not to. She didn't want to have a conversation with him. Not yet anyway. And she didn't want to act like everything was fine, because it wasn't. Her heart was still crushed by the massive loss of her mother, and she couldn't bring herself to see the man responsible. She wanted to thank him for her gift, and she did. So she left it at that and went to get ready for her last-minute cookout/party.

* * *

As she crawled into bed that night, exhausted and stuffed, she assessed the day. It was her first birthday without her mom. Morgan had little to no expectations for her birthday. If it were left up to her, she would have stayed in her PJs all day watching HGTV. Instead, she was surrounded by friends, great music, good conversation, and bomb funnel cake! *Not half bad*, she thought to herself. She reflected on how busy George was the entire day and felt good that 'the man who would remain nameless' got his money's worth. She also made it a point to make sure folks got George's information so he could get some repeat business. Morgan was always down for supporting black-owned businesses.

Chapter 11

Two months passed, and Morgan hadn't heard from or talked to Derek. On the one hand, she acknowledged that she told this man that she didn't want anything to do with him. On the other hand, she felt like if he really cared for her the way he said he did, he would fight for her. But there was nothing. Morgan began to second guess the feelings he had for her and the kismet connection that she felt down in the depth of her soul for this man. She was buried in grief, but what was his excuse for staying away? It seemed like every second of every day Morgan replayed the happiest moments of her life, which all stemmed from time spent with her mother or Derek. What she wouldn't do to have the opportunity to relive those moments with both of them. The lack of communication with Derek was a blessing in disguise because it allowed Morgan to put all her energies into executing the church's bake-off.

After months of planning, the big day came, and Morgan's anxieties were in full force. It seemed like everything that could go wrong, went wrong. First, the First Baptist Church of Gwynn Oak's celebrity coach, Bart Vimeano, canceled last minute because he came down with the flu. On such short notice, Morgan was only able to secure the local pastry chef of the Mandarin Oriental Hotel, Pastry Chef Preston St. Laurent. He was a skinny, long-legged, super uptight, seventy-something-year-old man with no sense of humor. Morgan was grateful that she was able to secure him but was even happier that she wasn't on the church's bake-off team because he ran things like a drill sergeant.

Then the venue that was supposed to host the event, the Institute for Culinary Design, had a pipe burst the week before the event, flooding the brand-new state-of-art wing of the school. They managed to move the bake-off to another building, but it was an older, drab, and dated facility. The kitchen was painted a pinkish salmon color, and the Kenmore appliances reminded Morgan of the ovens in the kitchen of the seventies television sitcom, *The Brady Brunch*. She wouldn't dare complain because it was better than having to cancel the whole thing. Still, this was not what she pictured in her head.

On a positive note, ticket sales surpassed the expected goal of five hundred, and the plan B space could accommodate selling another two hundred tickets at the door. A local radio personality agreed to MC the event and a news anchor from NBC4 was covering the event. There was a lot riding on this event going well, including the nearly twenty-five thousand dollars raised that would be split among the winner and runner-up teams. To engage the community, Morgan invited the local junior high school marching band and some junior varsity high school cheerleaders to perform. She also tapped the students from a local charter school that specialized in hospitality management to serve as hostesses to pass out sample baked goods.

The event was to start promptly at 5:00 p.m. The five teams representing Gwynn Park, Holy Trinity, Church of Peace, Greater Mount Washington and Highland Ridge were eagerly standing at their respective counters in their color-coded aprons. Several teams were getting pep talks from their coaches, but not Gwynn Park. Chef St. Laurent just stared at the Gwynn Park congregant team members, Ms. Betty and Ms. Diana, as they nervously fidgeted with the utensils placed on their counter.

All the judges were in place, except for one who was late. Morgan pulled all the stops to bring in the big names to serve as judges. The judges consisted of a socialite from the *Real Housewives of Potomac*, a player from the Washington Capitals, and a Grammy-award-winning home-grown R&B artist. Beyond frantic, Morgan kept looking at her watch, which currently read 4:50 p.m. Just then, in walked Tyrone Gill, the musical artist, and final person to round out the team of judges. Morgan rushed over to him, greeted him politely and quickly escorted him to the judges' table. Then she went over the program and the rules with all judges.

As the event began, Morgan's nerves began to calm down. Within the first 10 minutes, the MC revealed the mystery ingredient - jackfruit - and about half of the audience gasped. Morgan had never seen a jackfruit, let alone know how to prepare it, but the five teams were scurrying around the kitchen making meticulous moves. Obviously, they all had a plan. With an hour on the clock to complete their first dessert, the news anchor went around to the different teams to ask how their dishes were coming along. Morgan canvassed the audience to see people's reactions. Everyone seemed to be enjoying themselves, including Pastor Johnson, who did some trash-talking with the other teams' pastors. As Morgan's eyes scanned the dimly lit room, they stopped when they spotted a brown-skinned gentleman in a baseball cap. *Is that?* she thought to herself, but she couldn't make him out because of a giant guy, who sat in front of the mystery man, blocked her view. Her gut, which could sense that man from a mile away, said it was. Just then, the five-minute countdown clock began and Morgan got distracted.

To Morgan's surprise, the five baked dishes turned out well. As the judges deliberated over the entries, the students from the charter school handed out samples of the entries to guests. Morgan managed to snag a beignet. However, she quickly spit it out as it was hard as a rock and completely flavorless. She didn't know if it was the jackfruit, in particular, she didn't like, or the recipe. Either way, she decided that she didn't need to try any other entries for the entire night. The judges rated the beignet low as well, sighting that it was heavy, which was inconsistent with the texture of beignets which were light, airy, and fluffy. They unanimously scored Highland Ridge's upside-down cake a 9, which was the highest score given. Gwynn Park's cookie and ice cream scored a 6.6, coming in third place behind Greater Mount Washington' jackfruit tart which scored a 7.

The second round featured avocados. Morgan immediately thought about guacamole, which she loved to eat with tortilla chips, but remembered that this was a bake-off. She reminded herself, *this is why you are not in the contest.* While the teams prepared their masterpieces, the marching band performed, and judge, Tyrone Gill, took the mic and freestyled acapella. The audience got a kick out of that. They started chanting "blue jeans" and Tony obliged and sang the first verse of his noteworthy song. Gwynn Park ended up winning the second round with avocado and sweet potato brownies which got them a score of 9. Highland Ridge's avocado cheesecake was a close second with a score of 8.6, followed by Church of Peace's avocado oatmeal cookie sandwich.

For the final round, the teams were given free rein to bake whatever their hearts desired. Although Gwynn Park won four years in a row, Morgan couldn't remember if, in years past, the scores were as close as they were that day. She glanced over at Pastor Johnson who was now seated at the edge of his seat with his hand resting on his forehead. Morgan noticed his lips moving and assumed he was praying for a win.

* * *

There was no way to predict who would win the bake-off. Gwynn Park's Ms. Betty and Ms. Diana gave it their all, but their signature Sock-It-to-Me cake, which was the rave at all church functions, just couldn't compete with Highland Ridge's double-baked apple pie, which took first place. Neither could it top Greater Mount Washington's pumpkin cheesecake which was the first runner up. Morgan was bummed that their church lost in the end. She was grateful the event was a success because that was what she most cared about.

By the time she returned home, Morgan was exhausted. She turned off all the lights on the first floor because she knew she wasn't returning. As she crawled into bed, back aching from standing on her feet all day, she thought about heading downstairs to her mother's room to sleep in the heavenly bed, but she was too tired to move. Morgan immediately fell asleep. As she drifted to sleep, she kept replaying the bake-off in her mind, the audience's reaction to the secret ingredients, the news anchor's interview with team members, the guy in the baseball cap. *Was that Derek?* Her spirit said yes.

At about 4:00 a.m., she heard a chirping sound like an exterior door was opened. Morgan awakened. *What was that?* Did she really hear a chirping sound, or was it a dream? She replayed her steps when she first got home and realized that she forgot to put on the house alarm. She immediately reached for the taser in her nightstand drawer. *Lord, please help me. I don't want to have to kill anybody, but I won't be raped again.* She tried to be as quiet as possible but tensed up when the drawer squeaked. Morgan, being the Paranoid Patty that she was, had already played out this scenario in her head a million times. If someone ever broke into her house, she would play dead. She never understood why people got up and roamed the house asking if someone is there like they do in the movies. So, she laid as still as possible, with the covers up over her nose and taser gripped in her right hand and cell phone in her left. She managed to dial 911 quickly and whispered that someone was in her house and to hurry because someone was about to die. Thoughts began to flash through her mind of the happiest and worst days of her life. Derek appeared with his signature heartwarming smile, followed by observing Mrs. Barnes' cold, dead body at the funeral home. Morgan knew that this moment was not going to be her last. This would not be how her story ended. God had brought her too far. *Come through, Jesus, let whoever is downstairs have a change of heart and turn around. Jesus. Jesus. Jesus. Come on Jesus.* Although she had never been in a fight a day in her life, after watching *Columbiana* and *Salt* multiple times, Morgan definitely felt that she possessed the survivor gene. Although she was scared, she knew that the gene would kick in and take charge. For goodness sake, she was Mrs. Barnes' daughter. The thumping of Morgan's heart rang loudly through her ears.

As she lay still with eyes closed, Morgan began to take short quick breaths. *Get it together, Morgan.* Once she began to focus on her breaths, her ears began to take control. She could hear that the person was ascending the stairs because the stairs cracked one by one. Morgan said a quick prayer under her breath—"Jesus, please help me" - just when the bedroom door opened, and the intruder entered her room. She wasn't sure what they were doing as they hadn't approached her yet. She intentionally kept her eyes closed because she wanted to play sleep, but the anticipation got the best of her, so she peaked by opening one eye, and pulling the sheet down off her face ever so slightly. To her surprise, the person was standing over her, just staring at her. She couldn't make out who they were, but they were male and of large stature. He caught her eye when she peeked.

"Morgan, I know you are awake," said the man.

Morgan knew the voice, but in that split second, she couldn't make out who it was. *Oh, my God! How does he know my name? Who is this?* It was killing her to figure it out. She was perspiring profusely under the covers because she was trying her best not to hyperventilate as she tried to hold her breath to keep the blankets from moving up and down. Morgan began to think about all the men whose path she crossed who would want to do her harm. She was coming up empty. She continued to lay very still and not say anything, but the anxiety of not knowing who was standing over her, why, and what they were there to do was causing her to freak out. Morgan wanted to immediately lash out of bed and attack this big black blob that stood before her. Morgan's lip began to quiver and she fought back tears of fear. *Where are the police? They should be here by now.*

"Do you know what's it like to lose someone you love?" the man asked as he inched closer to Morgan. "I lost my best friend, my soulmate. Thirty-four years we spent together. I don't know life without her. The son, we never had, who brought her so much joy, you - you took away from me." This time, he slowly pulled the comforter back. "I got help. I got a job. I was doing better. But you didn't care. You told that judge to take my child away from me, anyway. It wasn't enough that I lost my wife. You had to take my son too. Everything I ever had is gone because of you." he said.

Just then, Morgan realized who was standing before her *—Mr. Stevenson.* Just when he pulled back the sheets, Morgan sat up and tased him in the neck. He jumped back, knocking the taser out of her hand. Mr. Stevenson charged at Morgan, grabbing her by her hair and pulling her down to the floor. As she was falling to the floor, Morgan grabbed the lamp from her nightstand and hit Mr. Stevenson over the head. It shattered into pieces and he immediately grabbed his head. Morgan jumped to her feet, and just then, she heard sirens down the street and prayed that they would hurry up. As she ran for the bedroom door, Mr. Stevenson lunged at her from the floor, attempting to grab her leg. Morgan started to have flashbacks of her senior year in college. She kicked him as hard as she could and ran downstairs and out the front door, barefoot, in her nightshirt, as the police were approaching the porch.

"He's upstairs in my bedroom! He attacked me. Get him! Get him!" she yelled.

* * *

One week later, Morgan was still on edge. The police apprehended Mr. Stevenson and confirmed that he was behind the drive-by shooting that occurred before Mrs. Barnes passed away, but that didn't make her feel any safer at home. She cleaned up the shattered ceramic lamp off her floor but was reminded of his invasion every time she went into her room. Renee and Stacy offered to let her stay with one of them, but Morgan was determined not to let that man ruin her life or her sanity. She knew without a shadow of a doubt that she was going to be okay, especially today, which would have been Mrs. Barnes' seventy-third birthday.

As Morgan got ready to visit her mom's grave, her cell phone rang.

"Hello?"

"Hey. How are you doing?" Renee asked.

"I'm okay. Getting ready to go to the cemetery. What's up?"

"Derek got suspended," Renee blurted out.

"What? What are you talking about?"

"Someone filed a sexual harassment claim against him at the hospital, and he got suspended pending an investigation."

Morgan heard the words that Renee just spoke, but they didn't make any sense. The Derek she knew was not capable of sexual harassment. "It's not true. It can't be," Morgan said.

"Girl, I agree. You know it's that stank of an assistant who's behind all this," Renee offered.

"Lauren?" Morgan said.

"Yeah. When Stacy and I went to see him, he told us that he fired her and…"

Morgan interrupted, "When y'all went to see him? When was this? Why didn't you say anything?"

"Morgan, it was shortly after you guys broke up. We needed to know what the deal was. It just didn't add up. And anyway, he told us he fired her. He was trying to be loyal to his mentor, who asked him to look after her, but after she ruined things between the two of you, he was done."

"I can't believe he's been suspended. I mean, his reputation, which I know he prided himself on, is in the garbage because of this chick." Morgan was in disbelief.

"So, what are you going to do?" Renee asked.

"What am I going to do?" In her head, Morgan thought, *I am going to go to Derek's place, wrap my arms around him, and beg for forgiveness. Only then will I find out where ol' girl lives and go give her a beat down for defaming my man!* Instead, Morgan continued, "I'm going to go see my Momma... and pray for Derek. I don't know what else to do at this point." *The man doesn't want anything to do with me, which is why he has fallen off the face of the earth.* "If I'm supposed to reach out, God will give me a sign. I just feel bad for him. I know how much he loves what he does." Morgan concluded her conversation and proceeded to get ready.

* * *

With everything going on leading up to the bake-off, Morgan hadn't made it to the cemetery to visit her mother yet. She picked up two dozen yellow and white carnations, Mrs. Barnes' favorite, packed a blanket and headed to the cemetery. It was a beautiful day with a slight overcast. The sun peaked its head out through the clouds. As Morgan walked down the hill to her mom's plot, she could smell the freshly cut grass. As she approached Mrs. Barnes' headstone, she noticed some dead red roses in the bronze vase atop the headstone. She dropped the blanket on the grass, knelt, removed the roses and replaced them with the fresh, vibrant carnations she purchased. She then stood up, took a step back, and assessed the headstone and the lovely flowers.

"Hi, Momma," Morgan said. "Long time, I know. There is so much to tell you. I don't know where to begin. I miss you," Morgan closed her eyes. "I miss you so much. Nothing is the same without you here. I got your birthday card. Thank you! How did you manage to do that? You were always ten steps ahead of everybody else... You know that taser you bought me a couple

Christmases back, I finally got to use it. It didn't work so well, but no worries, I'm your child, so I improvised." With the wind brushing across her face and the trees bristling back and forth, Morgan continued, "Momma, I messed up. I never thought of myself as a prideful person, but I definitely let my pride ruin whatever chance I had with Derek. I was just so angry with him because he just stood there and watched you take your last breath and he could have saved you. When that girl told me they slept together, I was so quick to believe her. I mean, how could I believe her? I knew she was thirsty. And more importantly, I knew him and the kind of man that he was. I just… thought it was all too good to be true. Yes, I know God answers prayers, but" Morgan started to cry, "I didn't think I was worthy. I mean, why? Why me? Why now?"

"Why not you?" Morgan, startled, jumped and turned around to see Derek standing before her with a bouquet of red roses in his hand.

"What? How long have you been standing there?" Morgan asked.

"Long enough to know that faith without works is dead. Mo, you believe that God is working miracles in everyone else's lives but not your own? He answered your prayer. He answered my prayer. He answered Mrs. Barnes' prayer. Don't question it. Claim it. Embrace it. Thank Him. Why now? Cause He said it ain't good for a man to be alone. Why you? Because He made you just for me. Because I love you with all my heart and the past couple of months have been hell without you," Derek stepped closer to Morgan and wiped the tears running down her face.

"Derek, I am so sorry to hear about your job. We can't let her get away with this," Morgan said.

"I agree. I worked too hard to build up my practice to let one person tear it down, but He got me. My practice will be okay. Can't no one tear down what He has elevated."

Morgan nodded.

"But, enough about me. Stacy told me about the break-in. Are you okay?" Derek asked, concerned.

"What's up with you talking to my friends? Apparently, all of you have been communicating behind my back!" Morgan rolled her eyes. Derek locked eyes with Morgan, and she mumbled, "I'm okay."

"You sure? I've been driving by at night and checking out the alley. It's good to see there's still police presence in the neighborhood," Derek said.

"You've been checking out the house?"

"Yeah. I was concerned. I wanted to do more, but I was trying to respect your wishes," Derek said.

"Wishes?" Morgan asked.

"You said you didn't want me contacting you. So, I tried to keep my distance," Derek explained.

"So, that's why you haven't called?" Morgan said.

Derek paused, "Yeah. That's exactly why I haven't called." He squinted and said, "You wanted me to call?"

"Well, yeah. I mean, not right away, but eventually. But when you didn't, I assumed I messed things up too bad, and, well, I couldn't really blame anyone but myself."

"Morgan, I'm right here. You didn't mess up anything. I'm just glad to know that there's still an us. There is still an us, right?" Derek leaned in to kiss Morgan.

She looked up at him, taking in his presence, and then turned his head to the right so she could see his profile. "That was you at the bake-off! With the baseball cap, right?" In true Morgan fashion, she knew how to ruin a moment.

Derek laughed and nodded, "Yeah, I was there. I wanted to support you. You did an outstanding job, by the way."

Morgan blushed, "Thank you. Although we got robbed of the win."

"I don't know. That double-baked apple pie was everything," Derek declared. Morgan smiled, reminiscing about the bake-off desserts.

"Ms. Barnes?" Derek asked.

"Hmm?"

"You didn't answer my question," he said.

"What? What was the question?" she asked.

"Is there still an us?"

She nodded with a big ole smile and answered, "Yes."

And Derek leaned in and kissed her. Morgan pulled back and looked deeply into Derek's eyes.

"I'm sorry for being so stubborn. I've wasted so much precious time that we can't get back."

Derek lifted Morgan's chin and said, "Babe, it's okay. You needed time to process your mom's death. You were completely caught off-guard. And all that other drama just added fuel to the fire. No regrets. We are here now and that's all that matters. Now, can we get back to where we were before you rudely interrupted me?" Derek laughed and began kissing Morgan again.

As they stood there, embracing in the middle of the cemetery, they heard a soft pop. They immediately looked at each other and then canvassed the cemetery. From where they were standing, they saw Morgan's car at the top of the hill.

"Is that a…" Morgan thought she saw a car beside her car, but it was so close she couldn't make out if it was really there.

Immediately Derek saw what she was saying and started running toward the car. It took a few seconds for Morgan to realize what was happening. Someone pulled up on her car and broke the passenger window to steal her wristlet that was lying on the seat.

"Stop! Stop!" she yelled as the gray sedan sped off. Derek took off after the car, but he was too late. He was only able to get the last three digits of the license plate as well as the make of the car. He pulled out his cell phone and called 911.

"What did they steal?" Derek asked.

"My wallet – it has my ID, my credit card…. My address. Who would do something like this at the cemetery?" Morgan was again in disbelief.

"Call the credit card company and let them know your card was stolen. We'll grab you a bag, and you'll stay with me. All this drama didn't follow you when you were with me, you know?" Derek said to make light of the situation.

"Well, why didn't you call and tell me that months ago? You could have saved me so much drama," Morgan replied.

They waited for the police to arrive and filed a report. A manager for the cemetery stopped by to apologize but indicated that it happened more than a few times, and the cemetery didn't know how to stop it. Before leaving, Morgan made room in the vase for Derek's flowers. He admitted to coming to visit Mrs. Barnes often in the past couple of months. They wished her mom a happy heavenly 73rd birthday and headed to the auto body shop to drop off Morgan's car.

Chapter 12

Today was a very special day. It marked the one-year anniversary of Derek and Morgan's first encounter. In honor of the occasion, Derek got them tickets to see Rome Devereux at the Fillmore in Silver Spring for a one-night-only special performance. Morgan loved herself some Rome Devereux and was so excited.

In the months since Mrs. Barnes' birthday, Derek and Morgan picked up where they left off before the awards dinner. She stayed with him for a few nights after the car break-in—in the second bedroom. However, that proved to be a little challenging since they both had gone so long without seeing one another that they couldn't keep their hands to themselves. Although they succeeded in not going all the way, after four nights, Morgan suggested that she head home, and they reaffirmed their commitment to remain celibate.

Things were falling back into place. The investigation into Lauren's claim of sexual harassment proved that Derek did absolutely nothing wrong and the charges were dropped. Derek was given an opportunity to file a defamation lawsuit against her but chose not to because he just wanted to be completely done with her. He was able to resume his practice and put all that nonsense behind him. Mr. Stevenson was sentenced to ten years in prison for two counts of attempted murder. Morgan was thrilled that Derek and Deitrick had bonded. He got joint custody of Deitrick and had him every other week. They routinely went fishing, and Deitrick even invited Morgan to tag along the next time they went. Deitrick couldn't stop talking about the big fish he caught. It was a "snaffer," as he called it. Morgan would kindly correct him with, "I think you mean 'snapper.'"

That night brought back so many fond memories for Morgan. She thought about her reaction to opening her front door and Derek standing there on the porch. She remembered her eye contact with Mrs. Barnes over the dinner table when she insisted that she invite Derek to go dancing with her. She thought about their first dance and how Derek commanded the dance floor. But it was how the evening ended, with Mrs. Barnes plopping down on her bed to inquire about the night's festivities that got Morgan a little emotional. If it hadn't been for her mother and her divine relationship with Jesus, Morgan knew she wouldn't be where she was today. So much happened in the past year, but she knew without a shadow of a doubt, that it all led her to be right where she was. She immediately remembered Mrs. Barnes saying, "All things work together for good, to those who love and serve the Lord."

* * *

The concert was everything. The Fillmore was a quaint venue with standing room only. It was packed, and as Morgan stood center stage just arm distance from one of her favorite male vocalists while wrapped in the arms of the man she loved, she thought life couldn't get any better than this. Song after song, she sang her heart out while leaning on and dancing with Derek, who sang along too, but just with not as much vigor. About an hour and a half into the performance, Derek excused himself to use the restroom. Derek was leaving on one of her favorite songs, but who was she to control his bladder? When Derek didn't return after another favorite, "Potion Love," Morgan was starting to get annoyed. Now she realized that every song was a favorite, but she couldn't understand what was taking this man so long. She started to look around the crowd to see if she could spot him, but he was nowhere in sight.

Rome transitioned to yet another song, "My Rib," and this time with the music down low, he said, "Fellas, how many of y'all know we can't play the field forever. When you meet the one, you got to man up and lock it down before the next brotha does. You can't let her go. You gotta pull out all the stops. You got to set the mood right. You get you some rose petals and candles, and of course, you gotta have Rome playing in the background. Wait." Talking to the audience, Rome said, "I need y'all to help me out real quick. Can I get Morgan to come up to the stage?" The house lights came up slightly and people started to look around. Morgan followed suit and canvassed the audience to see who Rome was talking to. Then he clarified, "Morgan Barnes," and pointed to her. Morgan pointed to herself as if she didn't just hear her name. She hesitated and then made her way to the stage where a chair was waiting for her. Nervous and confused, Morgan sat down and from stage left, Derek walked toward her with a fuchsia and white orchid. Placing the plant down beside her chair, Derek grabbed Morgan's hand and helped her to her feet as he got down on one knee. Morgan's eyes began to water, and her hand began to shake.

Caressing her hand, Derek said, "Morgan Elizabeth Barnes, it's been exactly one year ago today that I knew I wanted to spend the rest of my life with you. You are my everything, and I want to make this official. Will you do me the honor and marry me?"

"Yes!" Morgan bent over to kiss Derek as he placed a two karat Ascher cut diamond on her ring finger.

Rome said, "She said yes, y'all!" and proceeded to sing yet another one of Morgan's favorite songs.

Morgan and Derek remained on stage, hugging one another, and singing along, "I want you to be my rib, my rib, my rib…"

In this moment, Morgan could honestly say that the wait had been worth it. Here she was madly in love with a man that she was certain was sent by God. Forty was a year of self-discovery; of learning to truly love oneself, of falling in love, of being vulnerable, of stepping outside of one's comfort zone, of experiencing loss, and of strength and resilience. She was not the same person that she was this time last year. Everything that she experienced in life had prepared her for this very moment. Where would she be if she settled and married Justin, all to fulfill an arbitrary goal of being married before forty? Once again, she realized that God's plan trumped her own, and she had to thank God for His perfect will and timing.

Epilogue

After two weeks of flu-like symptoms with no relief in sight, and Derek insisting that Morgan was pregnant, she finally made an appointment with her obstetrician. Morgan thought the suggestion was ridiculous because even the news reported that the flu season was extremely bad this year, so she wasn't alone. However, to appease her husband, she made the appointment, and to her surprise, he took off from work to accompany her.

While they waited in the examining room, Derek read up on all of the literature posted in the room. It was his first time in an OBGYN office. Morgan sat anxiously, trying to decide whether she was ready to find out the results. She convinced herself that she was sterile and was okay with not having kids, but the idea that she could be pregnant brought some excitement. She loved Deitrick as her own and the idea of having someone for him to play with brought a smile to her face.

In walked Dr. Chao with her assistant. "Hi, Morgan, how are you doing? Oh, this must be your husband, Hi. I'm Dr. Chao"

Derek extended his hand, "Hi. I'm Derek."

"Well, congratulations. You are definitely pregnant," Dr. Chao blurted out as she reviewed the results from Morgan's urine sample. Pulling out the ultrasound machine, Dr. Chao said, "I'm going do an ultrasound so we can determine how far along you are."

Morgan looked at Derek, who was cheesing from ear to ear. He gave her that look of "I told you so," and she rolled her eyes. With a bunch of jelly on her belly and a cold prong moving across it, Dr. Chao looked at the ultrasound and said, "Well, my dear, you are thirteen weeks along…. Huh."

Morgan asked, "What's wrong?"

"Uh. Give me a second," Dr. Chao replied. She moved the handgrip around on Morgan's stomach some more and said, "Yup. I wanted to confirm before I said anything, but I guess double congratulations are in order. You are having twins!"

"Say what?!" Morgan looked at Derek and then at Dr. Chao. "Shut the front door! God and Momma got jokes."

Made in the USA
Middletown, DE
09 August 2020